DIRTY PUCKING TEASE

A FORBIDDEN STEPBROTHER HOCKEY ROMANCE

SPECIAL EDITION

MICHAELA SAWYER

Edited by: Kate Seger

Beta Readers: ME Cruz, Damara R. Hill

Cover Design by: Artscandare Book Cover Designs

To my readers: Thank you for taking a chance on my words. When you support an author you are supporting a dream! Thank you for supporting mine.

1

Kaia

"Jax," I roared, drawing out his name as I pounded my fist against the bathroom door. "Get out of the bathroom." I banged again, this time harder. "You've been in there for over an hour." Jaw clenched, I glared at the closed door, dropping my fist.

Clenching my fists at my side, I blew out a loud, exaggerated growl and dropped my forehead to the door with a thud. "Jax." His name came out as a dramatic whine. "Please, get out of the bathroom."

"Just use my bathroom," Harlow, my younger sister, yelled outside my bedroom door. That would be an easy fix, except all my things were in my bathroom—the one I was forced to share with my evil stepbrother, Jaxtyn.

Why my stepmother and father thought it would be a good idea for Jax and me to share a Jack-and-Jill bathroom was beyond me, but they did, and now we fought at least once a day over it. Well, to be fair, it was always me standing outside the bathroom screaming. My younger sister, Harlow, and Jaxtyn's younger sister, Syn, shared a bathroom. Trystan, Jaxtyn's older brother, got his own, and I had to share with an egotistical jerk who spent way too much time staring at himself in the mirror.

"Fuck this," I muttered, pushing off the door. I had my first date tonight, and I had less than thirty minutes to get ready. I stormed out of my room and straight into his. He always locked my side, but he never locked his. Throwing the door open, I walked straight in. He didn't even give me a sideways glance, like he'd expected it.

Letting my gaze fall, I noticed he wore nothing but a white towel wrapped low on his hips. Beads of water shined across his broad shoulders, toned chest, and tight abs. I watched the muscles flex as he moved to put his toothbrush back in the glass holder. He was infuriatingly annoying, but it was even more infuriating how stupid hot he was. Like the kind of hot that had girls begging to take their panties off for him, even if he'd been an asshole to them. What was even worse was that he knew it.

"Did you need something, Baby Cruz?" He smirked, his gaze flicking up to me in the mirror as he swiped his thumb across his full bottom lip. My jaw clenched at the stupid nickname he'd given me, reminding me why I hated him. He'd overheard my dad call me baby once years ago during a conversation when I was struggling with my mother's death. He added my last name, and now he only ever referred to me as Baby Cruz.

"I need the bathroom," I said cocking my hip to the side as I crossed my arms over my chest. "I have a date tonight."

He spun around. His amused gaze scanned me from bottom to top. "You look like a homeless person." He scoffed a sarcastic laugh, crossing his arms over his broad-tatted chest as he leaned back on the counter. He was referring to my three-day-old ratty ripped Kiss tee and two-size-too-big grey sweatpants.

"That's why I need the bathroom." I scowled. "So get out, or I'm getting ready with you in here." The look in his eyes shifted from amusement to something else. Something dark as his eyes lingered a little longer than normal on my lips. Something that, if I didn't know better, looked like jealousy.

Clearing his throat, he spun around, averting his gaze. He grabbed his phone off the countertop. "I would watch if I were into itty bitty titties and an overgrown bush." He sneered, bumping my shoulder on his way out. I rolled my eyes but decided not to engage. I had less than twenty minutes to get ready now. "You should make time for a shower." My eyes flicked up to see him through the mirror. He turned up his nose like something smelled bad. "You stink." He slammed the bathroom door shut.

Standing in front of the mirror, I sniffed myself. I didn't have time for a shower. Fuck! I'd just let him get into my head. Now I would be paranoid all night, thinking I stunk.

2

Jaxtyn

Standing on the second-floor balcony overlooking the narrow driveway, I watched as Kaia and Harlow strolled towards Kaia's new sleek black Lexus. A gift from my mother for Kaia's eighteenth birthday.

Before their father married my mother, they lived closer to the east side projects and attended an underfunded public school.

Now, they lived in a million-dollar mansion, drove a luxury car, and graduated from one of the world's best private schools, but Kaia spent her nights working in a bar on the lower East Side where she grew up, and everything about that annoyed me.

Kaia beeped the Lexus unlocked and tossed her purse into the seat. I knew she'd been lying about a date. No one was stupid enough to show up here to pick her up. No one was stupid enough to touch what was off-limits, and Kaia was off-limits to everyone, but just in case, I waited to see.

My gaze trailed down to her heart-shaped ass in her skin-tight jeans, and I bit into my bottom lip, picturing my hand curling into it as she rode my cock, but I immediately shook away the images. She was off-limits even to me. She was my step-sister, but that didn't stop her from teasing me, though I suspected it was unintentional.

She left the door open to her bathroom every night, and every night when she shoved the thin sheet off her, I had the perfect view of her perfect round ass. It was too bad she didn't sleep topless, too. It was hard to believe she didn't know that her bed was completely visible from my bed through the opened doorway. Or maybe she was just a dirty tease.

"Let's go, Syn," Harlow called out, brushing a strand of dirty blonde hair from her eyes. The sisters twisted to see a bright red Ford Mustang swerve down the drive. After parking next to Kaia, a tall, lean blonde appeared from the car. Kaia turned around, her eyes narrowing on the blonde, who was here to see me.

Carly flicked Kaia and Harlow a smile before situating herself and giving her face a once over in the reflection of her car window.

"Who are you?" Syn asked, pausing in front of the red Mustang. Syn was the same age as Harlow, but the two were complete opposites. Syn was the epitome of her name. The only similarities between them were their ages and their height. Harlow was a dirty blonde with almost no curves, while Syn's hair was jet black, and she was covered from head to toe in tattoos and piercings.

"I'm meeting Jax." Carly flashed a large white smile. "You must be Syn."

"Save it," Syn snarled, shoving her dark black hair over her shoulder, revealing her newest tattoo. "No need to make friends." Syn shrugged her narrow shoulders. "They'll be a new you tomorrow." Syn wasn't wrong.

My gaze flashed to Kaia, and when her piercing blue eyes flashed up to meet mine, I realized it wasn't Carly I wanted up here tonight, but she'd have to do because I couldn't have Kaia.

The girls slid into the Lexus, and Carly headed toward the house.

"Hey baby," Carly purred from behind me mere seconds later. "What do you want to do tonight?"

Curling my fingers over the railing, I replayed her question. What did I want to do tonight? My gaze followed Kaia's black Lexus as it pulled out of the driveway and into traffic.

Kaia.

Kaia was what I wanted to do tonight.

I wanted to follow her, drag her back here, and fuck her over this railing. I wanted to hear her scream my name as she came all over my cock. I wanted to rearrange the face of any guy who even looked her way, but none of those were an option. So, I turned around, a slow smile spreading across my face; Carly would have to do.

LOUNGING back against the leather chair in my bedroom, my gaze trailed over Carly's naked body and her attempt to tease me. Her large store-bought tits, tight perky nipples, and long, thin, tanned legs spread wide for me.

Her gaze locked on mine as she trailed her fingertips over her mouth and down to her tits. Then, licking her full red lips, she teased her nipples.

"Play with yourself," I ordered, watching as her hand slide down her stomach straight to her pussy. "Spread your legs wider." She did as she was told as her fingers circled her clit. Her eyes closed, her back arched, and her lips parted with a soft moan as she slid her fingers through her slick flesh.

"Oh fuck, Jax," she moaned dramatically; adding another finger, she pumped them in and out of herself. "I can't wait to feel your cock inside of me." Too bad she wouldn't get to feel me in her, ever. She was going to suck my dick and go home.

It had taken all night, but I was ready for her.

"Get on your knees," I demanded, and she did eagerly as her tongue swept across her bottom lip. Her fingertips trailed over my bare torso and settled on the waistband of my boxer briefs, tugging them down and setting my erection free. She curled her fingers around my thick cock as she started to stroke. Closing my eyes, my head fell back on a groan. Images of Kaia's tight little ass sprung forward, and now I was into this. She stroked me from root to tip, using the moisture to quicken her strokes.

She didn't stop when my phone chimed, echoing through the quiet room. I didn't bother looking. It could break my concentration. The phone went quiet as Carly leaned forward, running her tongue ring over the head of my dick. Fuck!

The phone chimed again. Damn. I snatched the phone off the stand beside the chair.

My eyes narrowed as I read her name. It was Kaia. She never called me.

Hitting the button, I brought the phone to my ear. "What is it, Baby Cruz?" I barked into the phone. I didn't try to hide the fact that I was in the middle of getting my dick sucked or my annoyance at her terrible timing. "I'm kind of in the middle of something." Carly placed her mouth over the head of my cock, slurping and sucking as her head bobbed up and down.

"I need you to come get me," she said, a sense of

desperation wrapped tightly in her words. "My date kicked me out."

"Holy fuck." I grunted as Carly pushed me to the back of her throat, holding herself deep until she gagged. I closed my eyes. Kaia's voice and Carly's mouth as images of Kaia flashed forward were exactly what I needed to get off, and since I couldn't have Kaia, this was the next best thing. Threading my hand through her hair as she slid up my cock, I tightened my grip, forcing her deep at the same time I thrust forward.

"Are you okay?" Kaia asked as Carly choked on my cock. I didn't answer just let the speaker fill with wet sounds of me fucking her mouth. "Jax?"

"Fuck yeah." I grunted, easing off as tears streamed down Carly's cheeks. There was nothing I loved more than messing up a pretty girl's makeup, and nothing did it quite like pushing past that throat barrier. I needed to keep Kaia talking. I was close. Carly gasped, and I shoved her back down hard and deep fucking the back of her throat. Fuck! "Why did your date kick you out?"

"I believe his exact words were put out or get out." She groaned. My eyes flashed open, and the face fucking stopped. Anger settled low in my stomach as I released Carly, who popped off, gasping for air. What the fuck? Someone was trying to fuck what was off-limits, to fuck what was mine.

"Are you fucking kidding me?" I growled, leaning up

and pulling Carly off my lap. This session was over. I was going to kill whoever this douche was.

"Uh, well, as funny as that would be, no. I'm not kidding you."

"Where's your car?"

"Harlow dropped me off and left with Syn," she said. "And now neither of them are answering their phones, and I'm kind of in the middle of nowhere."

"Drop me a pin," I said, shoving Carly out of my way and pulling my boxers over my throbbing erection that I would have to take care of later. "I'm leaving now." I disconnected, reaching for my pants.

"What's wrong?" Carly whined.

"I have to go pick up Kaia," I muttered, searching the floor for my shirt.

"What, like your step-sister?" She scowled, and I winced at the word step-sister. I was well aware of the fact that she was my step-sister, but hearing it from someone else made me feel dirty for the disgustingly filthy thoughts I had of her; I'd just pictured Kaia's mouth on me and not Carly's.

"Yes." I ripped the shirt from the floor, quickly pulling it over my head.

"I can go with you." She smiled, wiggling into her pants. Her large, round tits bounced as she hopped around. "And then we can finish what we started."

I snorted a laugh. "Yeah, no. You have to go, but

maybe another time." We both knew there wouldn't be another time.

Since the day Kaia and her family moved in, we had never been left alone. Never. Not purposely; it just never worked out like that. Eight of us lived in this house, plus houseguests and friends. The house was always full. So now I was going to pick her up by myself and bring her back to an empty house.

"Are you serious?" she snarled. I was one hundred percent serious.

"Yeah." I bolted for the door. "Let yourself out."

3

Kaia

It felt like I had been standing alone in the darkness of the groves for hours before Jax finally pulled up when, in reality, he'd made it in fifteen minutes. Which was impressive, but I assumed that was why he took the bike.

"Where is he?" Jax growled, pulling his helmet off.

"Jax, please." I stifled a groan, wrapping my arms around my chest to hide my humiliation. "I've already been humiliated enough for one night. I want to go home."

"Are you hurt?" He sighed as his gaze trailed over me, looking for any sign of injury.

"No." I shook my head. He nodded, twisting back to grab his other helmet.

"Don't waste your time, bro," the voice that told me

to put out or get out cackled from behind me. I cringed as Jax's gaze flicked up and over my shoulder. "She's a prude who thinks her pussy's made of gold." His gaze followed him as he passed us. Jax threw his long leg over his bike as the realization that this was the guy who left me stranded hit him.

"Jax," I warned, but he was already storming towards him. He tapped him on the shoulder, and when David whipped around with a huge grin plastered across his face, Jax's fist rocked him, sending him flying backward.

"What the fuck, man?" David scowled, reaching up and wiping the blood pooling from his split lip.

"Don't. Ever. Talk about her again," Jax growled. His entire body tensed as his fist clenched at his side like he might throw another punch.

"Jax, please," I pleaded, tugging on his shirt. We were drawing a crowd of party-goers curious about all the commotion. This was exactly what I didn't want to happen. I didn't want to draw more attention to this entire situation.

"I asked you for a ride," I hissed when we returned to the bike. "Not to defend my honor."

He kicked his leg over the bike, a cocky smirk tugging at the corner of his lips. "It's the same." He handed me a helmet. "Put it on, and let's get out of here."

"Hold on tight," Jax's voice boomed through the speakers inside the helmet. I grabbed his waist awkwardly and heard him laugh through the speakers as he grabbed each of my hands, pulling them tightly around him. Then, he revived the motor and zoomed off.

It wasn't exactly a cold night, but the wind on my hands was brutal. I balled them together, desperate for warmth.

"Are your hands cold?" he asked as he eased the bike to a stop at the red light.

"Yeah, a little," I said. "But I'll live."

Dropping his feet to the ground, he balanced the bike and grabbed my hands, prying them open with his thumbs. I couldn't see what he was doing over his shoulder, but I felt it. He pressed my flat palms against his bare, ripped torso, then pulled his shirt over them. The heat from his skin immediately warmed them when he pressed his hands over the shirt, holding them in place.

"Better?"

"Yea-yeah," I stuttered. His back bounced slightly like he was laughing as he pulled his legs up and surged forward, causing my thighs to tighten around his waist.

Jax and I had an odd relationship. It mainly consisted of rude comments, eye-rolling, sarcasm, and me screaming at him to get out of the bathroom. I had never touched him in all the years we'd lived together. I mean, sure, I ogled him, but who wouldn't? Look at him. He was fifty-shades of fucking gorgeous with his dark thick hair, piercing blue eyes, and chiseled jawline. But feeling the deep curves of his smooth, tight abs underneath my touch sent a rushing wave of heat straight between my legs.

Not that he felt the same.

4

Kaia

Turning over, I glanced at my alarm clock. Three-forty-five in the morning, and I was wide awake. I leaned up on my arms and peeked through the bathroom into Jax's room, but it was covered in darkness. He probably left to finish whatever he'd been doing before I called after I bolted to my room when we got home. Or maybe he was asleep.

My stomach growled, and I decided that I needed ice cream.

My father and stepmother, Liz, were out of town on their 700th honeymoon. Harlow and Syn were supposedly staying with a 'girlfriend,' and Trystan was gone with friends to what sounded like a massive orgy and wouldn't be home for the night. So that left me alone in the mansion.

Pushing through the door leading into the kitchen, I

froze at the sight of a half-naked Jaxtyn. Swallowing hard, I watched his tanned and toned back muscles flex with his movement. Something shifted between us tonight, and I thought it best to avoid him until I could wrap my brain around what.

"I was making some ice cream," Jax said, his back still facing me. It was too late to run now. If I bolted for my bedroom again, he'd know I was being weird. "Want some?"

"Yeah." I sighed, strolling up to the island in the center of the kitchen.

"You like it plain, right?" he asked, reaching into the cabinet and grabbing another bowl. "Vanilla?"

"Right." I was surprised he knew that, but we had lived together for a few years.

Biting my bottom lip, my eyes trailed over him. The way the muscles in his back and arms flexed as he moved, how his grey sweats hung low on his hips. He had dark ink scattered over his chest, arms, and back. His dark hair was wet, like he'd just gotten out of the pool.

"I can feel you eye-fucking me," he said, his tone arrogant. I choked on absolutely nothing, quickly averting my gaze to anything other than my stepbrother.

I cleared my throat. "Don't flatter yourself." I moved around the island to the counter, where he worked to put together two bowls of ice cream. He cut his gaze over to me, a slow smile spreading across his lips. He was missing spoons. "I'll grab the spoons." Spinning on my bare feet, I grabbed two spoons from the drawer.

He didn't hear me because he was twisting to grab the spoons when I spun back around. I bounced off his rock-hard chest.

"Woah!" He hooked an arm around my waist, pulling me flush against him. To keep me from falling... "Careful." The heat from his breath brushed across my lips. Frozen, my gaze snapped to his full lips when he swept his tongue across his bottom lip before biting it. My heart pounded against my rib cage.

Holy shit, this is wrong...He's my stepbrother.

Clearing my throat, I pushed firmly against his chest, but there was nowhere to go; my back was against the island.

"You okay, Baby Cruz?" His fingers curling around my waist. The room started to spin as the heat from his hands burned the sensitive skin through the thin tee I was wearing. *Omigod, what is he doing?* My breath caught as his bare chest brushed against my t-shirt. I yelped, gripping his strong shoulders when, in one swift jerk, he hoisted me up, dropping me on the cold granite countertop.

"So what was the deal tonight?" He spun around, grabbed the bowls, and handed me a small bowl of ice cream, unfazed at our contact. I shrugged off his question. "Baby Cruz?"

"It was nothing." I shoved my spoon into my ice cream.

"I think the least you owe me is an explanation," he muttered, his hand sliding down, gripping his dick. "Considering I was five pumps away from emptying my load down the back of Carly's throat."

I choked on my ice cream at his crudeness. I wished I had the confidence he had. How did I tell one of the most confident men I'd ever met that I had no idea what I was doing sexually, and it was terrifying? I almost had a full-blown panic attack when David tried to kiss me because I was so unattractive that I was embarrassed to be naked with someone.

"I think I need your help," I muttered, avoiding eye contact. Jax was arrogant, crude, rude, bold, and a man whore, but he was also someone I trusted who was shameless and had a lot of experience in that area.

"My help?" He narrowed his piercing blue eyes on me, setting his bowl of ice cream on the counter behind him.

Here goes nothing...

"I want to be more assertive and confident," I paused, pressing my lips into a thin line as my eyes sliced up, meeting his confused expression, "with men."

"And how exactly am I going to help with that?" he asked, crossing his arms over his ripped chest.

"Teach me."

"Let me get this straight," he paused, swallowing

hard, "you want me to teach you to be more assertive and confident with men because...?"

"Because I'm terrified of intimacy."

He froze, letting my words sink in. "Intimacy or sex?" he asked, drawing out the words. Everything about sex and intimacy terrified me. The thought of being naked in front of some stranger who would judge every one of my physical flaws was horrifying. I wasn't one of the pretty girls. I was smart, and sometimes I thought I was funny but super hot or sexy...Nope.

Growing up, it was always just my dad, who wasn't the best at teaching my sister and me how to be women or do womanly things. So I was beyond excited when my dad met Liz because I was desperate for that female role model I hadn't had growing up. She came at the perfect time when I was transitioning from child to woman.

"Both, I guess."

"Kai, how many guys have you been with?" Heat crept up along my neck, and my cheeks heated with embarrassment. I suddenly felt flushed at the bold question. I'm so embarrassed by the question that I didn't even pick up on the fact that it was the first time he'd ever said my name, not Baby Cruz.

"None."

"Fooled around with?" He furrowed his brows.

"None."

"Kissed?"

"One, but truthfully, it was kind of gross." I scowled, staring at my bowl of ice cream to try to hide my embarrassment. "Kind of sloppy."

"Gross," he drew out the word. I nodded, my gaze flicked up to meet his. "So you're a virgin?" I nodded again. "I—" He paused, frozen, eyes locked on mine in what seemed to be a form of shock. "I can't help you. Good night." He stormed out without a second glance back.

"O...kay." I hopped down from the countertop. "Great! This is just great. I will be the forty-year-old virgin."

5

Jaxtyn

Strolling through the empty house, I made my way through the darkness toward my bedroom. Practice had been brutal today, mostly because I'd had little to no sleep between my blue balls and conversation with Kaia in the kitchen; it left me wide awake.

I needed a shower, alcohol, a blow job, and sleep.

Pushing through my bedroom door, I dropped my gear on the floor, immediately drawn to the crack of light coming from the bathroom and the sound of water hitting the tile floor filling the silent room.

I was home an hour earlier than usual, but there was no way she left the door open to the bathroom while she showered. No fucking way.

Stepping in front of the cracked door, I peered in. It was her. My breath caught at the sight of her bare, wet back. My eyes trailed down her exposed body, following the water droplets as they cascaded down her naked round ass. Her eyes closed as she let the water hit her face. She reached up, running her hand over her long, wet blonde hair. My gaze dropped to the side view of her tits. Licking my lips, I could feel my cock twitching. Begging to break free from the gym shorts restricting it.

I wanted to join her. I wanted to pin her to the shower wall, wrap her perfect thighs around my waist and fuck her until the water ran cold.

This is exactly why I couldn't help her. There's no way I could help her fuck someone else.

Fuck...

Running my hand down my face, I realized I needed to get out of there before I did something I couldn't take back. So I'd skip the shower and go straight to the alcohol and a blow job.

A quick change and I was out of the house before she finished in the bathroom.

Twenty minutes later, I swerved my bike into the Eastside Edge parking lot, a shithole bar on the lower east side. I stormed straight for the bar, ordered two shots, threw them back, and ordered another.

"Woah, man," Owen slapped my back as he slid onto the stool next to me. "Rough day?" Owen and I had been friends since the first day of high school when we bonded over our love for hockey and women. After graduation, we'd accepted hockey scholarships to the same school close to home. He knew everything about me, including my contempt for my housemate.

"You have no idea." I reached for my drink and throwing it back before slamming it down onto the bar.

"What has your panties in a bunch?" Owen chuckled. "Or should I say who?" I rolled my eyes, twisting around to lean on the bar. "Does this have something to do with a pretty little blonde who lives with you?" I ground my teeth together, not bothering to answer. Nobody got to me the way Kaia did. "Where is she anyway? Tucker said she was on the schedule tonight." My eyes snapped up to meet his in a warning. Why would he even ask if she was on the schedule? "Chill, bro." He laughed, reading my facial expression. "I overheard him tell Max." Max was the bartender tonight.

"She was getting ready when I left." I groaned.

"In your bathroom." He laughed.

"She's driving me crazy."

"Fuck her." He shrugged. My eyes snapped up to his.

"She's my step-sister," I reminded him. "She lives in the bedroom next to mine. We share a bathroom."

"She's not your real sister." He smirked. "And you are both adults who are obviously hot for each other."

"I can't fuck a girl I can't escape from," I shook my head. "Plus, if my mom found out..." I sighed. "She asked me to behave, and so far, I think I have." I quirked a grin. Looking didn't count as not behaving.

"That was years ago," he stated. "When they moved

in. You're all grown up now, and you're not going to be able to hold the men back much longer." He jerked his chin forward, and I followed his line of sight to see Kaia walking through the front door, tying her apron around her waist. Every eye in the room followed her, well, the ones with cocks between their legs anyways.

I groaned, twisting back around the bar. Holding up two fingers, I signaled the bartender for two more shots; I leaned over the bar.

"Why do we come here?" Owen laughed. "There are tons of bars on our side of town. So why do we come to this shithole?" I didn't bother to answer his rhetorical question. We both knew why.

To be near her.

To watch her.

To protect her.

To keep the drunk men and their grabby hands off her.

"Don't you boys ever do anything else?" My jaw clenched, and I rolled my eyes at the sound of her voice directly behind me. I didn't bother turning around; I didn't need to. "Oh wait, Kai's working tonight, so, of course, you're here."

"Good to see you too, Cam." I twisted around, forcing a sarcastic smile. Camryn, also known as Cam or Cammy Young, was Kaia's best friend, and unfortunately, they were a package deal.

"You gonna buy me a drink, Jaxy Boy?" Cam smirked, sliding onto the stool next to me.

"Nope," I said dryly, staring off into the crowd. "I don't buy girls drinks."

"Good thing I'm not a girl." She chuckled. I knew she was referring to her womanhood, but I couldn't resist.

"Thanks for the confirmation." I laughed, cocking my head to the side. "I knew that was an Adam's apple." She rolled her eyes dramatically. Camryn didn't resemble a man at all, and she knew it. She was petite with short dark hair and deep brown eyes. She had an athletic body because she was a dancer at some fancy art school by day and a boxer by night.

"Hey, O." Cam smiled, leaning forward on her fore-arms on the bar to see past me. "Long time no see."

"What's up, Cam Cam?" Owen flashed an all-white smile. Cammy, Owen, Kaia, and I all grew up together. Owen and I were older, and we didn't run in the same crowds, but Cammy and Owen were always at our house growing up, and even in the massive mansion, there were only so many places to hang out, not to mention we all shared a bathroom when everyone stayed over. "I'll get you that drink."

"So, what brings you here tonight, Cam?" I muttered, crossing my arms over my chest as my gaze followed Kaia around the crowded room.

"I'm on a mission," she said. "To get your girl," she shoved a finger into my arm, "laid tonight." I rolled my eyes. "Someone needs to help her get past her insecurities." Camryn definitely wasn't the person for that job.

"Maybe she needs to move at her own speed." I scowled. "When she's ready."

"Maybe she just needs to be fucked," she said.

"Maybe she's not a whore."

The corner of her mouth quirked up. "Takes one to know one, man whore." My lips pulled into a smirk. That was the one thing I liked about Camryn. She gave as good as she got.

"Come on, Cam." Owen smiled, sliding out of his stool. "Teach me some new dance moves." Cam's face lit up as she hopped down from her stool and followed him.

My gaze searched the room for Kaia, finally spotting her in a dark corner, taking a drink order. My eyes trailed down the length of her to the short cut-off shorts that were part of her bar uniform. I hated her bar uniform.

Kaia was a mystery to me. She was incredibly sexy, but she didn't know it. How could she not know it? Was her lack of confidence the real reason she was still a virgin?

My gaze followed her around the room, making sure no one crossed any lines, and by lines, I meant putting a hand on her.

The song ended, and Camryn made her way back to the bar." You're totally giving off creepy stalker vibes right now." Cam laughed, leaning on the bar beside me. I rolled my eyes. "Why don't you just tell her you want to fuck her?"

"Fuck off, Cam." I whipped back around to lean on the bar. "You have no idea what you're talking about."

"You're not fooling anyone." Cam smirked. "The only person who can't see it is Kaia, and that's only because she's naive when it comes to sexual tension or anything pertaining to sex." She shrugged, throwing back a drink. "She has no idea how men see her." She laughed. "But you do, don't you?" My jaw flexed, but I didn't answer. I didn't need to. Every guy here had noticed her, but she was always utterly oblivious to it, and it wasn't just that. Flirting went over her head. She confused it for polite friendliness. "You're both fucking adults. For the love of god, just get it over with."

Camryn was one of those overly nosy bitches that you couldn't hide a fucking thing from. She paid way too much attention to everyone else's behavior. So trying to hide how much I wanted to fuck Kaia from her was almost impossible. On top of being nosy, she also had no filter on her mouth. She said everything she thought without hesitation.

"Where's Trystan tonight?" Cam asked dryly.

"With his girlfriend," I lied. Camryn's had a thing for Trystan for longer than I can remember, but Trystan is a free spirit.

She laughed. "Girlfriend?" She shook her head. "He

doesn't have a girlfriend." The song changed, and Cam jumped and pushed off the bar. "Catch ya later, Jax."

Camryn danced her way over to join Kaia, who was chatting with Owen and some tall asshole in the middle of the dance floor. The unknown asshole was a little too close to Kaia for my comfort, but I wasn't going to make a scene. Not yet, anyway. He dropped his head to her ear, and his hand slid up, settling just above her ass, and my eyes went wide as her body tensed. Owen's eyes flashed down to the asshole's hand and then back to me just as I pushed off the bar.

"Hey, man." Owen scowled, shoving the guy's hand off Kaia. "No touchy touch." The guy laughed awkwardly, throwing his hands up. Owen wasn't just protecting her; he was protecting me from killing him and going to prison. Which meant I would be off the team.

My gaze scanned over Kaia and the asshole standing next to her. There was no way I was going to let Camryn help her. That was the kind of guy she would send Kaia home with—or worse.

Twisting back to the bar, I held up two fingers to the bartender, letting her know I needed another round of tequila.

6

Kaia

The clock in my car flashed three a.m. when I swerved down the long, narrow driveway towards the house.

Something was blocking the driveway. Tapping the brakes, I leaned forward, flashing on my brights to try to make out the dark blob in the middle of the driveway.

It was a person... Fuck!

I threw the car in park, jumped out, and rushed to the person. Saying a silent prayer, whoever it was, wasn't dead.

"Are you okay?" I shouted, dropping to my knees beside the person.

"Go away," Jax slurred. He was trashed. I rolled back on my butt, annoyed that he scared me like that, and relieved there wasn't a dead person in my driveway.

"Seriously?" I rolled my eyes. "Why are you passed

out in the driveway?" I caught sight of something in my peripheral vision, and my gaze snapped over to his bike lying sideways in the grassy area just off the concrete driveway. "Did you drive home?"

"Is this where you pretend to care about me, Baby Cruz?" he slurred, rolling over to his back, giving the perfect view of the side profile of his perfect face, his sexy full lips, structured jawline and sharp cheekbones. "How else was I supposed to get home?"

"You could have waited until the end of my shift, and I could have given you a ride."

"And give you another chance to tease me?" He scowled, staring up into the starry night. "No thanks."

"Tease you?" I repeated, drawing out the words more as a question. Me, tease him? That was almost comical. He was obviously trashed. "Okay, buddy, we should get you to bed." I hopped up to my feet and leaned down to grab his hands.

"You think you're so slick, don't you?" he asked with a slight edge to his tone. I raised my eyebrows. "Always showing your ass like a little slut. Teasing and taunting." This was typical Jax behavior.

"You know what," I shoved his wrist away, "fuck this. Sleep in the driveway." I turned to storm off to leave him to sleep off his insanity in the driveway, but I didn't move fast enough. His long fingers curled around my wrist.

"Jax," I yelped when he jerked, and I fell straddling

his lap. I quickly moved to push off of him. Sitting up, he locked his arms around my waist. Chest to chest, his lips so close his ragged breath fanned my lips, and the sweet smell of liquor hit my nose.

This was a dream, right? I'd had this dream before—more times than I'd like to admit.

"Tell me I'm wrong," he breathed against my lips, sending chills racing over my body. This definitely wasn't a dream. "Tell me you don't leave the bathroom door open while you shower to tease me." The only time I ever left the door open was if he wasn't home, and I knew he wouldn't be home, though the thought of teasing him had my attention. The idea of being able to turn on a man who had girls falling at his feet was interesting. Not only was Jax stupid hot, but he was also the star college hockey player predicted to go pro. Girls came from everywhere for a shot with him, and he thought I was teasing him.

"You're wrong." I tried to hide the tremble in my voice.

A slow smile spread across his face. "I can feel your pulse racing." He smirked. "Does this make you nervous?"

"Jax," I breathed, eyes locked on his. My heart was pounding so wildly that I thought it might explode. "We should go inside." Pressing my lips into a thin line, I averted my gaze to look around the yard. Anyone could see us, and how would that look? My dad would flip. Jax's mom would definitely flip.

Jax was my stepbrother and not a new stepbrother. I was twelve when we moved in together. I was fourteen when we started sharing a bathroom. Now, we were both adults, and the chemistry had shifted, I thought.

I didn't know what this was, but it couldn't happen, and Jax would realize that, too, if he wasn't trashed.

"Jax," I hissed. "We should go inside. Now." His eyes lingered on my lips for longer than normal as he slowly started to nod. I blew out a breath, saying a silent thank you that he agreed with me. Jax was double my size, and if he didn't want to do something, there was no way I would make him. I gasped when he rolled, pinning me underneath him. "Jax."

"Chill, Baby Cruz," he said, pushing off me before pushing up to his feet. "I couldn't get up with you sitting on me." I hopped to my feet, quickly dusting myself off. "You're right. We should go inside." He leaned forward, charging me, scooping me up, and tossing me over his shoulder.

"What the actual fuck, Jax?" I growled, but he ignored the question, carrying me into the house, up the stairs, and into his bedroom. Jax wasn't as drunk as I thought he was. Had this all been a game? He tossed me onto his bed. "What are you doing?"

"Going to bed," he mumbled, dropping his pants before reaching back and pulling off his shirt. I was so confused. Biting the inside of my cheek, my gaze trailed over his thick muscular thighs, up to the very prominent cock outline underneath the thin material of his black boxer briefs, up to his tight, tanned and toned torso. When my gaze made it up to his face, a blush heated my cheeks when his lips curled up into that sinister smirk he wore perfectly. He'd noticed I was checking him out. He climbed onto the bed, and I shifted to get off, but he looped an arm around my waist, dragging me back up to him.

"Jax," I growled, shoving away his arm. "What the fuck are you doing?"

"Do you want my help or not?" he asked. I froze, narrowing my eyes at him.

"Help?" He nodded, and I realized what he was saying. I did want his help—no, I needed his help, and for some insane reason, I trusted him. "Yes."

"Then lay down," he muttered, holding up the blanket for me to slide underneath. The same blanket he was under, almost naked.

"What if someone sees us?"

"No one cares." He groaned. "We are both adults free to make our own choices." He was partially right, but if my dad came home and I was in Jax's bed, there would be a fight. "Lay down, Baby Cruz. Stop overthinking everything. This is why you're still a virgin. You think too much." He was right. I overthought everything, always, but I didn't know how not to.

"I don't get how this is going to help?"

"Have you ever shared a bed with a man before?" he asked, leaning up on his arm. I shook my head. "Then lay down. We are taking baby steps."

Sucking in a deep breath, I tried to steady my hands as I slid in beside him. He wrapped an arm around my waist, jerking me flush against him. Holy fuck, he felt good. I melted into him.

"Those can't be comfortable," he said, jerking on my shorts. They weren't comfortable. They were tight and short, but I wasn't going to tell him that. "Take them off."

"What?" I snapped.

"Kai," he groaned. "If you want my help, then stop questioning me. You're going to have to trust me." He'd said, Kai. Something about the way he said my name made my stomach flutter. "I'm not going to fuck you if that's what you're freaking out about." And the fluttering is gone. Of course, he wasn't going to fuck me. I wasn't his type. I wasn't pretty and skinny enough. I saw the girls he brought home, tall, thin, massive fake boobs. He flicked open the button, slid down my zipper, and I wiggled out of the shorts, kicking myself for wearing the tiniest thong I owned today. He pulled my bare ass flush against him, and I felt him. The hardness between his legs and I couldn't help but wonder was that for me? Because of me?

"Have you ever slept in the same bed with a woman?" I whispered as his hand trailed up the back of my shirt?

"No," he breathed against my neck as he popped my bra open. Holy fuck. I squeezed my thighs together to try to keep them from shaking. *Pull yourself together, Kai.* I pulled each strap of my bra off, sliding it through the armhole of my tank before tossing it to the floor. I was drawing the line at taking my shirt off. "But I'm not intimidated by intimacy either."

I sucked in a breath as his fingers teased the sensitive skin above my panty line. "Have you ever touched yourself?" A blush crept up, heating my cheeks, and I almost choked on the lump in my throat.

I cleared my throat. "Yes," I whispered, a heavy dose of embarrassment washing over me.

"Show me." The heat from his breath teased the sensitive skin where my shoulder met my neck. Something about this was so incredibly hot—his smell, his touch, his low, raspy voice, his boldness—but I didn't move.

"I think you had way too much to drink, buddy," I chuckled awkwardly, trying to hide the tremble in my voice.

"You're probably right," he breathed against the shell of my ear, sending a chill racing through me and heating my core. I squeezed my thighs tightly. "But you want my help, and I'm giving it to you." He slid his hand over mine, dragging it down my torso to just above my panty line. "Show me."

7

Jaxtyn

If Kaia wanted my help, she would get it, but it would be on my terms. Between the mixture of alcohol, my throbbing cock, and lust coursing through my veins, I was no longer thinking logically.

"Show me," I repeated in a low husky voice. I wasn't new to watching a girl play with her pussy, but already being hard for a girl before she'd touched herself was a whole new ball game for me.

Our spooning position wouldn't allow me to see much, but I didn't need to. I wanted to hear what she sounded like when she came. The arm under her head wrapped tightly around her, holding her close to me.

Her fingertips slid below her thin, lacy panties, and her legs shifted, allowing room for her hand.

"That's it, baby," I whispered, so the warmth of my breath fanned over the exposed skin of her neck. "Play with that tight little pussy." She gasped, and I wasn't sure if it was the dirty talk or if she'd found that spot. Maybe both. Her shoulder bounced in a slow rhythm. "I bet you're soaking wet. Dripping wet for me, aren't you, baby girl?" When she whimpered, I knew. "Does it make you hot when I breathe dirty, disgusting words in your ear?"

"Yes," she cried out as her legs quivered and my cock throbbed against her ass.

Closing my eyes, I listened to each little sound she made and cursed under my breath, realizing it might be harder than I thought not to participate, but that wasn't an option. I was only going to help build her confidence sexually and send her on her way, but the thought of this body, her body pressed against someone else, sent a wave of anger simmering low in my stomach.

"Don't stop," she whimpered. I slid my hand around her small waist, stopping underneath her wrist just above her panty line so I could feel every move she made.

"What do you want to hear, baby girl?" I whispered, trailing my lips up her neck as she arched her neck into me. "Do you want to hear how hard you made me right now?" I ground my erection against her bare ass. "Or how deep I want to bury my cock inside your tight little pussy right now?"

"Oh fuck," she moaned, and a slow smile spread across my face; little-miss-innocent liked it dirty, and knowing that would torture me for the rest of my life. Her stomach muscles tightened, and I knew she was close. She rolled her hips, working them harder against her fingers. Fuck I wanted to see it, but I knew it would be too much. I wouldn't be able to control myself.

Desire raced through me, and I clamped my eyes closed as a groan slipped free. My entire body ached, begging to touch her. It was almost too much now. All the blood in my veins rushed to the tip of my swelling cock, begging for a release as I ground it harder against her ass. Her moans grew deeper, and every nerve ending in my body was awake and on high alert.

"Fuck, Kai, I want to taste that sweet pussy." I groaned; every single word I'd said was true. Kissing and nipping my way up her neck, she arched her back, pressing her ass harder against me. "I want to know what you taste like when you come."

"Jax," she whimpered, her body vibrating against me. I wasn't done. I could have told her every single disgustingly dirty thought I'd ever thought about her, but that was all she needed. "Oh...Fuck!" Her body tensed, and I knew she was coming hard. Probably harder than she'd ever done alone, and everything about that made me hot, sending me spiraling over the edge. I exploded without even touching myself.

Holy fuck, that had never happened before. I'd never ever come so hard grinding myself against a girl.

"Omigod," she panted as she slid her hand out of her panties. I had to know, to know what she tasted like.

My fingers curled around her wrist. She rolled to her back, and her breath hitched as she watched me bring her soaking fingers to my lips. My eyes locked on hers, and my tongue slipped out and across her fingers before I sucked two of them through my lips, cleaning every ounce of her off them. Her gaze flicked to my lips as her mouth gaped open. She tasted even sweeter than I thought.

After tonight, she probably wouldn't be scared of intimacy anymore. I'd hoped she wouldn't because I was not sure if I could keep my hands off her if she ended up back in my bed again. I hadn't expected to feel like this after, like hearing wasn't enough anymore. Now, I needed to see her come like I needed to be the reason she came.

I was so fucked.

STANDING at the foot of my bed, freshly showered, I watched Kaia sleep peacefully in my bed. Last night, we'd crossed a line, and now there was no going back, and I wasn't entirely sure how to deal with it.

"Hey," I whispered, strolling around the side of the

bed. She didn't move. "Get up." Nothing. I didn't typically have to kick girls out of my bed the following morning because I never invited them to stay. I usually made it clear from the beginning that we fucked, and they left. For some reason, I didn't want Kaia to leave last night, but now I was sober, and she had to go.

Grabbing the pillow under her head, I jerked out from under her. "What the..." She shot up, her gaze flashing to me. She rolled her eyes, falling back onto the mattress.

"You weren't supposed to actually sleep in here." I tossed the pillow at her.

Leaning up on her arms and letting the pillow fall to the floor, she pinched her face. "You told me to."

"What if someone saw you?" I shoved my hands in the pockets of my sweats.

"Seriously," she hissed. "You told me to stay."

"I was drunk."

"Here I was," she growled, throwing the blanket off her, "worried it might be awkward this morning." She rolled out of my bed, only wearing her tank and tiny lacy thong. "But nope, you're still the same asshole." She reached down, ripping her shorts and bra off the ground, not bothering to cover herself. I fought the smile tugging at the corner of my lips. She'd never been a morning person.

"Do you still want my help?" I smirked.

"Are you bipolar?" she muttered, cutting through the bathroom to her room.

"Is that a no?" I laughed, following her.

Blowing out an exaggerated sigh, she spun around. "Yes, I want your help. I thought we established that last night."

"I was drunk."

"So you don't remember..." she trailed off. I remembered everything. The way she tasted, the way she sounded, the way she felt against me, but because that couldn't happen again, I decided to lie, making this all less awkward.

"No," I lied. Hurt flashed across her pretty face, and I wanted to kick myself. "Do you work today?" I quickly changed the subject. She shook her head. "I have classes this morning and practice after. We can talk about a plan tonight." She nodded. "Listen, this stays between us, okay?" Pressing her lips into a thin line, she nodded. "Even from Camryn." She hesitated for a moment but then nodded again. The last thing I needed was for everyone to know my business with Kaia, and Camryn already knew too much.

I SPENT the rest of the day unable to focus on a fucking thing. I failed the test I'd been studying for the past two weeks because the only thing I could think about was how Kaia sounded last night when she came.

Fuck...

My skates glided effortlessly across the ice as I skidded to a stop and dropped the puck, lining it up. I was early, but I needed to work off some pent-up energy before practice started. I slapped the puck with my hockey stick, using every ounce of built-up aggression to hit it as hard as I could, sending it soaring across the ice.

"Oh good," Owen muttered sarcastically. "You're in a good mood for once." I rolled my eyes. "Want to talk about it before practice? Before Coach benches you for the next game because you have anger issues."

I snorted a laugh. "Coach can't afford to bench me," I snapped, dropping another puck and lining my stick up with it.

"Seriously, man." Owen dropped a puck. "Kaia again?" I groaned as I sent another puck soaring across the clean ice. "What did she do now?"

"She spent the night in my bed." Owen's mouth gaped as his eyes widened. "And now I can't think about anything else."

"Did you..." he started.

"No," I cut him off. We didn't fuck, which was what he was going to ask, and he definitely didn't need to know what we did do.

"Well, that's why."

"She asked for my help," I said, twisting to see him. Cocking his head, he narrowed his eyes. "She wants me to help her lose her virginity. So she's less awkward around guys."

"I'm not understanding the problem. Sounds like a win-win."

"The problem is still the same." I shoved my hand through my hair. "She's still my step-sister. She still lives in the bedroom next to mine. We share a bathroom. I can't fuck her and never see her again."

"So, are you going to help her?" Owen asked.

"Yeah." I nodded. "I'm going to help her build her confidence enough to help her find someone else to fuck."

"Really?" Owen scowled. "So, you've spent the last few years keeping guys away from her, threatening anyone who gets near her, and now you're okay with her fucking someone else?" He threw his head back in laughter.

"Shut up," I growled.

"Look, that sounds like you'll be more sexually frustrated than normal," Owen muttered as our gazes flicked over to see Michael Moore, one of our teammates, hit the ice.

"Yeah," I said, watching as Michael skated towards us from the other end of the rink. "I'm supposed to start helping her tonight, but I think I need to get laid first."

"Nicole was asking about you today in class," Owen said, and I inwardly groaned. Nicole was that one girl who would drop everything and run to your side, hoping this time she'd get to keep you, but I knew it would never be more than a quick fuck and only when there were absolutely no other options. I didn't lead her on. She knew the drill, but it didn't matter. She'd still show up with hopeful eyes every time.

"I'll call and make plans with her after practice," I said as Michael slid in beside us.

"You guys going to the after-game party tomorrow," Michael asked. We both shrugged, knowing damn well we'd be going. "You should bring Kaia."

"Oh fuck," Owen scowled, his gaze flicking between Michael and me.

Michael threw up his hands in a white flag wave. "I know she's your sister, but..."

"Step," I growled, "sister."

"Yeah." He smirked. "I saw her and her friend here yesterday skating. She's hot. I was going to ask her out."

"Oh fuck," Owen shifted to standi between Michael and me. "Hey, um, Mike. Buddy, uh, why don't you take a lap before practice? We'll let Kaia know." He pushed off, gliding away. "Do. Not. Kill him today," Owen snapped, giving me a warning shove, but we both knew I would kill him before I'd let him get near Kaia.

"I won't kill him." An evil smile spreading across my face. "But I can't promise I won't hurt him."

"Yeah." Owen pursed his lips. "You let me know how that whole helping Kaia fuck someone else goes for you." He shoved off, skating away, and I knew he was right. How was I supposed to help her give someone else what was mine?

8

Jaxtyn

I had every intention of telling Kaia I'd made plans and didn't think I could help her tonight. That we'd try again after I'd fucked someone, anyone else, but walking into the room and seeing her changed my mind. I didn't want to go fuck someone else even though I knew I should.

Kaia was lying on the couch, staring at her phone while the TV played in the background. She was wearing the one thing I couldn't resist—my oversized Crestview University sweatshirt, her hair pulled up messily in a bun on top of her head, her black-framed glasses, and fuzzy socks.

"Nice sweatshirt." I pulled up her legs, sinking on the couch, and placing her tanned legs across my lap.

"I didn't think you would mind." She was right; I

didn't mind. It looked so much better on her. "Someone hung it in my closet."

"It's yours," I said dryly, trying to hide how fucking attracted I was to her.

"So what's the plan for tonight?" she asked, not seeming to notice. "Should I go get changed?"

"No." I sighed, shaking my head. "You need to learn to be comfortable with yourself before you put yourself out there."

"Okay." She smiled. "How do I do that?"

"Why do you think you have an issue with men?" I asked. A blush crept across her pretty face as she chewed on her bottom lip. "You have to be honest with me if you want this to work, Baby Cruz."

Releasing her lip, she rolled her eyes as she blew out a sigh. "Men don't find me attractive," she whispered. A laugh bubbled up, but I caught it, shoving it back down when I realized she meant it.

"You can't be serious."

"Jax, you've told me enough how unattractive I am," she said, and my chest tightened, thinking back to all the mean things I'd said over the years. I hadn't meant any of them; in fact, I'd said them to convince myself that I didn't think she was fucking gorgeous, but it never worked.

Realization sank in; I'd done this.

"Even this morning, you told me to keep all this a secret, and last night you said you weren't going to fuck me." She raised her shoulders. "I'm not sexually attractive, I guess."

I gaped at her. I didn't know what to say. Not only had I kept guys away from her growing up, but I'd also made her feel like she wasn't beautiful. I'd never meant for any of this to go that far, and now there was no backing out.

I was all in.

I didn't know how to fix this yet, but I'd figure it out.

"Kaia." I sighed. "I didn't ask you to keep this a secret because I'm embarrassed. I asked to keep it between us so it doesn't get back to my mom or your dad."

"Oh..." Her mouth formed into the shape of an o.

"And I told you I wasn't going to fuck you because you're a virgin, not because I didn't want to."

"So, you did want to?" She narrowed her pretty blue eyes on me. Fuck. I didn't want to answer that question because once it was out there, I could never take it back.

"Hey," Syn called out, and I blew out a breath when Kaia's gaze flicked up to see her and Harlow pushing through the kitchen door. "What are you two doing?" Syn and Harlow's gaze simultaneously flicked down to see Kaia's legs lying over my lap.

Fuck. I panicked. "We were," I jumped up, shoving her legs off me, "going to watch a movie."

"Fuck, yeah," Syn shouted. "We should rent that new horror movie. You know, the one where she's possessed that just came out."

"Sounds good," I said, thankful they wanted to hang out with us. I didn't trust myself to be alone with Kaia at the moment. My gaze flicked down to her, still sitting on the couch. "You in?" Kaia didn't watch horror movies. I didn't think she hated them; she was just easily scared. "Come on." I laughed, reaching for her hand and pulling her up. "I'll protect you."

"I'll grab the snacks and meet you in the theatre room." Harlow smiled.

A built-in home theatre was on the first floor, toward the back of the house. Syn claimed the two large recliners for her and Harlow, leaving the reclining loveseat for Kaia and me. The room used to have six large recliners until Trystan and his friends had a party and ruined them with cigarette and weed burns and bodily fluid stains. The love seat was behind the last two recliners but slightly elevated on the slanted floor.

"Trystan's band got their first big gig," Syn said, settling into her seat while I set up the movie.

"When?" Kaia asked, settling into the loveseat. I already knew when and where because Trystan texted me earlier today.

"Next Saturday," Syn answered, twisting around her chair to see Kaia behind her. "We are all going." She didn't say it like an invitation; she said it like a demand, letting us know we were all going. "Oh, it's that one." Syn pointed to the TV, twisting back into her seat when the movie appeared on the massive screen.

Harlow pushed through the door with a handful of drinks and snacks. Dropping everything on the table between Syn and her recliner, she settled into her chair.

"Did you want anything, Kai?" Harlow asked.

"No."

The movie's opening credits blared through the surround sound speakers, and I flipped off the lights before settling in next to Kaia on the loveseat.

"You're cold," I whispered when I noticed she was trying to use my sweatshirt to cover her entire body. The theatre was the coldest room in the house. "Syn, toss me that blanket." Syn yanked the blanket off the back of her chair and tossed it. I threw the oversized throw blanket over Kaia before settling back into my seat to watch the movie.

I couldn't remember the last time we'd all watched a movie together. We were all so busy now that none of our lives coincided anymore, or maybe I avoided being in such close proximity to Kaia because I was scared I wouldn't be able to control myself.

Within the first fifteen minutes, Kaia was curled into my side with her eyes squeezed shut. I closed my eyes as heat rushed over me, heading straight to my dick. A blood-curdling scream blared through the speakers, and Kaia thrust herself hard against me as her fingers curled into the thin material of my t-shirt. My dick swelled, straining against my shorts.

My mind flashed back to our conversation earlier.

She didn't think she was attractive. She didn't think she turned men on. She didn't know what she did to me. Shoving an arm under her head, I pulled the blanket to cover both of us. Tonight, she would know.

"You keep rubbing up against me like this," I whispered against the shell of her ear. "I'm going to show you how much you turn me on." She sucked in a ragged breath. "Do you want to feel what you do to me?"

"Yes," she whispered, the heat from her breath fanning my cheek. I loved how eager she was. There was no hesitation in her words. Tangling my fingers into hers, I guided her hand down my chest, only stopping when I placed her hand firmly on my dick through my shorts.

"Do you feel how hard I am for you?" I breathed.

"Can I?" she whispered, her eyes darting up to where Syn and Harlow were entranced in the movie.

"Touch it," I finished, and she nodded. "You can do whatever you want. That hard-on is for you." Swallowing hard, she slid her hand under the elastic of my gym shorts, and I hissed when her hand curled around me.

"Teach me," she said, and I narrowed my eyes slightly, distracted by the hand wrapped around my dick. "Teach me how to... you know." She couldn't even say the words.

"Jerk me off?" I answered, and she nodded. "Now?" She nodded again. Holy fuck, she was fearless, but I was so down. I shouldn't have been. I should have told her no and walked away, but I couldn't, not with her hand already wrapped around me.

Sliding my hand into the elastic of my shorts, I lifted my hips and slid my shorts down before I curled my fingers around hers, stroking with her from root to tip.

Her big blue eyes watched me as her hand moved up and down, and I wanted to kiss her. I wanted to slam my mouth against hers and steal her breath away, but I couldn't. Kissing was intimate; it meant more than a hand job or even a one-time fuck.

I released her hand as she got the hang of it, stroking it herself. Studying my face, she picked up her speed, rolling her wrist over the head of my cock. My head fell back as my eyes rolled to the back of my head. I pressed my lips tightly together to keep from moaning. Her strokes quickened, pumping hard as her grip tightened.

"Fuck," I groaned against her ear. "You're going to make me come all over that pretty hand of yours." Her grip tightened as she pumped harder and faster. My hand slid under the oversized sweatshirt, finding the bare skin of her stomach, and I couldn't help but wonder if she was wearing a bra, which was the last thought I had as my entire body tensed, my balls drew tight, and I exploded on her hand.

My gaze flicked over to Harlow and Syn, who were still fixated on the movie. Pulling off my shirt, we used it to clean up the evidence of what we'd just done. Grabbing her waist, I twisted her, pulling her body into mine. I slid my hand under the sweatshirt, pressing my palm flat against her toned stomach.

"You are so fucking hot," I purred against her ear, wrapping my arms around her. Tomorrow, when I came down for my high, I would probably panic, but at that moment, I didn't care who saw us.

9

Jaxtyn

My eyes eased open; everything was still dark except the large movie screen. It took me a minute to realize where I was and who I was wrapped around.

We'd fallen asleep in the theatre.

"Eww." Syn sneered, and my eyes snapped up. Syn and Harlow stood beside me. "You're cuddling with your sister."

Panic coursed through me as I thrust forward, throwing a sleeping Kaia off the opposite end of the loveseat, and jumped up. She hit the floor with a thud. "Eww," I repeated what Syn said, instantly wincing with regret. Kaia sat up on the floor, hurt flashing across her face. Fuck. My eyes squeezed shut as regret coursed through me. I didn't mean to say it. I'd panicked. It was not just because it was my step-sister but also because I didn't fall asleep with girls and didn't cuddle.

Fuck!

No wonder she thought she wasn't attractive... because I said stupid shit like ew after she jerked me off last night. "Kaia," I started, but she pushed to her feet and stormed out of the theatre.

"Damn, bro." Syn scowled. "I was kidding. She's not your real sister. I don't get why you're so mean to her." Swallowing hard, I shoved a hand through my hair as I watched Syn and Harlow leave.

I fucked up.

By the time I'd made it upstairs, Kaia had locked herself in her room, and I'd felt like the biggest jerk ever. Dropping my head to her door, I blew out a breath. Last night, I'd tried to convince her that men were attracted to her, only to tear her down again first thing in the morning.

I needed to get out of the house.

I needed space from Kaia to think straight, and since I didn't have classes today, I decided to get in a few extra hours of ice time.

THE MINUTE my skates hit the ice, I saw her. Camryn was at the opposite end of the rink. Along with dancing and boxing, she also dabbled in figure skating, mostly for fun, and most of the time, Kaia was with her. She glided my way the minute she spotted me, but not in the 'I'm happy to see you' kind of glide. The kind of glide that says, 'You fucked with my friend again, and I'm going to fuck you up.'

"What did you do?" Cam snapped, her eyes narrowing on me, her arms crossed over her chest as she skidded to a stop, spraying shaved ice on my skates.

"Good morning, Cam." My tone thick with sarcasm. "Great to see you too."

"What did you do, Jax?" she hissed.

"I don't know what you're talking about, Cam," I said, pushing off and gliding away.

"Kaia was upset." Cam sneered, sliding in beside me. "She refused to come to skate this morning. We skate almost every morning."

I drifted to a stop.

"I fucked up." I groaned. "I said something I didn't mean and..." I trailed off.

"So apologize," she snapped.

"I tried," I muttered.

"Look, I don't know what happened," she sighed, "but it's obvious you feel bad for whatever it was, and lucky for you, Kaia doesn't hold on to grudges, and she usually gets over things quickly."

One of the things I loved about Kaia was that she forgave so effortlessly. She didn't hold on to anger or hurt. She was resilient. "Are you going with us to Trystan's first gig on Saturday?" she asked, and the corners of my mouth curved up.

"You know Trystan is never going to settle down, don't you?"

"Every man will settle for the right woman." She laughed.

"And you think you're the one, huh?" She shrugged dramatically. "I'm the only girl in this town he refuses to fuck."

"Maybe that's because he's just not that into you."

"Or maybe it's because he's in love with me." She laughed again, skating circles around me. Camryn was obsessed with Trystan. She had been for as long as I could remember, but as far as I knew, Trystan hadn't noticed her. It could be because she was so much younger than him. After all, it was weird that with all the times she threw herself at him, he'd turned her down. It could also be because she was Kaia's best friend, and Trystan and Kaia were close, but most likely, it was because Trystan was a rockstar playboy who couldn't be tied down to only one woman.

"Kaia's going with me to the cages this weekend after Trystan's concert," she said, and my gaze snapped up, meeting hers as she slid to a stop. The cages were an underground illegal fighting ring. Camryn and Kaia had no business there. "You should come."

"What the fuck, Cam?" I growled. "Are you fighting?"

"I'm considering it." She shrugged, her tone defensive.

"You keep Kaia away from there," I growled, sliding into her space. I'd been a handful of times, and it wasn't a place for a girl to get caught alone.

She rolled her eyes. "Kaia's a big girl," she said, crossing her arms over her chest. "She can make her own decisions, but you're welcome to join us if you're worried about her."

"You have no idea what type of people you are getting mixed up with if you get involved in the dark side of fighting, Cam. I can't stop you, but I promise you will fight me if you take Kaia to that bullshit."

"Whatever, Jax." She rolled her eyes and pushed off, gliding away.

Camryn knew I'd never hurt her, but there was also no way in fucking hell I was letting Kaia go to the Cages, and I knew just how to keep Cam from wanting to go to them. I'd have to get Trystan to agree, though.

10

Kaia

Wrapping the large white pool towel around me to cover my solid black bikini, I strolled through the house toward the back patio.

Another night home alone.

I hadn't heard from Jax since this morning when he referred to me as 'eww.' He'd taken off quickly; if he'd returned home, I hadn't seen or heard him.

"What are you doing here?" I asked when I noticed Trystan sitting shirtless on the edge of the pool with his feet in the water, surrounded by a cloud of smoke.

"I'm heading to practice soon," he said before taking a deep drag of his blunt. "Want some?" He held the blunt out to me, watching me out of the corner of his eye. I'd never smoked before. Every time Trystan asked, I'd always said no, but today had been shitty, and I wasn't going anywhere tonight, so why the hell not.

"Sure," I said, taking the blunt and bringing it to my lips.

"Why are you home alone again?" Trystan asked as I inhaled deeply. Too deeply. I winced before I fell into a coughing fit. Trystan laughed, and once I caught my breath, I did, too. "Do you want to come with me to practice?" I went to Trystan's practices often, but it was always a pity invite. He hated that I was always home alone. Sometimes, even a pity invite was nice, but after being referred to as 'eww' this morning, I would rather be alone.

I shook my head. "No. I'm going to slip into the hot tub and then go to bed. I skipped out on skating with Cam this morning, and she'll flip if I do it again tomorrow."

"You coming to my gig on Saturday?" He brushed the long strand of dirty blonde hair off his forehead. Trystan was hot, but not in the same way as Jaxtyn. He was tall with dirty blonde hair and dark blue eyes, thin but not in a scrawny way. He was ripped and covered from neck to feet in colorful art, with a lip and nose piercing. He shared the same sharp jawline, full lips, and perfect white smile as Jaxtyn.

I nodded as I inhaled again, and it went down smoother this time.

"Yeah, Cam and I will be there with everyone else." I exhaled.

"Cool, there's an after-party," he said. "You and Cam should come."

"We kind of already have plans." I sighed, passing the blunt back to him. "I promised I'd go to the Cages with her."

"The Cages?" he repeated, raising a brow. I nodded. "Kai, the Cages can be dangerous."

"I know," I said, sucking in a deep breath, "but I'm not going to let her go alone, and you know Cam, if she wants to do something, there's no talking her out of it."

"Well," he said, passing the blunt back. "Tell her I personally invited her to the after-party to hang out with me."

"Are you actually going to hang out with her?" I asked, my brows pinching. Trystan had never shown any interest in Cam; actually, he went out of his way to avoid her.

His lips curled into a grin. "I guess you'll have to invite her and see." If he was only inviting her to keep her away from the Cages and planned to lead her on to do that, I didn't want to be part of that.

"You know you could call her and invite her."

"You know me better than that, Kai." He laughed. "I don't call girls."

We sat on the pool's edge until the blunt was gone, and I was higher than a kite. My sides and cheeks hurt from laughing so hard. Trystan and I always got along the best out of everyone, even Harlow and Syn. Trystan was hard not to get along with, though. He was so laid back and easygoing all the time. I'd only seen him mad once in all the years I'd known him.

He flipped his phone over, and the screen lit up. "Shit," Trystan muttered. "I have to go."

"Have fun," I said as my eyes rolled and I eased my back onto the concrete pool patio deck. "I'll be here." My gaze flicked up to the sky as I threw my arms over my head. "Counting stars."

"Yeah," Trystan said, drawing out the word. He didn't seem even half as high as I was. "I can't leave you here like this."

"I got her," Jax said. My head twisted, and my gaze flicked over to see Jaxtyn beside Trystan. It was like he appeared from thin air.

"She's high, man," Trystan said, pushing up to his feet. "Like really high."

"Go," Jax said, nodding towards the door. "So you're not late."

Trystan disappeared, leaving Jax and me alone.

11

Sucking in a breath, my gaze traveled down the length of her laid out on the pool patio. The white towel lay loosely around her, revealing a small amount of tanned skin and a tiny black bikini.

"How much did you smoke?" I asked, leaning over her and grabbing her hand.

"Um..." She chuckled. "I don't know."

"Come on." I smiled, pulling her to her feet. "Let's get you inside."

"Wait," she said. "I was getting in the hot tub."

"Well, then, let's get in the hot tub."

We walked around the pool, and she dropped her towel on the patio table. Biting down on my bottom lip, my gaze raked over her almost naked body. The curves of her waist, the roundness of her ass, her full tits in the tiny black top, every inch of her made my hands twitch with a need to touch her.

"What are you doing home?" she asked, climbing over the edge and slipping into the bubbling water.

"I was hoping I could hang with you tonight," I said, sinking into the water across from her. "I owe you an apology for this morning. I'm really sorry, Kai."

"It's okay." She smiled, shrugging her bare shoulders. "It's not a big deal."

"No, it is a big deal," I said. "It's a really big fucking deal. I panicked and said something I didn't mean, and I really need to stop doing that."

"I forgive you." She smiled. I knew she would because that's just how Kaia was. She didn't hold grudges. "So, did you have plans tonight?" I shook my head. I didn't have plans because I could only think about her. She literally consumed my brain at this point. "Can I ask you something?" Her face twisted with curiosity, and I could see the wheel spinning.

"Yep." I nodded.

"How do you know when you want to kiss someone?" she asked, her brows pinching together. "Like, I've heard people say they feel something, but I didn't feel anything when I kissed Craig."

So, Craig was his name, huh? I would store that for later.

"Sounds like you kissed the wrong person," I said,

the corner of my lip curving up. I knew he was the wrong person because he wasn't me.

"What does it feel like?" she asked.

How did I describe the feeling of desire and give it the credit it was due? I couldn't, but I could show her. Pushing to my full height, I stood directly across from her waist-deep in water. She was definitely high because she didn't even hide the fact that she was eye-fucking me like she normally did. Her gaze trailed over my naked chest as her tongue swept across her lips.

"Stand up," I ordered. "And close your eyes."

"Why?"

"Could you just do what you're told?" I fought the smirk pulling at my mouth.

"That's not really my thing." She laughed, and that was the truth.

"Just shut up." I smirked, reaching out and pulling her to her feet. "And do it."

"Fine," she said, blowing out a heavy breath as she closed her eyes.

"No matter what, do not open your eyes," I ordered.

"Are you going to tell me why?"

"No."

I stepped forward, my body mere centimeters away from hers as my gaze trailed over her full lips, down the delicate curve of her throat, and I realized that the desire I was trying to explain to her was vibrating through me.

I wanted to taste that spot on her neck where her shoulder met her throat.

Leaning down, I brushed my lips against the shell of her ear. "It's a hard feeling to describe in words," I whispered, letting the heat of my breath fan across her ear, and a grin spread across my face when I felt her shudder against me. My hands curled around her waist as I pressed my body flush against hers. "So, I'll show you."

She cleared her throat. "Okay," came out as a strangled whisper.

"First, your skin starts to tingle," I breathed, trailing my fingertips over the heated, wet skin of her shoulders trailing down her arms. My lips brushed along her cheek, hovering above her lips. "Then, your breathing deepens." I pressed my forehead against hers. "Next, your stomach feels like a million tiny little butterflies are fluttering." Her lips parted, and her breath hitched as my breath fanned across her lips. My lips brushed against hers, and my mouth watered to taste her. She sucked in a deep breath as my fingertips trailed over the curves of her neck. "Now, your entire body is consumed with want and need. Nothing else matters but that overwhelming desire and need to taste the other person."

"I feel it," she breathed, and I squeezed my eyes closed, letting the feeling take over.

"Kai," I said, my tone low and husky.

"Hmm," she hummed, placing the palms of her hands flat on my chest.

"I want to kiss you."

"Then do it," she said in a breathy whisper.

"There's no going back," I said, mostly warning myself.

What the fuck am I thinking?

I couldn't kiss her and not keep her, and being attached to one person terrified me. I dropped my hands and stepped back as her eyes flashed open.

"That's what it feels like. Do you need help into the house?" My tone was cold and clipped.

Her brows furrowed in confusion. "No," she said after several long seconds. "I'm fine."

"I'll see you tomorrow." I hopped out of the hot tub and stormed into the house, not bothering to grab a towel.

Slamming the door closed, I fell forward, grabbed my knees, and breathed heavily.

What the fuck is wrong with me?

Drawing in a deep breath, I stood up and exhaled while I turned to see Kaia getting out of the hot tub.

I did it again. I ran.

No woman had ever made me feel like she did, but she wasn't the kind of girl you only wanted for one night.

My tongue swept across my lips as I watched her stroll to the table and grab her towel. Her perfect body glistened under the moonlight. She wrapped the towel around her and strolled towards the house.

I should run upstairs and lock myself in my room, but I can't. I'm drawn to her by some electric force.

She pushed through the door, freezing when she noticed me. Our gaze locked as our chests rose and fell in sync. The only sound was our labored breathing filling the room.

"Fuck it." I stormed forward, my hands gripping her face. My mouth crashed hard against hers.

I wanted to be her first real kiss. I didn't know it until now, but I wanted to be her first and last real kiss. I wanted to be her first and last everything. I didn't want to share her.

I'd thought about this moment more than I'd ever admit, and she had no idea how badly I wanted her.

Her lips parted, and I took the opportunity to dive in, exploring every inch of her mouth. She tasted like heaven and strawberries.

A horn blew in the distance, and I pulled out of the kiss. We were in the middle of the kitchen where anyone could see us.

"What was that?" she breathed.

"A kiss," I panted, releasing her face. "Was it gross?" She shook her head.

I needed to put some space between us before I threw her on the counter and did something I knew she wasn't ready for.

"Good night." I smiled, turned, and walked away.

12

Kaia

Pushing off the ice, I twirled around. It was a little after five a.m., and the rink was empty. The way I liked it.

The ice was like a second home to me. It became my escape after my mother died, but three years ago, when my skating partner Matthias was killed in a car accident, I lost my passion for the sport. I would have stopped skating altogether if it hadn't been for Camryn, who forced me every morning to get back on the ice.

Although I still had no interest in the sport, I did love skating again.

Most mornings, I wasn't alone, though. Camryn usually came, and by the time she picked me up and we got here, there were already hockey players using the ice. But this morning, Cam wasn't here, and the only sounds were my skates slicing through the fresh ice and my labored breathing.

That lasted for twenty whole minutes before the sound of a second pair of skates slid through the ice.

Jax pushed off the ice skating effortlessly towards me.

"You're here early this morning." I smiled as he circled me.

He shrugged, skidding to a stop in front of me. "I wanted to get in some ice time before classes this morning. Where's Cam?"

"She twisted her ankle last night," I said. "She's okay but wanted to rest this morning, so she's ready for Trystan's gig tonight."

"So you're alone?"

"Yes, do you plan on murdering me?" I laughed.

"Not today." He smirked. "Owen told me about Olga."

My smile faded. Olga Petrov was a skating coach. One of the best skating coaches I'd ever met, and two days ago, she'd approached me about getting back into the sport. Owen was there talking with Cam.

She wanted to train me and get me back into the sport, hoping to make it to the Olympics, but I told her I wasn't interested because I really wasn't. I wanted to skate for fun now, not for sport. Even if I wanted to, I hadn't skated like that in so long that I wasn't even sure I still had it in me.

"I knew he couldn't keep his mouth shut." I pushed

off and skating away. I already knew where this conversation was going. He was going to tell me I should do it, but I didn't want to skate without Matthias. He was the only person I'd ever skated with, and even if I wanted to find a partner, it was hard because it wasn't just a matter of finding someone who could skate. You had to have chemistry with the person.

"Stop, Kai." Jax groaned, sliding in beside me. He shifted to skate backward in front of me. "Please stop and just talk to me."

I slowly slid to a stop. "What do you want to talk about, Jax?"

"Were you in love with Matt?" he asked, and my gaze snapped up, meeting his.

No one had ever asked me that. Matt was one of my best friends, but he was in love with Camryn, and Camryn was in love with Trystan.

"I loved Matt, but I wasn't in love with him." I sighed. "He was my best friend, and I trusted him, and that's hard to find."

"Matt wouldn't have wanted you to give up the sport you love."

"Figure skating is hard," I said. "And working with a new partner is even harder. I have to trust that person to lift me, and that's not something that happens overnight."

"Do you trust me?" he asked.

"Yes, but you play hockey." I smiled. "You don't figure skate."

"I skate," he teased. "How hard could it be?"

"It's harder than you think."

"Teach me."

"Is this some kind of trick?" I narrowed my eyes suspiciously.

He shook his head.

"Okay," I said apprehensively. "Skating with a partner is a feeling. You have to be in sync. It's not easy to do, and if there's no chemistry, it will show in your performance."

"Do we have chemistry?" he asked, skating circles around me as his hand slid around my lower stomach. He slid to a stop behind me. One hand was on my thigh, and the other arm wrapped tightly around my waist. My eyes squeezed shut as I let the feel of his touch and the heat of his body consume me. "Do we, Kai? Do we have chemistry?"

We did have chemistry, but it wasn't the same chemistry I had with Matt. This was so much more intense. The kind that made me squeeze my thighs together to settle the throbbing his touch caused.

Clearing my throat, I nodded as his lips trailed down my throat. "Yes." I pulled out of his touch so I could think straight. "But I don't know if that's the same thing you need on the ice to make a good performance."

His lips curled into a smirk as I glided backward, and he followed me.

We skated side by side for what felt like forever, and our chemistry spilled over into our skating. I hadn't realized how much I'd missed this.

I hadn't skated like that with someone since the morning of Matt's death, and my legs felt like jello.

Jax skated backward, and I skated forward, hand in hand, as we slid to a stop, spinning around. My legs slid out from under me as I fell to my knees.

"My legs are done for the day." I chuckled, dropping Jax's hands and placing my palms flat on my thighs. "They haven't had a workout like this in a long time."

Jax laughed. "Maybe I can work with you in the mornings until you decide if you want to get a new partner and skate again."

"Yeah." I sighed. "That would be fun." He smiled.

"You need a minute?" He nodded to my legs.

"Just drag me to the wall," I said, reaching my hands up to him.

He leaned down, looping his arms under mine and wrapping my arms around his neck. He lifted me to my feet. His grip tightened around my waist as he lifted my skates off the ground, and I wrapped my legs around his waist.

"What are you doing?" I whispered, my mouth near his ear.

"Skating." He smiled against my cheek. He pushed

off the ice, carrying me around the rink, spinning and gliding across the ice. He leaned his head back so he could see me. "I may not be able to do all the fancy lifts, but I got this one down." He brushed a loose strand of hair out of my face.

"Yeah." I smirked. "How many girls have you done this with? I heard you were really popular with the skaters."

"None," he said, his tone so earnest I believed him. "This requires intimacy, and if you haven't noticed, I struggle with that kind of stuff."

"I've noticed," I said. "But you're doing it now." I wanted to know if this was considered intimate to him or if it was part of him helping me overcome my awkwardness with men.

"What's going on here?" Owen shouted from across the rink. Jax and I head snapped to see his skates hit the ice as he pushed off, heading towards us.

I expected Jax to freak out and drop me, but he didn't.

"Kai and I were talking about her conversation with Olga this morning," Jax said when Owen slid to a stop in front of us.

"And that requires you to carry her around the rink." Owen laughed.

"No," Jax said, our cheeks nearly pressed together. "But she's teaching me to figure skate."

"Sweet," Owen said. "Maybe Cam will teach me." His gaze darted around the rink. "Where is Cam?"

"She's home," I said. "Twisted ankle."

"Ahh," Owen said. "Well, are you ready to practice, or are you still figure skating."

"Let me take Kai up to the benches," Jax said. "And then we can smack the puck around."

"Wait a second," I snapped. "So I teach you to figure skate, but you aren't going to teach me hockey."

Jax's lips curled into a smirk. "That would require your legs to work, Baby Cruz. Unless you want me to carry you."

"You're at all of the games," Owen muttered. "You don't know how hockey is played?"

My eyes went wide as Jax's grin widened. I had never missed one of Jax's games, just like I'd never missed one of Trystan's performances or Harlow's violin recitals, but I didn't know they saw me.

"I think I should call it a day." I forced a smile. "But I'll see you guys at Trystan's show tonight."

Jax skated to the far side of the rink and stepped off the ice. My legs released around his waist, dropping to the ground, but his grip didn't loosen.

"I want to kiss you right now," he whispered against the shell of my ear.

"Owen is here," I whispered back.

"I'll see you tonight, Baby Cruz." He smirked, stepping back onto the ice and gliding away.

13

Jaxtyn

The bass of the drums and lead guitar rattled the walls of the nightclub as Trystan belted out the lyrics to his newest song. Strobe lights danced across the stage, lighting up as the crowd of screaming girls went wild. The venue was packed tonight, standing room only.

Kai, Syn, Harlow, and Cam were all dancing at the front of the stage while Owen and I hung back with our teammate, Brandon.

I ordered another round. I loved my brother, but he and I had very different tastes in music. Thank god, this was his last song, and by the time he wrapped everything up, I'd be done with my beer.

"Are you ever going to tell me what's up with you and Kai?" Owen asked before bringing the long-neck bottle to his mouth and drinking.

"Nothing to tell," I shouted.

"Oh no, man." He smirked, cocking a brow. "I saw you two this morning. I saw the way you looked at her."

"To be continued." I flashed a grin as I shrugged my shoulders. To be continued meant I didn't know. She didn't know, but we'd figure it out later. My gaze flicked to the front of the stage and straight to Kaia's perfect ass as she swayed her hips to the beat of the music. Her dark, ripped denim jeans hugged her feminine curves, not leaving much to the imagination. Her top was almost completely backless, and her long, blonde, wavy hair fell down her bare back. "I'll catch you guys later," I muttered, my feet already leading me to her.

She tensed when I pressed my body flush against hers just as their lead drummer started his solo. I slid my hand around her hip, digging my fingertips into the sensitive bare skin right above her low-rise jeans, holding her in place.

"It's just me, baby," I whispered against her ear, letting the heat of my breath and the stubble of my five o'clock shadow tease her skin, and I smiled when I felt her relax into me. I loved that she was so comfortable with me. Her hips swayed, and even though I hated dancing, like loathed it, I couldn't help but move my body with hers.

I suddenly wished I didn't have a beer in my other hand and I could use it to hold her harder against me.

As the rhythm picked up, so did the movement of

her hips, each sway getting the attention of my dick. I knew she could feel me. I knew she could feel what she did to me.

The music stopped, and I immediately released her, snapping back to reality and realizing we were in the middle of a crowd, not just with strangers but also with my sister, her sister, my brother, and our friends.

"Chill out," I mumbled to myself. There was no reason to panic, I reminded myself, and for the first time, I made myself relax and not freak out.

Trystan and his band packed up as the club's DJ took over.

"That was fucking awesome," Syn screamed once we made it back to the bar where I'd left Owen and Brandon. "They are definitely getting a record deal."

"God damn, girl." Owen sucked in a breath. His gaze raked over Syn. "Could that dress get any smaller?" Syn wore a tiny, tight, strapless black dress that somehow stood out against her pasty white skin. Her black hair was pulled back into a loose ponytail, showing off all her artwork.

On Syn's eighteenth birthday, she started interning at a tattoo parlor with a friend who did all my tattoos. He was the only one I trusted not to take advantage of a naive young girl trying to get into the field of tattooing. Since then, she'd covered most of her body in different pieces of art she'd designed. Some of the art was tattooed by her, and others by him.

"You like it, don't you?" Syn spun for him, and I rolled my eyes.

"Hey," Kai said, tugging my shirt. I raised a brow, lowering my head so I could hear her. "How about tonight?"

I leaned back to look at her, my brows furrowed. "What about it?" I asked, my gaze lingering on her lips.

"You know." She scowled before relaxing her face. "Teach me how to tell if a guy is flirting."

My mouth remained closed, but my jaw dropped. I almost blurted out, 'Are you serious?' But I knew she was. She didn't know I'd watched every move she'd made all night. She didn't realize the way I touched her was flirting, which made me smile.

I couldn't explain why I loved that about her, but I did, and I didn't want her to lose that.

I leaned down. "Not here," I whispered. "It's too loud and crowded." I lied. I had zero intentions of helping her hook up with someone else, but I'd show her what flirting was. I'd lay it on so thick she wouldn't be able to miss it.

"Hey," Cam shouted. "Let's go. We're all heading to the party."

My plan had worked. Trystan personally invited Camryn and Kaia to his after-party, and I knew Cam wouldn't be able to say no to him. He was her weakness.

We all loaded up in our vehicles, the girls in one car and the guys in another. I let the girls pull out first and followed them to Trystan's bandmate's house about twenty minutes from the venue, and by the time we got there, the house was already packed with partiers.

14

Jaxtyn

We all unloaded, and most of us went our separate ways.

"I'm going to go find Trystan," Cam said, flashing Kaia and me a smile.

"You want a drink?" I asked when we managed to push through the crowd into the large kitchen.

"No," she shouted, shaking her head. It was hard to hear anything between the music and all the people. "It's a little crowded in here. I'm going to go outside." I nodded and followed her toward the back door.

The backyard was massive, with a large inground pool, an enormous pool house, and a lot more open space than the inside.

"So, tell me, Jax," she said, twisting to face me. "How do I know the difference between someone being friendly and flirting, and is there a difference between I only want to fuck you flirting and I want to date you flirting?" My tongue swept across my bottom lip as I watched her, contemplating what I wanted to say. I opened my mouth but snapped it shut when Cam bolted by us, visibly upset.

"I'm leaving," she muttered as she passed.

"Wait," Kaia said, stopping her. "What happened?"

"Trystan." She sniffled, pointing toward the pool house. "He's screwing some girl in the pool house right now. He didn't invite me because he wanted me here. He invited me because he wanted you here." She stormed off. I'd never seen Cam so upset in all the years I'd known her.

"I—" Kaia started until she noticed Trystan stumbling from the pool house, situating his pants as he stormed toward us.

"That's fucked up, Trystan," Kaia hissed. Hurt flashed across her pretty face. "You know she likes you, and you led her on." She whipped around, ready to storm off, but he caught her by the arm.

"Kai," he snapped. His tone was sharp and clipped. "I would tell you I'm sorry, but the truth is I'm not. I would do it again if it meant keeping you away from the cages. That place is dangerous, and truthfully, I didn't want Cam there either."

"Let me go, Trystan," she snarled. We were starting to draw attention, not that either of them cared.

"You're not going to the cages," he ordered. His tone commanding.

"It's two against one," I said dryly. "You're not going to the cages."

"What the fuck, Jax?" she growled, attempting to shove me out of the way. "Move." I shook my head. "This is bullshit. If anything happens to her, I'll never forgive you."

"She's not going either," Trystan mumbled. "Now, if you can handle her, I'll deal with the other one."

"No," Kaia snapped, surging forward, but I hooked an arm around her waist, holding her back. "You stay away from her. You're not going to manipulate her and then hurt her."

"I'm not going to hurt her," Trystan said over his shoulder as he strolled away disappearing into the house.

"What the fuck just happened?" She scowled. "This was all some big ploy to keep me from the cages, and you thought using Cam was the way to go?"

"Maybe you haven't realized it yet, baby," I whisper-hissed, leaning into her. "I will use anyone to protect you."

She snorted a sarcastic laugh. "I will never trust you again," she spat out, crossing her arms over her chest. I didn't believe her, but even if I did, it wouldn't matter because I would give up everything to keep her safe, including her trust.

"Thanks for the warning." I chuckled. "Next time, we'll lock you in your room." She rolled her eyes, and if she wasn't so mad, I'd kiss her, but she'd probably slap me. Blowing out a heavy sigh, I grabbed her shoulders, twisting her to look at me. "Look, Kai, I don't know if Trystan likes Cam or not, but I know he cares about her, and he didn't want her at the Cages either. In fact, he had a whole backup plan in case our original plan didn't work, and it wasn't just for you. It was for her, too, but Trystan is a free spirit, and he's not ready to be tied down." I dropped my hands and shoved them into my pockets. "But I don't think he intended to hurt her."

She blew out a heavy breath. "He chased after her," she said, her lips curling into a grin. "Rock god, Trystan West, chased after a girl." We both fell into a fit of laughter at the thought.

"He left his blow job for her. That has to mean something, right?" She nodded.

"I'm sorry." I sighed after a few seconds.

"It's okay." She shrugged. "But you could have just asked me not to go."

"You wouldn't have listened."

"Touché." She laughed.

"Come on, Baby Cruz." I smirked, sliding an arm around her shoulders and guiding her toward the door. "Let's get you a drink and teach you a thing or two about flirting."

15

Standing in the kitchen of the main house, my eyes narrowed as I followed Jax's line of sight.

"Pick one." He smirked, pointing to a group of guys across the room. "And show me what you got."

"So, you enjoy watching me embarrass myself," I snarled, rolling my eyes. I cocked my head to the side as he brought his beer bottle to his lips. "I can't just walk up to guys and say, 'Hey, would you like to fuck me.'" Jax choked on the beer, spraying it across the room. Luckily, no one was in his path. Jax wiped the spilled beer from his face.

"What's going on?" Owen smiled as he and Brandon Benson slid up beside Jax.

"Jax is teaching me how to flirt."

"How do I get in on that?" Brandon teased, and my cheeks heated. My gaze flicked to Jax, who was piercing

Brandon with a threatening glare. Brandon's smile faded, and he cleared his throat. "I mean..."

"He means nothing," Jax cut him off, his gaze flashing to me. "Was he flirting or just being nice?" My brows pinched. How the heck was I supposed to know? Brandon Benson was hot. Like the kind of hot that made a girl nervous, and I probably would be too if I hadn't grown up with him. He was tall, with dark hair and eyes, a sharp jawline, full lips, and a perfect white smile, and I was sure he was sporting some rock-hard muscles under his clothes. He could have any girl he wanted. I'd seen them throw themselves at his feet. So why would he flirt with me? "Come on, Baby Cruz? Was he flirting or not?"

"No." I smiled, confident with my answer. "He was being nice." Jax huffed out a groan as his gaze flicked up to Brandon.

"Were you flirting, man?"

Brandon's brows pinched as his gaze met Jax's, and his lips pressed into a thin line. Owen's head began to shake 'no' slowly. I was pretty sure I was missing something, but I had no idea what. "Just answer the question."

"Yes," Brandon said hesitantly, his gaze never leaving Jax's. "I was flirting."

"Were you flirting to be nice or because you like me?" I asked, curiosity twisting my face. "Or because you want to fuck me?"

"Holy shit," Jax cut me off, jumping out of his seat.

"Do not answer that!" He pointed a threatening glare Brandon's way, but Brandon couldn't hide the smirk twitching at the corners of his lips.

"What?" I snapped. "How am I supposed to know if I don't ask, and who better to ask than a bunch of guys I grew up with?"

Jax's brows knitted together as he glared at me. His mouth opened, but before he could say anything, everyone's attention was drawn to the commotion behind me. None of us had time to register what was happening before everything erupted, and the room went crazy.

"Fight," someone chanted. I whipped around but was shoved hard by two massive men throwing punches and not caring about the people they took out in the process.

"Fuck," Jax muttered, moving to shield me from the fight that had gone from two men to eight. "Go find Tryst and Cam." I wasn't sure who he was talking to. Jax leaned forward, tossed me over his shoulder, and stormed out of the house.

"What happened?" I mumbled when Jax dropped me to my feet in front of my car.

"That's what happens when too much testosterone and alcohol are mixed." He groaned. Owen and Brandon strolled out of the house, but Trystan and Cam weren't with them.

"Where's Cam?" I asked.

"They are," Owen paused, "busy." He drew out the word.

"Busy..." I said, mocking his tone. "Doing what?"

"Let's get out of here," Jax said. "You guys leaving now, too?"

"I'm not leaving Cam," I said.

"Trystan is giving her a ride home," Owen said. "But we are going to hang out. We'll make sure she gets home."

"Here," Jax said, popping the trunk to his car before tossing Owen the keys. "We'll take Kai's car. You guys can take mine. We'll meet you at my house later." Owen nodded before following Brandon back into the house.

I texted Cam quickly, ensuring she was okay, while Jax grabbed his bag from his car.

Kaia: Are you okay? There was a fight inside.

Cam: Yes, I'm with Trystan in one of the back rooms.

Kaia: Are you behaving?

Cam: Absolutely not...

I smiled at the phone. I was glad she was happy, and I hoped Trystan wasn't going to hurt her.

"Give me your keys," Jax said, holding his hand out.

"It's my car." I narrowed my eyes at his hand.

"And I'm going to drive it." He smirked. Why did that

turn me on? Was it the fact that he was telling me what he would do or that he was driving? Maybe both. I hadn't had much experience with men. In fact, growing up, it was almost like I had some contagious disease that only affected men because they always steered clear of me. So, I was still learning what I liked and didn't.

I dropped my keys into his hand, and he jerked open my door.

"Where are we going?" I asked once we were on the road and definitely not heading toward the house. He didn't answer. "Is this where you take me to some deserted location and kill me?"

"Or maybe it's where I take you to a deserted location and have my way with you!"

My breath caught in my throat as heat flooded my body, shooting straight down between my legs. I squeezed my thighs tightly together to alleviate the pressure building. He was teasing, I knew he was, but it didn't change the way he made me feel.

"And what way would you have me, Jax?" I purred, trying my hand at teasing. His jaw clenched, and his hand tightened on the steering wheel as he eased to a stop at the red light.

His hand still white-knuckling the steering wheel, he twisted up on the arm propped on the armrest, leaning over into my space. "Do you want me to tell you all the dirty things I'd do to you?" He ran his tongue across the bottom of his top teeth as his heat gaze raked over my body before slowly coming back and lingering on my mouth. My tongue swiped across my dry lips as my heart pounded erratically. I was out of my league, and we both knew it. His hand slid off the center console, and his large hand wrapped around my upper thigh. "Do you want me to tell you how badly I want to spread these thighs?" His voice was low and raspy. I sucked in a sharp breath when his fingertips dug into the tender flesh, jerking my thighs apart. "And all the things I'd do between them?"

I swallowed hard as the heat pooled between my legs, and I was pretty sure my panties were drenched. His heated breath brushed across my lips, and I literally felt like I might come undone right there in my passenger seat in front of him.

I yelped, nearly jumping out of my seat when a horn blew behind us, and Jax released me, snapping back in place at the wheel as he eased off the break and surged forward. My body and mind were still reeling, but he seemed completely unfazed as he swerved the car into the skating rink parking lot.

It felt so real, but it was all part of the lesson, and I needed to keep reminding myself of that.

"You have your skates?" Jax asked, pulling up to the front entrance. The rink was closed to the public this late at night, but Jax's grandfather was the owner, so we had keys and our own personal locker room. Even though he wasn't actually my grandfather, he'd always treated me like one of his own. All of Jax's family did, even his father.

"I have a pair in my trunk." I smiled. "What are we doing?"

"Skating." He smirked, pushing his door open. "Oh, wait." He reached into his pocket and pulled out two tickets. "Before I forget." He handed me the tickets.

"What is it?" I asked, my eyes narrowing on the tickets.

"My first game is next weekend," he said. "It's an away game, and I thought you and Cam might like to view the game from good seats for once."

"Omigod, these are ice level." My gaze snapped up, meeting his. "How did you get these? Cam and I have tried to get tickets like these since we started going to the games."

"I know people that know people." He laughed, sliding out of the car. "Come on, Baby Cruz. Let's skate."

FIFTEEN MINUTES LATER, Jax flipped on the arena lights while I laced up my skates. I couldn't hide the grin spreading across my face. The arena was my favorite place, especially when it was empty.

Jax stepped onto the ice, twisting to offer me his

hand like I was new to the ice, and I couldn't help but wonder if this was his play when he brought girls here.

"So what are we doing here?" I asked when my skates hit the ice.

"We are going to play a game." He smirked, gliding around me.

"What kind of game?" I asked as my gaze followed him.

"I'm going to teach you to play hockey," he said, and I couldn't fight the smile pulling at my lips. I'd asked him to teach me when we were younger. He always said no. "And any time I flirt with you, you get to call a penalty."

"Do I get to throw you into the penalty box?" I asked, spinning.

"Only if you plan to join me inside naked." This was going to be so easy. Jax said what was on his mind. He had no filter. He wasn't like other guys who beat around the bush.

"You're definitely going down." I laughed, running my fingers through my hair before gathering it together and pulling it into a ponytail.

"You think?" He laughed cocking his head and raising his brows as his lips curled into a smirk.

"Uh, no offense, Jax, but your flirting isn't exactly subtle."

He glided into my personal space, placing a hand on my waist as he circled behind me. "Flirting because I want to fuck you," he breathed against the shell of my ear, "and flirting because I like you are two very different things, Kai." My breath caught in my throat.

I knew he was right, and it was definitely something I was struggling to tell the difference between. I didn't want to end up with another guy who expected me to put out or get out again.

So, Jax's bluntness equated to fucking, then what did his flirting look like?

"Do you flirt with a lot of girls?" I asked, gliding around him as he reached into the black bag he'd been carrying and pulled out black pucks, tossing them across the ice.

"No, only the ones I like."

"I've never seen you with the same girl." How could you tell if he liked a girl if he never saw the same girl twice?

"Fact." Did that mean he didn't flirt with girls? Jax was a complete mystery to me. Sex came easy to him, but intimacy seemed to scare him away.

"Tell me how the game works," I said when he tossed the black bag over the wall.

"If you think I'm flirting, you can call a penalty, but if you're wrong, you have to complete a dare."

"And if I'm right."

"Then I'll complete a dare, but if you miss me flirting with you, you'll also have to complete a dare."

"Let's do this."

He spent the next hour showing me how to hit the

puck and skate with the puck, and I was so focused on the stupid puck I forgot why we were actually there.

"I've flirted with you several times, and you've missed all of them," Jax muttered.

"I guess I can't do two things at once." I shrugged. The corner of his lip twitched.

"Dare time."

Shit. "Hit me with it."

"I dare you to take Petrov up on her offer and train with her."

"What?" I snapped. "Jax, no."

"Just train," he said. I shook my head. "For a couple of months. If you decide you don't want to skate after that, I'll never say anything about it again." He glided into my space, and I shifted to move away, but I wasn't fast enough; he caught me by the waist, pulling me against him.

"I want a different dare," I said, rolling my eyes.

He cupped my face, pulling my gaze up to meet his. "Will you at least think about it?" Sucking in a deep breath, I sighed before I nodded.

"Wait." I narrowed my gaze. "You're flirting." His lips twitched, and I knew I was right. I pulled out of his grasp and did a happy skate around him. "My turn."

"Hit me with it," he mocked me.

"Hmm," I hummed, pursing my lips. He pushed me outside my comfort zone, and I wanted to do the same.

"I dare you to text Cam and tell her your real feelings for her."

"What if I really do hate her?"

"You don't; nobody hates Cam." Everyone loved Cam.

He froze, narrowing his eyes on me. "Kai, do you think I have romantic feelings for Cam?"

"Doesn't everyone?"

His lips parted as he stared blankly at me. "Do you think I would leave Cam with Trystan if I liked her like that?" I raised my shoulders, pursing my lips. "You really don't get it, do you?" He opened his mouth like he was going to say something but then snapped it shut.

"What?"

"Never mind." he skated away. He was shutting down on me like he always did.

"Jax," I snapped. "Don't do that." I pushed off the ice, speeding up behind him. "Don't shut me out like that." He spun, twisting to face me and continuing to glide backward. "What's going on?"

"You really want to know?" I nodded, and he slid around behind me before sliding in front of me, his hands wrapped around my waist, pulling me up so that my legs wrapped around his waist, and I slid my arms around his neck as he glided to a stop just before we hit the glass wall of the penalty box. "I'm not interested in Cam or any other girl." Pressing me tightly between him and the glass, he brushed his lips against mine, and I wasn't sure if we were still playing the game anymore. "You, Kai," he breathed. "I like you." My mouth went dry. If this was part of the game, it was so many levels of fucked up, but I didn't care.

His heated, labored breathing fanned across my lips, sending chills soaring over my skin. My heart pounded, and my stomach fluttered with anticipation. I thought he was going to kiss me, but he didn't. His grip loosened, and he dropped my skates to the ice.

He spun and skated away, leaving me completely confused. Was that real? Or was he still playing the game?

I should have let it go, but I couldn't. I was tired of the game. I was tired of feeling confused when it came to him because anytime he opened up to me, he shut down just as fast.

"No," I growled, shoving against the ice and racing toward him. "You don't get to do that anymore, Jax." I circled around him.

"What is that, Baby Cruz?" He groaned. Wow, we'd gone all the way back to Baby Cruz.

"Don't do that," I snapped. "Don't say shit like that to me and then push me away."

He slid into my space, pressing his face against mine. "What should I do, Kai?" he breathed, but his tone was colored with both anger and lust. "Should I tell you every disgustingly dirty thought I've ever had about you?" He dropped to his knees, pulling my skates out from under me but caught me before my ass hit the ice and pulled me onto his lap. "Or should I rip your clothes off right here and fuck you like I've dreamed of for years." I sucked in a sharp breath as heat bloomed over my chest and face. He leaned forward, laying me on the ice and climbing over me. The cold, wet ice seeped through my clothes.

"Jax," I croaked.

"What, Kai?" he breathed against my lips, pressing his hips into mine. My fingernails dug into the thin material of his t-shirt. "Should I tell you how badly I want to taste every inch of your body?" His lips raked over my jawline and down my throat. I whimpered when he pressed his hip harder into mine, letting me feel every inch of him. "How badly I want to see what you look like when I make you come."

"Jax," I moaned.

He stopped, pushing to his knees. "This can't happen, Kai. We live together. We will be in each other's lives forever, and if this goes bad, there's no escaping each other. Imagine how our parents would feel."

At that moment, I realized what I needed from Jax.

"Jax," I said, leaning up on my elbows. "I'm not looking to get married. I'm not even sure I want a boyfriend. I want to lose my virginity to someone I trust because I'm scared."

"That's what this is about?" he asked, his gaze softening.

"Until a few days ago, I'd never done anything with a

guy," I said. "And with you, everything is so easy." He always took control, making me feel so comfortable. "I know I could have lost it with some random stranger, but I'm scared." I blew out a long, dramatic sigh as my chest and cheeks heated with embarrassment. "It's okay if you need to think about it."

"You want me to fuck you, no strings attached. So that you can lose your virginity and fuck other guys?"

"Yeah, basically." I shrugged.

"Why me?" he asked, his brows pinching together.

"Because you're so confident with yourself and so comfortable with casual sex. I trust you."

His gaze lingered on me for a long, uncomfortable moment.

"Come on." He sighed, pushing to his feet and pulling me with him. "Let's go home and sober you up, and then we can revisit this later."

"I'm not drunk, Jax. I didn't realize it before, but this is what I need. I need to be with someone who will teach me." He ran a hand down his face.

"I don't know, Kai." Sighing, I nodded. "Let's go home."

16

Jaxtyn

It was game day, the first game of the season.

Coach Tomas was pumping the team up, and all I could think about was whether or not Kaia and Cam made it. Sitting on the wooden bench in front of my locker, I pulled out my phone and clicked on Kaia's name.

Jaxtyn: How do you like the seats?

I stared at the phone, my leg bouncing as I waited for the bubble to pop, and it did almost immediately.

Kaia: I can almost smell the sweat and blood.

A smile spread across my face.

Jaxtyn: What are you wearing?

Kaia: #53

My jaw clenched. Whose fucking jersey was that? It wasn't anyone on my team. My gaze flicked around the room to my teammates huddled around the coach. It had to be someone on the opposing team.

My hand buzzed with another incoming text.

Kaia: Just kidding, #32.

She was wearing my jersey. Why did the fact that she was wearing my jersey make my chest swell with excitement?

Kaia: Cam is wearing #87.

She was wearing Owen's jersey.

Kaia: Oh, and Trystan is meeting us back at the hotel tonight. He said to tell you he's sorry he has to miss the game.

I didn't care if Trystan was here or not. Kaia was, and she was wearing my number.

Jaxtyn: Make sure you scream my name loud today. I want to hear what you sound like when you're screaming my name.

I smiled as I pictured the perfect shade of pink flushing across her cheeks as she read the text.

"Let's go, Jax," Coach Tomas shouted. I shoved my phone in my locker and followed the team.

It was time to get my head in the game.

The announcer introduced the teams as my skates hit the ice. I fought the urge to look over to her. She was a distraction. The best kind of distraction but nonetheless a distraction, and I needed my head in this game.

We all took our starting positions, the buzzer blew, and it was game on. We weren't even five minutes in before penalties were flying, and the first fight broke out, and for once, it had nothing to do with me.

Going into the second period, we were on fire. The Blackhawks didn't know what hit them.

Owen cut off #45, Preston, and stole the puck. I pushed off the ice, sliding in to help Owen dodge their defensive measures to protect their goal and steal the puck back. Owen passed the puck to Dallas, and Dallas took his shot, sinking the puck into the goal.

The crowd went wild, and I couldn't help but do a victory skate by Kaia. I knew how much she loved being on the ice, but I never realized how much she loved hockey. The excitement in her eyes as I passed was apparent. If this made her smile like that, I would ensure she had the best seats in the house for the rest of the season.

The TSU Blackhawks didn't know what hit them. By the end of the third period, we were so far in the lead they didn't stand a chance of catching up.

We'd be on fire if this game was any indication of how our season would go.

The buzzer sounded. GAME OVER!

I'd made it through my first game without a single penalty or fight. Kaia was my good luck charm.

"Yo, West," Colton Hunt, the Blackhawks goalie, said, gliding to a stop in front of me. I knew Colton from high school. We graduated from the same class and played in the same league, but after high school, he was recruited by Tennessee State University, and I decided to stay local. "You bringing Kaia to Broadway tonight?" Colton knew Kaia was my weakness. My junior year, the guys went crazy over the new pretty ice skater, Kaia Cruz. I hated it. I didn't know why back then, but it was pretty clear now. She was mine. I spent the entire year fighting over her and almost got kicked off the team, but it was worth it.

"Why?" I snarled, my fist clenching at my sides.

"Oh," he smirked, "I was hoping I could rip that ugly ass jersey off her tonight right before I fuck her." Owen wasn't around to stop it this time. My clenched fist reared back before I slammed it into his face, and it was all downhill from there. That punch in the face turned into a massive team brawl that took way too long to break up.

When we returned to the locker room, we were scolded, but I couldn't hide the smile twitching at the corners of my lips because it didn't matter what the consequences were. It was worth it.

17

Jaxtyn

I didn't get to see Kaia and Cam before they left the arena to check into the hotel, but I'd sent them a text to get ready because we were bar hopping down Broadway tonight.

By the time we were all dressed and our feet hit Broadway, it was after eleven p.m.

"First round is on me," Owen said. "What does everyone want?"

"Surprise me," I said.

"I'll go with you." Cam smiled.

"I'll take a water," Kaia said, and everyone's heads snapped to her. "What? I'm the responsible one for the night."

Kaia and Cam weren't technically old enough to drink, but you'd be surprised what a low-cut top and a pair of cutoff shorts could do to a man, and Kaia's cutoffs made me want to stay in tonight.

"What's up, Kai?" Colton sang from behind us, and my jaw clenched. Kaia and I turned to see Hunt and his teammate Berkley strolling up to us.

"Colton." Kaia smiled. When he leaned in for a hug, his eyes locked on mine with a fuck you smirk plastered on his face, I thought my head might explode.

"Damn, girl," Colton said, his gaze raking over Kaia. "You are even hotter now than you were in high school." Kaia's cheeks flushed as a smile spread across her face.

"I'm Dexter Berkley," Colton's friend said, but the way he licked his lips as his gaze raked over her made my blood boil, not that she even noticed. Too bad he was wasting his time. She was mine, and she was leaving with me.

"Holy shit," Cam screamed. "Colton fucking Hunt."

"Camryn," Colton said, rushing and jumping into Colton's open arms. My lip curled into a snarl. I just wanted Colton to fuck off. Camryn lost her virginity to Colton when Colton was a senior and Cam was a sophomore. They broke up shortly after the event but remained close friends until graduation. "I thought I saw you at the game today. You should let me buy you a drink." And just like that, Colton had moved on from Kaia.

We met up with both teams and partied until we closed the bars down.

My phone buzzed, and I pulled it out of my pocket and narrowed my eyes at the screen, waiting for the fog in my vision to clear up.

Trystan: You still on Broadway?

Jaxtyn: Yes, but we closed the street down. Headed back to the hotel soon.

Trystan: Cam with you? She's not answering the phone.

Jaxtyn: Kind of...

Trystan: What does kind of mean?

Jaxtyn: It means there's a possibility she's crashing with Colton Hunt tonight.

Trystan: I'll be there in five.

I shoved my phone into my pocket and threw my arm around Kaia's shoulder.

"Did Cam spill the juice on what happened between her and Trystan the other night?" I asked Kaia as we stood off to the side while everyone said their goodbyes.

Kaia shrugged. "She said it was bad timing and said something about them revisiting the situation later."

"Trystan is on his way here to get her now," I said, and Kaia's eyes flashed up to meet mine.

"She's with Colton," Kaia said. "Should I tell her?"

"Nah." I smirked. "Let's see how this plays out." Trystan needed a taste of his own medicine. If he liked Cam, he should lay his claim and make her his. At least he didn't have that whole issue of being step-siblings. My gaze flicked over to where Cam and Colton stood side-by-side. Cam had about three drinks too many and was far past the legal limit. "I'll let Colton walk her back, but she's not staying with him anyway. She's too drunk to consent." And I hoped he knew that.

18

Jaxtyn

Our hotel was within walking distance of Broadway, and the Blackhawks were staying in the same hotel, but we were all on different floors. My team was on the 8th floor. Kaia and Cam were on the 6th floor, and the Blackhawks were on the 11th.

Security started to clear the streets, and all of us staggered our way toward the hotel. Cam stumbled, and Colton swooped in and threw her over his shoulder.

"Hey, is that Trystan?" Colton narrowed his eyes at the tall figure walking towards us. "It is."

"Put her down," Trystan ordered, and I knew Trystan would make sure she was safe.

"She's crashing with us tonight," Colton said.

"Does she really look like she is capable of making that decision?" Trystan growled, reaching for her waist and pulling her from his grasp. Colton released her, and Cam practically collapsed in Trystan's arms, and he scooped her up. "How much did she drink?"

Kaia rushed to Trystan's side to check on Cam. "Should we take her to the hospital?" Colton took a step back, a look of horror flashing across his face. My guess was he didn't realize how trashed she was, but the question was when he would have figured it out.

"Cam," Kaia said, gripping her jaw and shaking her face.

"Wha..." Cam slurred, swatting Kaia's hand away, and I watched as Kaia visibly released a heavy breath. "Why is the room spinning?"

"She's okay." Trystan sighed. "But we should get her back to the room and sober her up some." Trystan's gaze flicked up to Colton. "If you ever touch her again, I'll break your fingers." I'd never heard Trystan threaten anyone over a girl before other than Kaia, Syn, or Harlow. I guess I had my answer as to whether or not he liked her.

Trystan carried Cam into the hotel and onto the elevator. "Cam is crashing in my room tonight so that I can keep an eye on her. Do you want to stay too, Kai?"

"I'm crashing with Kai," I said. "Owen is... Occupying my room." And by occupying, I meant he had a girl in there.

"I'm in 6578 if you want to come to check on her," Trystan said as the elevator doors chimed open. Cam was in good hands. If anyone knew how to sober someone up, it was Trystan.

"Call me if anything changes," Kaia said as Trystan rounded a corner going left, and we went the opposite way.

Kaia scanned her card across the door, and when it beeped green, she shoved it open.

"One king bed, huh?" I smirked, standing at the end of the bed.

"It was the only room they had left," Kaia said, pulling open a dresser drawer. "I don't mind sharing with Cam."

"Do you mind sharing with me?" I smirked.

Her gaze flicked over her shoulder, and her cheeks heated. I curled my fingers around her arm, twisting her around to me. "No." She smiled. "I do not mind sharing with you."

"You seem nervous." I brushed a loose strand of her blonde hair out of her face and left it behind her ear. Her gaze locked with mine as she pressed her lips into a thin line. "Are you nervous about something, Kai?" She shrugged.

I thought a lot about her proposal of taking her virginity with no strings attached, but I also knew she made that offer thinking that's what I wanted. The truth was there was no way I could fuck her and not keep her.

"Kai," I whispered. "Talk to me."

"We are alone," she said. "And we are going to share a

bed, and you haven't exactly said anything about my proposal."

"How about this," I said as the corners of my lips curled into a smirk. My hands cupped her face, forcing her to look at me. "How about we just let it happen? No labels, no expectations, whatever happens, happens." I brushed my thumb across her bottom lip. "Tell me if you are curious about something, and I'll help."

"So..." She trailed off.

"So, I'm not going to just fuck you just to fuck you, Kai." I shrugged. "When we crawl into that bed, who knows what will happen, but it will not be because I'm planning to fuck you for the sake of taking your virginity." The corner of her lip curled up, and she nodded. "Go change, and I'll meet you in bed."

I flicked off most of the lights before slipping out of my clothes, leaving on my boxer briefs so I didn't freak her out before sliding under the covers.

When the door to the bathroom opened, and Kaia stepped out, every ounce of air from my lungs was sucked out. She wore a long black t-shirt that fell off one shoulder, her hair was pulled up messy on top of her head, her tanned legs were bare, and her makeup was washed away. She was so hot.

Clearing my throat, I held up the remote, trying not to stare and make her more nervous. "Did you want to watch TV?" She shook her head as she climbed into the bed. I twisted to flick off the light, and the room went black.

Shoving my hands under my head, I stared at the ceiling, allowing my eyes to adjust to the darkness.

"Jax," Kaia whispered, a hint of curiosity in her tone.

"Hmmm," I hummed, closing my eyes.

The bed shook as she shifted to her side, facing me. "Are all orgasms the same?" My eyes snapped open. That was not where I expected this conversation to go.

I rolled onto my side to face her, propping my hand on my hand. "I'm not sure I understand the question."

"Is there a difference between giving myself an orgasm and someone else giving me one? Like does it feel better or the same? Or does it depend?"

Someone else, hell. Her question required an experiment.

"Run your fingertips up your thigh," I whispered, sliding into her side of the bed. "There's no one that knows your body better than you." I wrapped my hand around her tiny wrist and guided her hand to the side of her upper thigh. "So, use your fingertips and run them over your skin."

She traced her fingertips over her thigh. "Okay," she said. "I don't get it."

"My turn," I whispered against her lips as my fingertips brushed against the heated skin of her thigh. "And you tell me if there's a difference." My hand curled around her thigh as I pulled her thigh over my leg and leaned into her. I brushed my lips across hers as my fingertips caressed the soft skin of her thigh. Her lips parted with a moan, and I knew she had the answer to her question. "Is there a difference?" I breathed, trailing my lips across her jawline.

Her eyes closed as she leaned into my touch. "Yes," she whispered.

"The night you touched yourself," I said, "while I whispered in your ear, how did that compare to when you touched yourself alone?"

"I thought you didn't remember," she cut me off.

"I remember everything," I said. "Every sound you made, the way you tasted, and how badly I wanted you."

"It was the best orgasm I'd ever had," she breathed, hooking her leg around my leg, flipping me to my back, and straddling me with a sudden burst of confidence. Dropping her chest to mine, she was taking control. My hands curled around her thighs, squeezing tightly. "I want to know what it feels like."

"What feels like?" I asked. I knew what she wanted, but I needed to hear her say it.

"When someone else makes me come," she breathed against my lips.

Shooting up, I wrapped my arms tightly around her, holding her flush against me. "Don't play with me, baby," I whispered, my tone low and raspy.

She wiggled out of my grasp, pressing her hand flat against my bare chest; she shoved me to my back. "I'm not playing anything," she said, grabbing the hem of her shirt and pulling it over her head.

I inhaled a deep breath as my gaze raked over her perfect, delicate curves.

"We shouldn't do this," I whispered.

Dropping her chest to mine, she brushed her lips across mine. "We should." I wasn't sure where this courage came from, and I didn't care. I was so here for it. My hand gripped her ass while my free hand fisted tightly into her hair, pulling her mouth tightly against mine.

19

I couldn't explain what came over me or the sudden burst of confidence surging through me like a bolt of lightning, but I knew it had more to do with him and how he made me feel than anything else.

I wanted to feel the difference between my own touch and his. I needed to be touched, and I wanted it to be him.

"Are you asking me to make you come, Kai?" he breathed. I nodded. "Say, please."

I dropped my lips to his ear. "Please, Jax," I purred, grinding my hips into his. His hand tangled into my hair, and his arm around my waist tightened, holding me in place. My nipples pulled tight as they brushed against the heated skin of his bare-toned chest.

"Please, what?" He breathed against the shell of my

ear. His tone was both commanding and seductive. "Say it."

"Please, Jax." Fire zipped through me as I could feel his length between my thighs. I wanted to feel all of him. "Will you make me come?"

He smiled against my cheek. "How do you want me to make you come, baby?" His grip tightened around me as he leaned up and flipped me underneath him, settling between my thighs. His hungry gaze locked on mine. "Do you want me to touch you?" he whispered as his teeth grazed my throat. A strangled moan ripped from my throat as I tried to answer him. "Where do you want me to touch you, baby?"

His large hand covered my breast, his thumb brushed over my taut nipple, and I arched into his touch. "Here?" A soft moan pushed past my lips. "Holy fuck," he groaned. "If you keep making noises like that, I might be the one coming."

My belly clenched as his mouth moved down. The stubble on his jaw left a trail of heated fire in its path. His mouth covered my nipple, drawing the sensitive flesh into his mouth, sucking and teasing the taut bud with each flick of his tongue.

His mouth descended to my stomach, sucking, nipping, and licking his way down until his lips hovered over the thin black lace of my panties. "Do you want me to kiss you here?" he breathed, the heat of his breath feathered across the sensitive skin, summoning a breathy, desperate whimper.

"Yes," I panted as his hands snaked around my thighs, holding my hips in place.

"Do you want to come all over my face, baby?" His tone was a low, raspy whisper as his lips grazed the inside of my thigh. A bolt of electricity zipped through me, and my blood heated as he ran his nose over the length of my soaking wet panties, inhaling deeply. "You're soaking wet, baby." He groaned against my panties, and I rocked my hips into his face. "Oh, my baby is so needy." Releasing his hold on my thigh, he reached further, hooking a finger into my panties and pulling them to one side. Chills raced over my skin in anticipation as he teased me, scattering kisses along my thighs and pussy.

"Jax," I cried out as my fingers curled into the sheets. It was a desperate plea to put me out of my misery and alleviate the throbbing between my thighs. His tongue swiped up the length of my pussy, tasting my wetness. My heart pounded like a drum as his tongue found my clit circling slowly. His tongue dropped to my entrance, circling before delving inside of me.

"Holy shit." I moaned as his heated tongue pumped in and out of me, making my insides turn to liquid heat.

"You taste so fucking good, baby." He grunted as his fingers curled tighter into the curve where my thigh met my hip, and he continued to fuck me with his tongue. I gazed down as he glared up through his dark lashes, watching me intently.

His mouth covered my clit, and my thighs flexed around his head as I rocked my pussy against his face. His hands jerked my hips back to the mattress, holding me in place as he used his shoulders to spread me wide. His tongue flicked my clit with slow, deliberate, and precise motions that made my legs quiver. My fingers slid in his hair, and my back arched as his speed increased with just the right amount of pressure that nearly sent me diving over the edge. He sucked my flesh into his mouth, teasing the swollen bud. "Omigod, Jax." My grip tightened in his hair as I held him in place, rocking my hips harder into his face.

"That's it, baby, fuck my face." He moaned, his voice a deep rumble. "Come all over my face." My toes curled, and my abs clenched. "I want to know what you taste like when you come." And that's what sent me spiraling uncontrollably over the edge, the combination of Jax's dirty words and perfect mouth. My eyes squeezed shut, my body vibrated with ecstasy, and my lips parted as I cried out from a mind-altering orgasm. I came so hard the air from my lungs expelled on a violent exhale. My body twitched as his tongue found my entrance again, taking his time to taste every ounce of the orgasm he'd caused.

He climbed up, hovering over me as my body floated on a high.

"Was it better?" he asked, his lips mere inches from mine, but I couldn't form words between my labored breaths, so I nodded. His mouth curled up into a smirk. He knew it would be better, and now there were so many other things I wanted to try.

20

Kaia

It had been three days since I'd spent the night with Jax in my hotel room. Three days since he'd given me a mind-blowing orgasm and then disappeared like he always did. I was starting to get used to it. This was just how Jaxtyn worked.

I pushed through the kitchen door and froze.

"Morning," he said, not bothering to look up at me as he poured the mixed contents of his protein shake out of the blender and into a cup. "Do you want to ride with me to the rink?"

Two days ago, I started working with Petrov early in the morning because Jax asked me to give it a try, and I couldn't lie, it felt good to be back on the ice, but today Petrov was introducing me to a new partner. Of course, I hadn't had the chance to tell Jax that because he'd been avoiding me.

"No, thanks." I scowled. "Cam is picking me up." I wanted to ask him what his problem was, but I already knew. Jax never saw the same girl twice, and that wasn't possible with me.

"See you later," he said, bolting out the door so fast you would have thought someone was chasing him. I rolled my eyes. Jax was so hard to figure out. He told me he liked me, but he freaked out and ran whenever there was any type of physical intimacy between us. Of course, the whole 'I like you' thing could have been part of the game. Shit, I didn't know what was real anymore, and I was starting to get irritated with the entire situation.

Cam blew her horn, and I grabbed my bag, threw it over my shoulder, and bolted toward her car but froze when I saw Trystan getting out of Cam's passenger side.

"What's up, Kai?" He smirked as he strolled toward me.

"I don't think I've ever seen you up this early." I narrowed my eyes at him. "Well, unless you've been up partying all night and haven't been to bed yet." He shrugged, a silly smile pulling at the corner of his lips, and I rolled my eyes. "You know she's going to tell me, right?" He shrugged again.

"Catch ya later, Kai," he said, pushing past me. "Oh, and good luck today. Cam said you were meeting your new partner."

"Thanks," I muttered, sliding into the passenger side of Cam's 2022 black Lexus. Sinking into the seat, my gaze flicked to her, and my lips pursed as I crossed my arms over my chest. "I thought you two decided it was the wrong time."

"It is, but I'm not supposed to tell you why," she squealed, her eyes lighting with excitement.

"We don't keep secrets, Cam," I reminded her, pulling my seatbelt across my chest.

"I know, but he really wants to tell you," she said, putting the car in reverse. "And it's his news, so I'm not going to ruin that for him."

"Okay, then tell me," I said. "Did you two spend the night together again?"

"Not exactly," she smirked, swerving out into traffic. "He needed a ride home."

"He has a motorcycle and a $70,000 truck," I said. "He didn't need a ride. He wanted a ride. He also has a brother, a sister, and two step-sisters. So he wanted that ride from you."

"We just talked." She smiled.

"I just don't want you guys to end up hurt," I said. "You're both my family, and things get complicated and messy when feelings get hurt in families."

"It's fine," she said. "Plus, I have a date with Owen tonight."

"Owen," I repeated, my brows pinching. When did that happen? "As in Jax's best friend, Owen?" She nodded. "Does Trystan know about this date?"

"No." She shrugged. "We agreed that we weren't

together and that whatever we did wasn't the other person's business."

"You agreed to that, huh?" I frowned.

"It was his idea." She laughed. "But I'm good with it." She might be, but for some reason, I didn't think he would be, but that was between the two of them.

She swerved into the parking lot, and I spotted Jax's empty car. He was already inside.

"Good luck today," Cam said as we walked into the building.

"Thanks."

Cam and I got our skates on and hit the ice together. She went one way, and I went the opposite way when I spotted Petrov and... Omigod. Parker Brooks, one of the best professional ice skaters, stood towering over Petrov. Parker lost his partner, Cassidy Morrison, to a severe injury last season that left her unable to skate. The pair had been inseparable. They started skating together at the age of seven. I assumed he would retire, and then it dawned on me that he was here to skate with me. Panic rose into my throat. I wasn't good enough to skate with Parker Brooks, not even close.

Not only was Parker an amazing skater, but he was also gorgeous. He was tall with dirty blonde hair and deep brown eyes. He had a smile that could melt a girl's panties off and a body constructed by the Greek gods.

"You're late, Kaia," Petrov scolded in her deep Russian accent.

I wasn't late. I was actually on time, but Petrov considered that late. "I'm sorry. It won't happen again."

"Parker, this is Kaia." Petrov smiled. "She's the one I've been telling you about." His deep brown eyes raked over me, but not in a good way. More of an assessing the product he was considering buying kind of way. "I want to see you two together. See if there is potential for chemistry."

"Chemistry isn't something that just happens, Petrov," Parker snapped, crossing his arms over his chest, his deep voice laced with annoyance. "You know this."

"Just skate," Petrov ordered. He didn't want to be here, which made the nerves twisting low in my stomach worse. "I want to see how well you pair skate together."

"What do you want us to do?" I asked, trying to lighten the mood.

"Skate in a circle around the rink," Petrov said. "Hold hands and introduce yourself to each other." My gaze flicked up to catch the end of Parker's eye roll.

"Let's just get this over with," he muttered, stepping onto the ice. He was being an ass. He reached for my hand, and I jerked it away from him.

"Actually," I snapped, "I'm good. I didn't get up early this morning to skate with someone who isn't in this. I get it. You lost your partner, and you think you'll never find that connection on the ice again, and maybe you're right, but maybe you're not. I lost my partner, too. At least you can still visit Cassidy because I can't. Regardless, you don't need to be a dick." I pushed off the ice and skated away. "Call me if you find someone who actually wants to skate with me," I shouted to Petrov over my shoulder.

I was done being pushed around by jerks. I was done dealing with Jax's shit, and I damn sure wasn't adding another asshole to the mix.

"Hey," a deep voice called behind me as I stepped off the ice. "Wait up." I twisted to see Parker glide up behind me.

"What?" I snapped, rolling my eyes.

"You were right." He smiled. "I was being a dick. I'm sorry."

"You were being a massive dick," I corrected him.

"I was." He laughed. "Do you think you could give me one more chance?"

He sounded so earnest that I believed he was sorry. Sucking in a deep breath, I exhaled slowly. *I guess we all have bad days.* "Yes."

"Care to take a spin on the ice with me?"

He offered me his hand, and I accepted, stepping back onto the ice. We pushed off the ice hand-in-hand. My gaze flicked to the stands to see Jax sitting in the stands, his gaze following us.

"So your name is Kaia, right?" Parker asked, following Petrov's orders to introduce himself.

"Yes, but everyone calls me Kai," I said, my gaze blinking back to Parker.

"I'm Parker Brooks," he said, and I laughed.

"Yeah, I know who you are." I smiled as we glided around the curve of the rink. "I've watched you and Cassidy skate together for years. You two were amazing together."

Without letting go of my hand, he spun to skate backward in front of me.

"Petrov told me about your partner," Parker said, his eyes softening. "I'm sorry."

I shrugged, swallowing hard. I never knew what to say when someone apologized for my loss, regarding my mother or Matthias.

"She said you two were amazing on the ice. Do you think you could have that kind of chemistry with someone else?"

"Like you?" I asked.

He nodded.

I'd skated with Matthias for years to get the kind of trust you needed at our level of skating. We knew each other's every move on the ice, and it was hard to believe I'd get that level of trust for someone else in a matter of months or even weeks.

"I think there has to be a friendship."

"Okay." He smiled. "Kaia, would you like to be my friend?"

I laughed. He was incredibly charming when he wasn't being a massive dick.

"How about we hang out tomorrow night? We can decide after that if there's a chance."

"Are you asking me out?" I asked.

He was silent for several long minutes as his dark brown eyes flicked from my eyes to my lips.

"Yeah," he said. "I guess I am."

"Are you and Cassidy..." I started.

"No," he cut me off. "We were never a couple, even though everyone thought we were. Do you have a boyfriend?"

My teeth raked across my bottom lip as my gaze flicked up to Jax, still standing in the same spot, his gaze still fixed on us.

"No." I smiled. "No boyfriend here."

"So, I'll pick you up at eight," he said as he glided to a stop where he'd picked me up.

"You two move beautifully," Petrov shouted. "I'll see you tomorrow morning."

"We should probably move it up to tonight." Parker laughed. "Petrov moves quickly."

"Tonight," I repeated.

"Do you have plans?" he asked.

"No." I smiled, shaking my head.

We exchanged numbers, and I texted him my address.

"I'll pick you up at eight." I stepped off the ice, and he skated off.

I had a date tonight. Omigod, I had a date tonight.

I swapped out of my skates and headed to the parking lot, but Cam's car was gone.

"She left me."

"I told her I'd give you a ride home," Jax said behind me, startling me.

"Why?" I groaned, following him to his car. I didn't want to ride with Jax. I was irritated with him. He shrugged, popping his trunk open and tossing his gear inside.

"Who was that you were skating with today?" he asked, sliding into the car.

"My new partner," I said. "And he's taking me out tonight."

21

Parker showed up precisely at eight to pick me up, and thankfully, I was the only one home, even though I expected Jax to be here. I wasn't sure what was going on with him, but I was done trying to figure him out. I was going to enjoy my night.

We decided to go to the bar Dirty Habits, one of the best bars in the area. They had live music, and it usually wasn't super crowded during the week.

"You grab a table, and I'll grab some drinks," Parker said when we pushed through the bar doors. "What do you want?"

"I'll just have water." I smiled.

"Water?" He laughed. "We came to a bar for you to have water?"

I shrugged. "I'm not much of a drinker, but I love the music."

The corners of his lips curled up. "Water it is."

Parker took a right toward the bar, and I took a left to find a table, spotting Owen and Cam at a high-top table.

"What are you guys doing here?" I laughed, strolling up to their table. This wasn't their typical bar of choice.

"Kai," Owen smiled, "we are on a date. What are you doing here?"

"I'm here with Parker," I said. "My new skating partner."

"I didn't know you had a new partner," Owen said. "Good for you."

"You guys should join us," Cam said.

"Oh, no." I scowled. "I don't want to interrupt your date.

"Don't be silly," Owen said. "Plus, Jax is our third wheel anyway." He nodded toward the bar, and I spotted Jax smiling at a pretty redhead. Jealousy bloomed in my chest, and I wasn't sure where it had come from. It wasn't like I'd never seen Jax with a girl before. I couldn't count the number of women I'd seen him with, but for some reason, seeing him tonight with her created a weird mixture of irritation, jealousy, and hurt within me.

"Is he on a date?" I asked.

Owen and Cam both laughed. "Jax doesn't date," Owen said. "Jax takes girls home, fucks them, and never talks to them again."

"I guess she's the lucky one tonight." I frowned.

Owen shrugged. "I don't think I've ever seen her

before, so he's probably feeling her out right now to see how easy she is. He was also already drunk when he showed up, so he may end up going home alone tonight with a whiskey dick."

"What the fuck is a whiskey dick?" I flashed a look of horror, and Owen and Cam erupted with laughter.

"It's when you drink too much, and your dick stops working," Cam said. "But it's better than sloppy drunk sex that never ends." I laughed, not because I'd experienced what she was talking about but because it was something she'd given me a visual of with a guy she was dating last year.

"There you are," Parker said, and I twisted to see him carrying a beer in one hand and a bottle of water in the other.

"Parker, these are my friends Cam and Owen." I pointed between them. "Guys, this is Parker."

"What's up?" Cam said. "You guys should join us."

"Sure," Parker said, handing me my water.

"Water, Kai. Really?" Cam rolled her eyes when she spotted the water. "Let loose and have some fun."

"Looks like I'm the DD again."

"We'll get an Uber," Owen said. "If that's what you're worried about."

Parker's gaze flicked to me. "Do you want something else?"

"What the hell." I threw up my hands. I was always the responsible one; I was always the one who took care of everyone else, and tonight, I just wanted to have fun. Plus, alcohol would help me care less about how Jax was smiling at the redhead.

"You ready for a refill?" the same redhead Jax had been talking to asked Cam. She was our waitress. Wonderful.

"Four Jolly Ranchers," Cam said. She knew I loved Jolly Rancher shots.

"And a whiskey," Jax said, sliding onto the stool beside Cam.

"Actually, make that two whiskeys," Owen said.

"Anything for you, darlin'?" the redhead flashed her perfect white smile to Parker.

"Nope," Parker said, raising his beer.

"I'll grab your drinks and be right back." She winked at Jax, but Jax's gaze was zeroed in on Parker.

"Who the fuck are you?" Jax asked in his fuck off tone.

"This is Parker, my new skating partner," I answered for Parker. "Parker, this is my stepbrother Jax."

"What's up, man?" Parker said, extending his hand, but Jax was being an ass. His less-than-amused gaze flicked to Parker's hand before it cut to me. Parker's brows pinched as his hand dropped to his side.

"Don't mind him." I smiled at Parker. "He's an ass." My gaze cut to Jax, flashing him a warning look.

Jax didn't take my warning look seriously. "I'm only an ass when I don't like someone." The tone in his voice was lethal, his fuck around and find out demeanor came through loud and clear, and the daggers he was shooting from his icy blue eyes were aimed directly at Parker.

Parker stood across from Jax, beer in hand, as he blinked in confusion, his stare flicking between Jax and me.

"Can I talk to you for a minute?" I clenched my teeth. Jax's gaze didn't waver as his jaw ticked. "Now, Jax!" He rolled his eyes but pushed out of the chair at the same time I did. I stormed out the front door, whipping around once I heard the door shut behind Jax.

"What the fuck is your problem?" He shrugged. Exhaling, I rolled my eyes. "What's going on, Jax?"

"I don't know what you mean, Baby Cruz." My jaw clenched at the stupid nickname.

"I mean, you've been avoiding me since the night in the hotel, and now you're acting like an overprotective dickhead."

"Kai, this is who I am." He took a step forward, crowding my space. "I fuck around with women, and then I avoid them forever. The problem is I can't avoid you forever."

"Why, Jax?"

"There doesn't have to be a reason for everything, Baby Cruz." He shrugged. "It's just who I am, and you can't fix me."

I knew this was who he was; I just didn't think this was who he was with me.

"You know what, Jax." I held my hands up, surrendering. "I'm done playing these stupid high school games. Grow up, or just stay away from me. I can't keep up with you, and to be honest, I'm starting to get whiplash."

"Kai." He sighed, suddenly apologetic.

"Save it, Jax." I held my hand out like I could physically stop his words. "Lay off my date and go fuck yourself." I spun on my heel, storming back into the bar and back to the high top where I'd left Cam, Owen, and Parker. I froze, my eyes narrowing. And apparently, Trystan— who was in Jax's seat shooting daggers at Owen and Cam on the dance floor.

"Not you, too," I grumbled, sliding into my seat next to Parker. "Seriously, you and Jax need to get your shit together."

I flashed Parker an apologetic smile before glancing over my shoulder to see if Jax had come in after me. He hadn't.

"I don't know what you're talking about," Trystan muttered.

"Yeah, funny, neither did Jax." I was over this night. I was over these commitment-phobic brothers, at least for tonight, anyway. I slid back out of my seat. "Parker, do you want to get out of here?"

"Yes." He nodded, his tone laced with relief.

I shoved my chair in as my gaze landed on Trystan,

who was obviously mentally plotting Owen's death. "I'll meet you at the car." I forced a smile, and Parker nodded. My gaze followed him until he was out of sight, and then I whipped around. "Trystan." His gaze snapped to mine. "Get. Your. Shit. Together. Or go the fuck home." His brows pinched in confusion. "Make her your girlfriend or leave her alone. You can't have it both ways."

His entire body slumped with defeat on a heavy exhale. "I can't," he said after several long seconds.

"Why not? Why do you and your brother have the same commitment issues."

His lips curled into a smile. "I don't have commitment issues, Kai. I'm just not ready to settle down, and I don't want to end up hurting her." He swallowed hard as he flicked a glance back to the dance floor before returning to me. "I was going to tell everyone tomorrow, but the band got a spot at Rock Fest, and then we will be touring with Wicked Sinners as their opening act for the following six weeks."

"Oh my God, Trystan," I squealed. "That's amazing!"

"Since she has too much going on here and she can't go with me, it wouldn't be fair for me to tie her down, especially when we both know that in the back of her head, she'll be wondering if I'm being faithful."

My gaze flicked out to Cam on the dance floor. He had a point. Trystan was a playboy, and he was about to go on the road where thousands of women would be throwing themselves at him every day. It would drive

Cam crazy. "Fair enough." My attention snapped back to Trystan. There was no hiding the jealousy etched on his face. "So you told her she could date other people, but that's not what you want, is it?"

He shook his head. "No." His throat bobbed on a hard swallow. "I want to rip out his throat." Owen and Trystan were friends. We'd all grown up together, and I had a feeling if Trystan did rip out his throat, he'd regret it later.

"Come on, Tryst. Don't sit here and torture yourself."

He slid out of his seat and followed me to the door. "Can I give you a ride home?"

"I came with Parker."

"Okay, let me rephrase that. Will you ride home with me?"

I was over tonight. Between Jax showing up and acting like an ass and everything going on with Trystan, I wanted to call it a night. It also wasn't very often that Trystan asked me to ride with him, so I assumed he either didn't want to be alone or he wanted to talk.

"Yeah, give me a second to let Parker know, and I'll meet you at your truck."

I met Parker at his car, and apparently, he'd had enough of the evening, too, because he seemed like he couldn't leave fast enough. We agreed to give the skating thing a try in the morning, but neither of us mentioned another date.

"You ready?" Trystan jerked the driver's side door open.

"Are you sober?"

He huffed out a laugh. "I don't think I've been this sober in a long time."

We climbed into the truck in silence, neither of us speaking until we were in traffic and headed toward the house.

"So, why did you want me to ride home with you?"

"Because you looked like you needed someone to talk to." He swerved the wheel to the right. "So, spill."

Slouching in the seat, I grunted as my lip curled into a snarl. I didn't even know if I wanted to talk about it or, if I did, where to start.

"Come on, Kai." He flicked a glance out the corner of his eyes.

No one knew Jax better than his brother, so if I were going to talk to anyone about Jax, it would be him.

"What's Jax's deal?" His head twisted to me, and his brows furrowed. "I mean, where do his commitment issues come from?"

"So, this is about Jax." I shrugged, hoping he wasn't going to ask questions. "Have you tried talking to him?"

"Yeah." I sighed. "He's so closed off."

He eased to a stop sign. "I think a lot of it comes from our parent's divorce." Leaning forward, he looked both ways before surging forward. "It was a pretty nasty divorce, and unfortunately, they didn't keep us out of the middle of it. We had to watch the fights, and they wanted us to choose. Like I said, it was nasty, and Syn and Jax took it hard."

"Do you think that's why he keeps himself and his feelings at a distance?"

"Probably. Be patient with him and give him time to work out his struggles with his own feelings. He'll figure out what he wants. Hopefully, it's not too late."

"It would be nice if he trusted me enough to talk to me."

"Kai, I don't think he even understands the reason he is the way he is." I nodded. He swerved into the driveway and stopped in front of the garage.

"What about you? You going to have a conversation with Cam?"

He shrugged. "I don't know."

"You should probably figure it out. Rockfest is next weekend." Then it hit me. "Holy shit! Rockfest is next weekend." He nodded. "We will never get tickets now."

"I already got them." A rueful grin split his face. "I have six tickets. You can invite your new partner if you want." Rock Fest was a three-day rock festival. I wasn't sure if Parker and I were ready to share a tent yet.

"Yeah, maybe."

Trystan and I strolled into the house, and he headed out back; I assumed to get high, and I headed upstairs to see if Jax was home.

22

Standing outside Jax's closed bedroom door, I chewed on my bottom lip. Jax never closed the door from my bedroom through the bathroom to his bedroom. So, either he had company or didn't want to be bothered. Blowing out a heavy sigh, I twisted around and sulked back to my room. I wanted to talk to Jax, but it would have to wait.

I stripped out of my clothes and pulled on a fitted purple tank top before climbing into bed and snuggling in with my back to the bathroom door I left open so I could hear if Jax came out.

Everything made so much sense now that I talked to Trystan. Trystan, Jaxtyn, and Syn had issues when it came to dating, and it made sense that those issues stemmed from their parents' divorce. I knew that Liz and

Bryan had a nasty divorce, and even after all these years, the two couldn't be in a room together for more than a few minutes without fighting, but I never realized what an impact that would have on their children.

The door handle from Jax's room into the bathroom jiggled, and I sucked in a breath, praying that it was Jax, not some girl using the bathroom after their late-night sex. I didn't bother rolling over to see because I didn't want to know.

A few seconds later, my bed sank in, and Jax slid in behind me, wrapping his arms tightly around me.

"I'm sorry, Kai," he whispered, the heat of his breath brushing the shell of my ear. I didn't move a muscle. "I've been an ass, and I'm really sorry, but I don't want to leave you alone. I said I would help you, and I meant it."

"That's the problem, Jax." I shifted out of his arm and flipped over, facing him. "You're not helping me. You're giving me a complex. You're building my confidence just to turn around and shatter everything you built."

"Kai." His tone was thick with sorrow as he reached out, cupping my face.

"No, Jax." I cut him off. "I don't want your 'sorry.' I need you to be all in or all out."

"And what does being all in entail?" His gaze lingered on my mouth.

"You let me explore the wide world of sex with you and a friendship. It means if you need space from me, you talk to me. You don't ghost me like I'm another one of your Puck Bunnies."

"You're not."

I shrugged. "I wouldn't know because that's how you act."

His throat flexed on a hard swallow. "I'm a dick."

"Yeah, a little bit."

"So, you're proposing friends with benefits, no strings attached?" His thumb grazed over my bottom lip. "Is this friendship exclusive or open?"

"That's the other thing we should discuss." He raised his brows. "You can't act like a jealous boyfriend whenever I go out with someone, especially when we both know you're not. I know you think you are protecting me, but I need to date to learn to navigate the dating world."

"How about this?" He propped his head up on his hand as his other hand dropped from my face. "As long as we are exploring the wide world of sex with each other, we do not have sex with other people, but if or when you think you are ready, let me know, and I will step down as your sex toy."

I laughed. "And dating?" I propped my head up on my hand to match him. "Will you continue to insult and threaten my dates?"

"No," he gritted out. "As long as you agree to no intimacy without letting me know first."

"Intimacy?" The word had gone from sex to intimacy. Intimacy was a lot more than just sex.

"Yes." He leaned forward, his breath fanning across my lips. "No one touches you until we are done. No kissing, no sex of any kind, no intimate touching." I honestly didn't think that would be a problem, especially considering that before Jax, I'd only been kissed once, but Jax brought a different girl home every other night. This agreement might be more difficult for him.

"And you're okay with following the same rules?"

"I don't date, Kai."

"But you do have sex, a lot."

He laughed. "The rules apply to me as well. I will not fuck anyone until we agree our deal is over."

"Let me make sure I understand your proposal. If I decide to have sex with someone else, I need to end it with you first?" He nodded. "And if I agree to this, we will have sex?"

"We will go as far as you are comfortable with." He was letting me set the pace.

"And if sex doesn't happen for months, will you find it from someone else?"

"What?" He scowled, shaking his head. "No. The rules apply to me, too. If, for some reason, I want to end this agreement, you will be the first to know." His hand curled around my waist. "But I need you to be honest too."

"About?"

"What you want?"

"So, if I wanted to learn how to give a blow job, I would say..." His lips twitched into a sexy smile that made my insides melt.

23

Jaxtyn

I wanted Kaia, but the thought of commitment or relationships freaked me out. Like panic attack level freaked out. I had zero intention of letting Kaia end up in someone else's bed, but I needed to somehow fool my mind into believing this was a friendship to get past my commitment phobia. Hopefully, with me, she wouldn't need anyone else.

Kaia and I stood at the foot of the bed, our gazes locked.

"Are you sure you want to do this?" I pressed my thumb to her bottom lip. Her brows raised as her chest rose and fell with deep, ragged breaths. I dropped my mouth to her lips so she could feel my words. "Do you want my cock between these pretty lips?" Her cheeks flushed as she swallowed hard. I loved everything about Kaia, but I couldn't lie; her innocence did something strange to me. I brushed my lips across hers. Her breath hitched, and her eyes closed. "I want you to suck me into this hot wet mouth and pull me deep into that tight little throat. Is that what you want to do, Kai?

"Yes," she breathed. "I want to learn how to please you."

Fuck! I bit down hard on my bottom lip as all the blood rushed to my cock. She didn't want to learn how to give a blow job. She wanted to learn how to please me.

Gripping the back of her neck and pulling her mouth flush with mine, I kissed her so hard it suffocated both of us until she jerked back, gasping for air. Grabbing the hem of her tiny tank top, I ripped it over her head, tossing it to the bed. I let my gaze rake over her perfect curves. Fuck, she was hot.

"Get on your knees, baby." She slowly sank to her knees. Heat swirled through my groin as I peered down at Kaia on her knees, eager to please me. "Tell me what you want." I needed to hear those filthy words come out of that pretty mouth. Staring up through her lashes, she pressed her lips into a tight line. "Say it, baby."

"I want to make you cum." And those six little words would be my undoing.

"Do you want me to fill your throat with my cum?" Her cheeks grow an even deeper shade of pink. "Answer me, Kai."

"Yes, I want to taste you." She had no idea what her words did to me.

"If you want it, take it." I took a step forward. Staring up through her long dark lashes, she slid her fingers into the waistband of my boxer briefs, hesitating briefly before slowly guiding them down my thighs. My dick sprang free, and her eyes widened. I couldn't tell whether they widened out of excitement or intimidation. She pushed my boxers past my knees, dropping them to my feet, and I stepped out, flipping them across the room.

Her heated gaze flicked from my cock to me as one hand flattened on my thigh and her other small hand wrapped around my thick girth.

My gaze lowered to her bare tits. Her perky nipples pulled tight, and I could only imagine how wet her pussy was for me. I'd fantasized about this moment an embarrassing number of times, and now that it was happening, it felt unreal. She was my deepest hidden desire. She was my dirty little secret. The one thing I wasn't supposed to want, but I did. I wanted her so fucking bad it hurt.

"Do I just put it in my mouth?"

"You do whatever feels right." Her tongue swept out, wetting her dry lips before pressing the tip of my dick to her lips. "Fuck, Kai, you have no idea what seeing you like this does to me." Her lips parted, sliding the tip of my cock through her full pouty lips, and my head fell back on a groan as the heat of her mouth surrounded me.

Her grip tightened as she rolled her tongue over the tip of my swollen cock. "Fuck," I choked out. Her mouth sealed around my head as she slurped, sucking so hard her cheeks hollowed. I wasn't sure how long I could handle letting her explore my cock. I wanted to fuck her face. I wanted to slide my fingers into her hair, hold her in place, and pump in and out of her throat until I filled it with my cum, but I couldn't. This was her show, and I'd let her have it for now, anyway.

"Like that?" She didn't look up at me this time. Her gaze was fixed on my cock. My hand slid into her hair at the back of her head, and I tugged so she looked up at me.

"Just like that." My lips curved into a grin. "Open your mouth, baby. Open wide for me and take me as deep as you want me." Her tongue swept across her lips as her eyes lit with excitement. My grip loosened, giving her the control back. Her hand tightened around my base as she opened wide, guiding me back through her lips and pushing me deeper into the heat of her mouth. My eyes closed, and my muscles clenched. I fought the urge to feed her my cock. The urge to rock my hips into her face and force myself deep. She gagged a bit as I hit the back of her throat, and I groaned. She pulled back and then slid me back in deeper. She moaned, sending vibrations through my cock and I thought I might lose it.

"Kai." Her name came out as a warning plea that I needed more.

She pulled off. "Fuck my face."

My grip tightened in her hair, and I jerked her head back to look me in the eyes. "Kai?" It was a question. This was her show, and I didn't want to take that away from her if she didn't want me to.

"Do it, Jax." Her lips curled into a smirk as her heated gaze locked with mine. "Fuck my mouth."

She hissed as my grip tightened in her hair, and I guided her back to my cock. "Open for me, baby. Let me feed you my cock." She eagerly did as she was told. "I'm going to fuck your face." I slid my cock through her lips. "I'm going to start slow, but then I'm going deep and hard." I slid to the back of her throat, watching her eyes as she gagged around me. "If you want me to stop, slap my thigh hard." I held myself deep. "Do you understand, Kai?" As she nodded, her gaze darted down. "Keep your eyes on me, baby. I want to see those pretty blue eyes when I cum down your throat." Her eyes flared as they met mine, her chest heaving as I slowly pulled myself out of her wet heat.

I started slow, giving her time to learn my rhythm as I thrust my hips forward, sliding in and out of her. My speed increased, and I released a deep groan as I shoved myself deep, pumping in and out faster. She formed a suction around me, deepening the friction, and that only made me increase my speed. I bucked my hips forward, holding myself deep as a tear streamed down her pretty face. I expected her to stop me, but she didn't. Her tongue curled around the bottom of my cock.

"Do you like gagging on my dick?" I murmured, our heated gazes locked. "Do you like feeling me in the back of your throat? I bet that pussy is soaking wet." I jerked out of her, and she gasped for air. She opened wide, staring up through long dark lashes, and I fed her my cock again. She took control back, pumping up and down, sucking hard.

"Fuck," I cried out. "I'm about to come." Releasing her, I let her continue to fuck my cock with her mouth until my body tensed and my muscles clenched. She shoved me to the back of her throat. Her fingertips dug into the skin of my thighs as I emptied myself down the back of her throat with her pretty blue eyes locked on mine.

She drew back, swallowing before drawing in a deep breath. I dropped to my knees.

"Are you okay?" Cupping her face, I swiped my thumbs across her cheekbones, wiping away the wetness under her eyes.

"Yes," she panted, nodding slowly. "That was fucking

hot." A huffed laugh escaped me as I pulled her into me. I was worried I'd gone too far. There was no way in hell I was letting someone else touch her.

Kaia Cruz was mine.

24

Jaxtyn

Laying in Kaia's bed naked except for the thin sheet draped over my dick, my gaze followed Kaia's almost naked body as she strolled through the bedroom; stopping in front of the full-length mirror, she reached up and pulled the band from her hair, letting her long blonde wavy hair unravel down her bare back. I loved how comfortable she was with me, but she was making it hard not to put her back in bed and pin her underneath me.

Kaia had her first practice with her new partner, Peter or Preston, or something like that. His name was irrelevant because, as far as I was concerned, he was irrelevant. I doubted he would ask her out again, but if he did, I knew it wouldn't go anywhere because Kaia wasn't one to go back on her word.

"I'll take you to practice today," I sat up in bed and

kicked my feet over the edge. "Are you working tonight?"

"Yes. I'm working a double today. I had to switch a shift so that I could go to Rock Fest this weekend." Her gaze met mine through the mirror. "You're going, right?"

"Yes." I leaned down, ripping my boxer briefs off the bedroom floor. "Family meeting tonight to discuss it. We need to figure out where everyone is sleeping and what we need before we go."

"Family meeting." She chuckled. "Owen and Cam are going too."

"Yeah." I pulled on my boxers before strolling to her. I wrapped my arms tightly around her naked torso and pressed my lips to her shoulder. "They are part of the family." I hummed against her heated skin.

Her head fell back against my shoulder when I straightened, and I couldn't stop myself from letting my gaze rake over her naked flesh, her round perky tits and pink nipples pulled tight like they were begging to have my mouth on them and up to her full pouty lips. My chest swelled as memories of last night flashed forward, and the feel of those pouty lips and the heat of her mouth wrapped around my cock.

"I thought you didn't have to be at practice until after classes today." She pulled me back to the present, and I dropped my arms, even though I didn't want to, as she wiggled free.

I didn't have to be to practice until later today, but I wanted to make my presence known in front of her partner today. I was pissing on my territory. Kaia wouldn't know it, but her partner would. "I figured I'd get in a little ice time before class this morning. Do you need a ride to work?"

"Nah." She smiled, pulling a shirt off her dresser. "Cam will be there. She can drop me off at work."

"I'll pick you up tonight after your shift. Trystan will be home tonight so that we can figure out everything for Rock Fest."

"Sounds good. Now go get dressed so I'm not late." She was cute when she barked orders.

An hour later, we were dressed and walking into the arena. She went left to meet up with Petrov and her new partner, and I went right to get my skates out of my locker. By the time I got my skates on and hit the ice, Kaia and her new partner were already twirling around the ice while Petrov shouted orders to them. Jealousy bloomed in my chest at the sight of her hand in his, and I reminded myself she wasn't his. I didn't know much about ice skating, but even I knew the two of them moved beautifully together.

I had zero intentions of putting in ice time this morning. My first class was at 7:00 a.m. It was 6:20 a.m., but before I could leave, I needed him to see me, to see I was here with her. I needed him to know she was mine.

I leaned against the wall, my arms crossed over my chest as I watched them glide by, and when my gaze met his, I knew he got the message.

25

Jaxtyn

Kaia got off at ten, and I pulled the bar door open at exactly 9:50 p.m. I liked to be here on the nights she worked, but tonight, I'd gotten caught up with helping Trystan and lost track of time. Her day shifts didn't bother me, but I didn't like her on this side of town after dark. The bar was located in the part of town with the highest crime rate. It was known for drugs, gangs, and violence. Since she started working here, I'd always been here when she left, even if she didn't know it.

My gaze scanned the busy bar for her. "What the fuck?" I muttered when my eyes landed on her sitting at the bar with Parker. My lip curled into a snarl as my fist clenched at my sides. Apparently, he hadn't gotten my message today, or he did, and he didn't give a fuck. Anger surged through me, but I controlled it, remembering she was leaving with me this weekend for Rock Fest.

"I thought you got off a ten," I said, not bothering to hide my annoyance. Parker and Kaia twisted to look at me.

"What's up, man?" Parker smirked, leaning back against the bar cockily, and I felt the anger still simmering in my veins. Kaia didn't know what that smirk meant, but I did, and that answered my question; he didn't give a fuck. I couldn't act stupid here with Kaia. If I punched him in the throat right now, he won because she would be pissed at me. So I had to live with the fact that she'd be sleeping in my tent tomorrow night.

"I got cut an hour ago," Kaia said. "And Parker was here, so we were hanging out." They were fucking hanging out? The quirk of his lips told me he was satisfied with my irritation, and the quirk of mine told him he didn't stand a chance.

"Let's go," I snarled, refraining from snatching her off the stool, throwing her over my shoulder, and carrying her out like she was mine.

Kaia slid off her stool, and I twisted to leave. "I'll see you tomorrow night, Kaia," Parker said.

I was stunned, but I didn't stop walking. Did he say, 'I'll see you tomorrow night'? Because tomorrow night we would all be at Rock Fest. Did she invite him? I shoved through the door so hard it slammed into the outside wall. He was wrong if he thought he was sharing a tent with her, and I'd be happy to correct him.

"Wait up, Jax," Kaia called out. I didn't stop, but she did catch up. "What's your problem?"

"Get in the truck." I jerked open the passenger side door, but she didn't move. "Kai, please get in the truck." I'd said please, but my tone said to get in the truck, or I'll throw you in the truck. It had been one day since we'd made our agreement, and it was already over. She was going to invite him into her tent.

Kaia climbed in, and I slammed the door before running around the front of the truck and climbing in.

"What's wrong, Jax?" Kaia asked as I pulled the truck into traffic.

"Did you invite him to Rock Fest?"

"Yeah," she said, confusion twisting her face. "Trystan said I could."

"Did he?" She nodded. "And will he be sharing your tent?"

"What?" His brows knitted tightly. "No. He's bringing his own tent." She cocked her head. "Wait, is that what this is about? You thought I was going back on our deal?" I shrugged, keeping my eyes on the road, afraid if I looked at her, they'd give too much away. "Jax, no offense but your communication skills suck."

I huffed out a laugh. "Yeah, no shit."

"Parker and I are just getting to know each other. I'm not ready to share a tent with him."

"Do you like him?"

She shrugged. "I don't know. He's attractive and easy to talk to, but I've heard about his reputation with the ladies, and I'm not interested in being just another notch in someone's bedpost." It didn't sound like I had much to worry about. "I want someone who makes me feel like..." She trailed off.

"Like what?"

"Like you do when you're not a commitment-phobic asshole."

I laughed. "Well, your communication skills are on point." I swerved the truck into the driveway, parking in the darkness. Hitting the button to unbuckle my seat-belt, I lifted the center console and clicked her belt loose.

"What are you doing?" she asked as I slid into the center of the truck. I looped an arm behind her, wrapping it around her waist, and hooked my hand under her knee on the opposite side, and with one swift pull and a tiny yelp, she was straddling me.

My hands curled around her bare thighs just below her ass. Maybe I liked her work shorts more than I realized. Her hands slid around the back of my neck.

"What are we doing?"

"I need to feel you on top of me."

"Everyone is home and waiting on us. They could see us."

My hand slid around the back of her neck, pulling

her to me. "Let them watch," I breathed against her lips. I pulled her mouth flush with mine, savoring her sweet taste. She moaned, thrusting her tongue into my mouth as my grip tightened in her hair, holding her in place.

I wanted to lay my claim to her. I wanted to fuck her but not here like this in my truck. "We should go in," I panted, breaking from the kiss. Our gazes met, and I saw the disappointment pointed back at me. I leaned up straighter, pressing my body into hers. I'd seen that look before in women, but it had never affected me the way it did right now. I stood strong, though, because her first time wasn't going to be in my truck. "Come on, baby. I'll feed you!"

Her eyes lit up. Apparently, feeding her made her happier than the possibility of sex.

26

Jaxtyn

I didn't think Trystan thought it through when he invited us to Rock Fest together. Trystan had a thing for Cam, and Cam was obsessed with Trystan, but because Trystan was emotionally unavailable, she had a thing for Owen, and Owen had a thing for her. I was into Kaia, but Kaia's attention was on Parker, and I wasn't sure whether Parker was really into her or just into pissing me off.

This was going to be a train wreck.

We'd managed to work out sleeping arrangements fairly easily, but I seriously doubted that's where anyone would end up sleeping. Kaia and Cam were bunked together, and Owen and I would share a tent. Parker and Trystan had their own tents, and Harlow and Syn were sharing.

It was day one of Rock Fest, and I was already irritated by Parker's presence, but I promised Kaia I wouldn't interfere with her dating life if she promised that there was no intimacy and I had to keep my end of the deal if I wanted her to keep hers. So instead of pounding his face in, I sat stewing on the opposite side of the fire, trying to watch them, thankful the music was done for the night and everyone would be ready to pass out soon.

Rock Fest was a massive stage set up in the middle of several thousand acres of open land, and the show went on regardless of weather status. There was a large designated area for fans to watch their favorite bands and a designated camping area. There were porta potties around the property and three large restrooms equipped with showers. On the opposite side of the camping area, hundreds of food trucks sold anything you could want 24 hours a day, and of course, it wouldn't be Rock Fest without the vendors selling the bands' shirts.

"I'm going over to the north restrooms," Kaia said, pushing to her feet. "And then I think I'm going to call it a night."

"That's a long walk." I scowled. Kaia preferred the northside bathrooms because they were so far away that no one used them, and they were cleaner.

"I'll go with her," Parker said, pushing to his feet. I refrained from rolling my eyes. Of course, he would take her.

My gaze followed them as they disappeared into the darkness, and my knee bounced rapidly as I fought the urge to follow them. It wasn't that I didn't trust Kaia. I wanted to be near her, and even more than that, I hated that he was with her.

"Jax," Cam said. My eyes snapped to hers. "Did you hear me?" I hadn't heard her or anything else for that matter. My need to follow Kaia drowned out everything around me.

I pushed to my feet. "No, sorry." I shook my head. "I'll be back." She nodded, and I stormed after Kaia and Parker.

By the time I made it to the northside restrooms, they were both already inside.

Shouldering the wall, I hid in the darkness around the corner of the restroom building, waiting for Kaia like some kind of creeper, but I didn't care. I needed a minute alone with her.

Kaia stepped out of the restrooms, and before she had a chance to register what was happening, I swooped, wrapping my fingers around her wrist and jerking her into the shadows with me. She squealed out, and I clamped my hand over her mouth, pressing her tightly between my body and the wall of the building.

"It's me," I whispered, and she visibly relaxed. I dropped my hand.

"What are you doing?" she asked, amusement laced in her tone.

I decided to show her instead of telling her. I swooped in and claimed her lips. I kissed her fiercely, suffocating both of us.

"Kaia," Parker called out just around the corner from us, and Kaia yanked back, gasping for air.

"Shhh," I breathed against her ear before brushing my lips over the shell and trailing down, kissing, tasting, and nipping at her throat. A soft whimper pushed past her lips. "Shhh." Knowing that he was on the other side of that wall waiting for her while I had her in my hands and tasted her with my mouth made my dick throb painfully against the denim of my jeans.

I didn't bother looking to see if he was still there because I knew he was, and I was about to make her come just to remind her who she belonged to. "I'm going to taste you right now." I breathed against her lips. "And I'm going to make you cum so hard you see stars." She inhaled sharply. "But you can't make a sound."

I dropped to my knees in front of her.

"Jax," she whispered, a breathy plea wrapped tightly with excitement and panic. I placed my index finger to my lips, reminding her to be quiet.

Leaning forward, I skimmed my nose up the length of her pussy through the thin material of her tiny sleep shorts.

"Uh, Kaia?" Parker called out again, and a slow smile spread across my face as I hooked my finger in the crotch of her shorts. Her breath hitched as I slowly pulled them to the side. God, I loved these shorts. I couldn't wait to taste her, to feel her squirm under my mouth. I slid my tongue through her soaking wet flesh, slowly grazing over her swollen clit. Her breath whooshed out as her fingers threaded into my hair.

I wanted to say so many dirty things to her, but I couldn't. Thankfully, several people were still partying in the area, so our labored breathing and whispers weren't echoing through a quiet night.

Flicking her clit, I swirled my tongue slowly around the bud as I pulled one of her legs over my shoulder to give me better access to her entire pussy. My mouth closed over her pussy as I sucked her into my mouth, swirling my tongue slowly over the sensitive bud. Her body vibrated against me, and I groaned, completely forgetting we needed to be quiet, but at that point, I didn't care.

Her grip tightened in my hair, and she pushed my face hard into her pussy, coating my mouth with her arousal. She wanted more, so that's what I'd give her. I increased my speed until her entire body tensed, and she rocked her pussy into my face.

I was going to need a private tent tonight because there was no way this throbbing in my pants was going anywhere without some attention.

Her fingers curled tightly into my scalp, holding me in place as her abs tightened, and she moaned the softest, sexiest moan I'd ever heard as she came all over my face.

By the time we corrected ourselves and caught our breath, Parker was gone, and I wasn't mad about it. Had he heard us? I didn't know, and I didn't care. By the end of the weekend, he would know Kaia was mine.

27

The crowd roared as Trystan and his band, Twisted Rage, took the stage. The music started, and the bright lights flickered across the dark stage, illuminating the band. Trystan belted out the lyrics, and I pulled my phone out of my pocket. I held it up to snap a picture as Trystan owned the stage. I snapped the picture, making sure to get the entire stage and the full moon behind them.

Everyone was at the front of the stage but me. Seeing Twisted Rage up close was an experience, being able to feel the lyrics as they sang and smell the sweat dripping from their bodies, but you didn't get the full magic of everything that happened on the stage being so close.

My hips swayed with the heavy beat as the music's bass increased. A flash of lightning lit up the sky, and rain started to trickle down.

Long fingers curled around my waist as he pressed his front flush against my back, moving his hips with mine. I could feel the heat radiating off him as I melted into him. My head fell back on his chest, twisting slightly when he dropped his head to my ear.

"I can't keep my hands off you," Jax whispered against my ear. "Especially if you're going to move your hips like that."

"Someone will see."

"Let them watch." He pressed his lips to the spot on my neck just behind my ear, and chills rippled through me.

"Them?" I asked as he mapped kisses down my neck to the curve of my shoulder. "Or Parker?"

"Are you insinuating I'm jealous?"

"Are you?"

Our bodies moved in sync as Trystan belted out the lyrics to his newest song. "The thought of him touching you makes me insane." He breathed against my neck.

"I thought we agreed to date other people."

"I changed my mind."

I opened my mouth to ask more questions, but he dropped his hands, and his heat was gone.

"There you are," Parker called out.

"Hey." I swallowed hard, trying to control my breathing as I forced a smile and resisted the urge to see if Jax was still behind me.

"What are you doing back here?" Parker asked, and

when his gaze didn't flick over my shoulder, I knew Jax was gone. A twinge of disappointment hit me, but I fought to keep my facial expression normal. "Everyone is up at the stage."

"I like it back here." He cocked a questioning brow. "I like to be able to see the entire stage."

My phone vibrated in my hand. Flipping it over, I smiled. It was Jax.

Jax: He can't give you what you need.

I reread the text. Was Jax insinuating he could give me what I needed? Did he know something I didn't? Because I wasn't even sure what I needed.

Kaia: And you can?

The bubble with three dots popped up immediately, like he already knew his response.

Jax: He would bore you to death.

Kaia: And you wouldn't?

Jax: He's not what you need.

Kaia: Tell me what I need, Jax.

Jax: Come find me, and I'll show you.

My gaze flashed up to Parker, who was watching the band. Parker and I were friends. There was a physical attraction, but that was where it fizzled out, and we both knew it. He was my new skating partner, and we were building a friendship, but there was no chemistry between us. Maybe there could have been if our first date hadn't gone so drastically bad, but that bridge had burned.

Trystan's band finished their last song, and the crowd went wild with excitement. They announced their tour with Wicked Sinners and exited the stage for the next band.

"I'm going to grab a bite to eat," Parker shouted over the crowd. "You wanna come?"

I shook my head. "No, I'm going to head back to camp." I didn't give him a reason because I didn't want to lie.

"Do you need me to walk you?"

"No, go eat. I'll catch up with you later."

Parker disappeared into the crowd, and I headed toward the campground.

Kaia: Where are you?

This was a big place, and there was no way I could find him if he didn't tell me. I stared at my phone, waiting for a response, but it never came. He'd left me on read.

Fingers wrapped around my wrist, and I balled my fist, ready for a fight, but when he jerked me around, slamming me into his chest, a smile spread across my face. "I'm right here." It was Jax. "Dance with me."

My skin prickled as his fingers skimmed the bare flesh of my waist, and I closed my eyes as heat flooded my body, settling between my legs. How did he have so much power over my body? He made me feel things I didn't know I could feel.

His hips swayed to the music as one hand slid down, gripping my ass tightly and pulling me flush against him. We were lost in the middle of a massive crowd covered in darkness.

"Are you going to tell me what I need?" I couldn't help the curiosity lingering in my thoughts.

His hand wrapped tightly around the back of my neck with his thumb under my jawline, holding me in place. Eyes locked on mine, he dropped his lips to mine as his thumb stroked my throat. "You need to be kissed so hard that you can't breathe, your body trembles, and your knees buckle."

I opened my mouth, but his mouth slammed into mine, literally siphoning the air from my lungs. His mouth moved slowly, like he was savoring the taste of my lips. His tongue slipped through my parted lips, tasting and teasing mine, and my heart pounded against my chest as the kiss turned desperate and frantic. His hand tightened around my jaw as he kissed me greedily, thrusting his tongue in and out of my mouth in intense, passionate strokes. My body trembled against his, and my knees felt weak. He drew my bottom lip between his teeth, sucking on the tender flesh.

I pulled out of the kiss, gasping for air as his lips trailed over my jawline. "You need to feel a flutter here," he whispered as his fingers trailed over my stomach, moving down slowly. "And heat here." His hand cupped me through my pants. My thighs clenched tightly to try to alleviate the pressure building.

My phone vibrated, and I pulled it out as his teeth raked down my throat. It was Syn, and they were looking for us.

"It's Syn," I breathed. "They are looking for us." He groaned against my heated skin before his head dropped to my shoulder.

"Let's go," he mumbled. "Before they hunt us down."

28

Kaia

After three rounds of shots celebrating Trystan and his band's success, I called it a night, and Cam decided to stay with Trystan. I didn't blame her. Tonight was our last night of Rock Fest, and Twisted Rage would be leaving tomorrow to tour with Wicked Sinners for eight weeks. There was no telling when the next time she'd see him would be or who he'd be when he came back. The world of fame could change a person.

Staring into the darkness of my tent as I listened to the raindrops trickle around me, I settled into my side, adjusting my pillow until I was comfortable. My phone vibrated next to me, lighting up the tent.

It was Jax.

Jax: Are you awake?

Kaia: Yep!

I half wondered what was going on. Jax was in the tent right next to mine. We could probably whisper through the walls and communicate with each other unless he wasn't back to the tent yet.

Jax: What are you wearing?

I couldn't fight the smile pulling at the corner of my lips. Was he sexting me?

Kaia: Clothes.

Jax: The tiny little sleep shorts?

I looked down like I couldn't remember. I usually slept in just panties and a tank top. I was only sleeping in these shorts as a courtesy to Cam, not that she'd really care, and because the bathroom was a mile walk and not connected to my bedroom.

Jax: You know, the ones that make it so easy for me to taste that sweet pussy.

I choked on my breath. Even if he wasn't here with me, Jax's words did something to me. I decided to try my hand at sexting back.

Kaia: No shorts.

Jax: Fuck.

I couldn't stop the flashback from earlier tonight and the night before from flooding my brain. My eyes closed, and I bit down on my bottom lip, remembering how it felt having his lips on mine as my finger traced circles over my bare stomach. I squeezed my thighs to help alleviate the building pressure as I remembered Jax's hands on me, but it wasn't enough.

Jax: Do me a favor?

Kaia: What's that?

Jax: Run your fingers through your sweet pussy and tell me how wet you are for me right now.

My cheeks burned, and my heart rate kicked up. Were we really doing this?

Jax: Are you dripping wet for me, baby?

My nipples pulled tight against the thin material of my tank top.

I was alone. No one would know.

We were really doing this!

My hand slipped lower, dipping beneath my panties as my pulse raced. Touching myself in the privacy of my tent wasn't half as risky as Jax going down on me in the middle of the woods with hundreds of thousands of people around us, but this felt so much more intimate.

Sliding my fingers through my soaking flesh, I teased myself as images of Jax flashed forward. Spreading my thighs, I arched my back, and a small moan escaped my parted lips as I circled my clit, imagining it was Jax's strong hands touching me. His insanely intense kiss, plus the three shots of tequila, had my entire body on fire, and it wouldn't take much to send me soaring over the edge.

Jax: Are you touching yourself, baby?

Kaia: Yes. I'm soaking wet.

I needed more, more of his filthy words.

Kaia: Tell me what you're doing.

I hit send and then mouthed, 'What the fuck.' What did that even mean? Why didn't I just say 'talk dirty to me."

Jax: You need me to talk dirty while you play with that sweet pussy?

But Jax knew what I wanted.

Kaia: Yes.

It was crazy how quickly he'd learned me, and he knew how hot his words made me. Or maybe that was just a thing all women liked. I pushed the thought out of my mind before I lost my focus—the focus of an orgasm.

Jax: Right now, I can't get the image of you on your knees in front of me with my cock stuffed down your throat out of my head.

Fuck. A rush of heat surged through me, settling between my thighs.

Jax: Your big blue eyes begging for more.

Jax: Begging for me to fill your throat with my cum.

Holy fuck. I slid my fingers down to my entrance, slowly pumping them in and out. My entire body trembled as my back arched, and I gasped. I could end this quickly. I knew my body, and I could get myself off in seconds, but I didn't want to.

Jax: You have no idea how badly I want to come to your tent.

Kaia: And what would you do?

Jax: First, I'd kiss you until I sucked all the oxygen from your lungs.

Kaia: And then?

I bit down on my bottom lip as I added another finger to add to the slow torture.

Jax: I would taste every inch of your perfect body. Starting with your mouth and working my way down to your soaking wet pussy.

Jax: I already know how sweet you taste.

I whimpered as my fingers stroked my clit.

Jax: I would hold you down and torture your clit until your body vibrated against my mouth.

Jax: Until you cum all over my face, and then I do it again, but this time I'd use my finger to stretch that tight little pussy.

Jax: To get it ready for my cock.

I was so close. He grunted.

He grunted.

I could hear him, and that only added fuel to my fire. I rubbed my clit as I pictured him stroking himself.

Kaia: And then?

Jax: And then I would grab your hips and force you to take every inch of my cock.

My abs clenched, and my breath hitched as I cried out his name. As my body went limp in satisfied exhaustion. Jax grunted, and I knew he'd finished, too.

Kaia: Good night, Jax.

Jax: Good night, Kai.

29

Kaia

Leaning forward, I tugged at the laces of my skates as Cam dropped into the seat beside me. "How was practice?" She asked, slumping back into the seat and crossing her arms over her chest.

"Brutal." I groaned as I peeled my skates off. My gaze flicked to her feet. No skates. It wasn't like Cam not to skate. She skated every morning. It was part of her exercise routine. "Have you heard from Trystan?"

"No." Cam shook her head. "But I didn't really expect to." She forced a smile as her gaze flicked out to the rink at the same time Owen and Jax hit the ice skating toward us.

Cam was different since Trystan left. There was always a light around Cam. In all the years I'd known her, I'd never seen her truly sad, but Trystan left a week ago, and the minute he disappeared on that bus, the light left her eyes. I wished I knew how to make it better.

"What do you want to do tonight?" I smiled. "Just me and you."

"Anything?" she asked, tilting her head and raising her brows, and I somehow knew, at that moment, I was agreeing to trouble. But if it made her happy, I'd do it. I nodded. "There's a fight at the Cages tonight. I want to go."

My expression faltered. I knew nothing about the Cages other than that Jax didn't want me going and Trystan didn't want her going, but they never really explained why. Jax also had a tendency to be overprotective and dramatic. "Are you fighting?"

"No," she said. "I want to check it out before I agree to fight." Cam was an adrenaline junkie who lived for the thrill, and I was not. It was why we made the perfect pair. We balanced each other out. I knew if Trystan were here, he'd stop her from going, but she needed this because he wasn't here.

"If I say no, are you going to go anyway?"

"Probably." There was no way I was letting her go alone.

I shrugged. "I'm in." What was the worst that could happen?

"Be ready at eight." She ran her fingers through her short, dark hair, pushing it out of her face.

"Should I invite Jax?" My gaze flicked out to the rink where Jax and Owen were slowly skating toward us.

"If you do, he'll lock you in your closet so you can't go." I knew she was right, and I also knew that wouldn't stop Cam from going alone, so I nodded, but I couldn't help but wonder what was so terrible about the Cages.

"Hey," Owen shouted from the ice up the five rows to us. "What are you two doing tonight?" My gaze flicked down, locking with Jax's.

"We are having a girls-only night," Cam said, her lips quirking to one side. Jax narrowed his eyes, and I broke eye contact. I was a terrible liar. I mean, technically, we weren't lying. We were having a girls-only night, but if he asked any other questions, my face would give it all away, and we both knew it.

"Sounds like my kind of night." Owen leaned forward on the wall.

"Girl's night." Cam rolled her eyes. "Hint hint, no boys allowed." She shrugged. "Sorry."

"What are you two doing tonight?" I asked.

"Boys night," Jax answered, the corners of his lips curved up. "No girls allowed."

Jax and Owen skated off when their coach shouted for them.

"Why do you think Jax and Trystan didn't want us at the Cages?" I asked as my gaze followed Jax back to his team.

She shrugged. "I don't really think it was about us

going. I think it was about me fighting. There aren't any rules, and it can be dangerous, but I'm not fighting tonight."

"So we're doing this?" I asked, making sure Cam really wanted to do this.

"Trust me." She smiled. "It will be fun. There will be tons of hot single guys, too."

30

Kaia

Cam swerved her car into the dirt parking lot of an old abandoned warehouse in the middle of nowhere, and I suddenly felt over-dressed in the little black dress and black strappy heels Cam told me to wear. I wasn't sure what I was expecting, but it definitely wasn't this—a dark and dirty old abandoned building in the middle of nowhere surrounded by old farm fields. A chill raced up my spine as my gaze surveyed the vacant property.

"Is this illegal?" I asked, crossing my arms over my chest as we strolled toward the warehouse. I don't know why, but it never crossed my mind before now that this might be illegal. Was it illegal to even be here? Everything about this felt illegal.

"Technically, yes," Cam said. "But we are so far off the grid we will be fine." She said it so confidently that I almost believed her. My dad would kill me if I got arrested. "Listen, if anything happens, just run. Call me when you are away safe, and I will come get you."

"What the fuck, Cam?" I whisper-hissed. Now I was worried.

"It's fine, Kai," Cam said. This was a normal thing between us. I freaked out about everything, and she worried about nothing and believed that everything would work out, and I did not have that belief. Typically, we balanced each other out, but I couldn't shrug off the bad feeling I had.

The parking lot was quiet enough to hear the announcer as we got closer to the door. My heart pounded with anticipation and fear of the unknown. What was I walking into?

Two large bald bouncers wearing all black stood guard at the entrance.

"What's up, guys?" Cam smiled.

"What's up, Cam?" the tallest of the two said. "We were starting to think you chickened out."

"You fighting tonight?" the other bouncer asked.

"No, just checking the place out. Any sure things tonight?"

"All newbies tonight," the tallest bouncer said, and Cam's lip curled into a snarl. I had no idea what they were talking about, and I didn't really care. My pulse thrummed so hard in my ears that I found it hard to focus on the conversation.

"Kaia," Cam said, and my gaze snapped up to her. "Are you coming?"

Well, I damn sure wasn't staying out here by myself. "Yes." I followed her through the main entrance and into a crowd of people, and I suddenly didn't feel over-dressed anymore. Everyone was dressed up. Not suit and tie dressed up but nightclub dressed up.

The smell of sweat and cigars overpowered the massive, dimly lit area. The only brightly lit area was the caged fighting ring in the middle of the floor, with crowds of people around it shouting as the two men in the cage tore each other apart. This wasn't my thing. The sight of blood made me queasy, but this was what Cam lived for.

"Do you want to hang back here?" Cam shouted over the crowd. "Or do you want to get closer?"

"I'll just hang back here."

"I'm going to go place a bet and then see if I can get closer."

I forced a smile and nodded. "Have fun. I'll be right here." Everything about this place gave me bad vibes. Cam disappeared into the crowds, and I jumped when my phone vibrated in my hand. I was definitely on edge.

It was Jax.

Jax: How's the girl's night going?

Holding my phone with both hands, I stared hard at

the screen, trying to figure out how to respond. I could confess where I was, but I knew he'd be pissed, and he would probably drop everything to get here. Or I could pretend to be having a great time and not in the middle of an illegal fight club.

Pressing my lips into a thin line, I decided pretending was safer. I started clicking out a vague response, being careful not to actually lie.

Something big slammed into me, knocking me to the ground. "Ouch. Shit."

"What the fuck, man?" a deep voice growled. I shuffled to my feet as my gaze flicked between two massive men.

"Do you have a fucking problem?" the other man snarled. His fist clenched, and his nostrils flared.

"You should watch where you're fucking going."

Fuck this. I hadn't been here for five minutes, but there was too much testosterone pumping through the air, and I wanted to leave.

Kaia: I'm sorry. We are at the Cages.

I hit send and waited as the tension built between the two men. I was going to find Cam and get out of here.

My gaze flicked up to gauge the situation, and one of the guys shoved his fist through the other man's face. "Fuck." I tried to move, but there was nowhere to go as the crowds surrounded us. Someone bumped into me, sending my phone flying and me to my knees. The one-on-one fight turned into a massive brawl, and I was right in the middle of it.

I was so fucked!

31

Jaxtyn

Whipping my truck into the dirt parking lot, my truck kicked dirt up behind me.

"Are you sure this is the place?" I snapped at Owen. The Cages were never in the same place. They moved after every fight to avoid attracting unwanted attention. Luckily, Owen was invited by friends who were going, so he knew where it was or how to figure out where it was.

Spotting Cam standing by her car in the darkness, I slammed on the brakes behind her, threw my car in park, and jumped out.

"Where's Kai?" I growled, my tone laced with venom. I didn't have time to jump down Cam's throat right now. That would have to wait.

"Jax, I'm sorry." Cam wrapped her arms tightly around herself.

"Cam," I shouted. "Shut the fuck up. Where is Kaia?"

"There was a fight, and she never came out."

"Cam," I snapped, grabbing and squeezing her shoulders. "I don't need the whole fucking story right now. I need you to tell me where Kaia was so I can find her."

"I'll show you."

"Let's go." I released her and followed her into the old abandoned warehouse.

The cage fights were still going on, but the warehouse was less packed than it usually was on a fight night. The fight that Kaia disappeared into must have cleared it out some. I followed Cam to the right of the door.

"I left her here."

"You left her?" I assumed they got separated during the fight, but she left her. She brought her here and then left her. That made my blood boil a little hotter. She opened her mouth, sorrow covering her face. I threw my hand up, stopping her apology or excuse or whatever was about to come out of her mouth. "Never mind. Owen, take Cam home, please."

"No, I need to..."

I twisted, stepping into her personal space so quickly she flinched. My fists balled at my sides, and my nostrils flared. She felt the anger radiating off me because she stepped back, and Owen put a hand on my shoulder. I would never hit Cam, but I wanted to throttle her right now. "You need to leave. Now." Anger colored my tone.

"Come on, Cam," Owen said. "Jax will let me know when he finds her." I nodded. Owen slipped his hand into Cam's and led her away. Twisting around, I ran a hand down my face, and when my eyes opened, they landed on Kaia's phone on the ground. I knew it was hers because it had the same pink cow print cover. Kaia loved anything cow print.

Grabbing her phone off the ground, I shoved it in my pocket. I had no idea how I was going to find her or if she was even here. She had no phone, and then it dawned on me. Her watch. If she had her Apple watch on, I could track her location. I pulled her phone out, punched in her passcode, and pulled up the find-my-phone app. After about thirty seconds, it found her watch.

She was still in the building.

It didn't give me exact locations, but it would hopefully get me close enough to the area she was in. With her phone in my hand, I pushed through the crowd to the opposite side of the Cage, and the phone indicated I was getting closer. I stopped in front of a set of double doors with no windows. My gaze flicked from the doors to the phone. It looked like I needed to go through these doors. I pushed through one side and stepped into a dimly lit long hallway.

According to her phone, she wasn't far from me. I

picked up my pace, stopping at each doorway to check for her.

"Owwww..." My heart clenched. That was Kaia's voice. I bolted to the doorway where the voice was coming from, swinging around the corner into the open doorway. Kaia was sitting on a stainless steel table with a tall, topless man standing in front of her.

"Get the fuck off her," I growled, surging forward, ready for a fight.

"Jax," Kaia called out. "No. Stop. Jax." I didn't stop.

"Woah, man." The man was obviously a fighter because he was still dressed in his fighting shorts and wrapped in tape. He threw his hands up in surrender.

"He was helping me, Jax."

I stopped.

"She got knocked down in a fight, and I pulled her out." He pointed to her ankle. "I tried to talk her into going to the hospital to have that looked at, but she's stubborn."

I blew out a heavy sigh. She was okay. "Thank you," I said my head to him as I moved to kneel in front of Kaia to check her ankle. "I'll take it from here."

"It was nice to meet you, Kai," the fighter said as he backed out of the room, and I rolled my eyes. I kept my gaze on her ankle because if I looked up and she was smiling at him, I was angry enough that I might have killed him.

"Are you okay?" I asked once we were alone as my

gaze scanned her ankle.

"I'm okay."

"Your ankle is pretty swollen. I'm going to take you to the emergency room to have it checked out."

"Jax, I'm really okay."

"You're going," I said, pushing to my full height. I scooped her into my arms, and she wrapped her arms around my neck.

She didn't say a word until we stepped into the darkness outside.

"Jax, I can't leave Cam."

"Owen is taking Cam home," I muttered as I dropped her into the passenger seat of my car.

Neither Kaia nor I said a word most of the ride to the hospital. I was too angry to talk, and I imagine she didn't know what to say.

"Are you mad at me?" she asked when I swerved into the emergency room parking lot.

"Yes." I threw the car into park and killed the engine.

"Like never talk to me again mad or..." I pushed open the car door, got out, and slammed the car door shut before she could finish. I was murder-someone-level mad, and I couldn't have this discussion with her.

It took us an hour and a half before we made it to the back, got the X-rays, and saw the doctor.

"The good news is you only twisted it," the doctor said. "The bad news is you still need to stay off it for a couple of days so you don't cause more damage."

"I'm a skater," Kaia said. "I have practice tomorrow."

"No, you don't," I said dryly. "You have five days off your feet."

"He's right." The doctor smiled, shrugging. "Take it easy, and you'll be back to normal before you know it."

"Thanks," I said, forcing a smile. The doctor left, and my gaze flicked up to Kaia. "Play stupid games, get stupid prizes."

"Jax..."

I threw a hand out, stopping her. "No." I shook my head. "I'm going to help you into the wheelchair, and we are going home. I don't want to talk to you about anything right now." She nodded.

From that moment until I dropped her on her bed, it was silent.

"Jax," Kaia sighed. "Can we talk about this?"

"No." I shook my head. "I'm going to bed, and maybe we can talk about it when I'm not furious."

Kaia's phone rang.

"That's probably Trystan."

Her jaw clenched. "You ratted me out?" I didn't call Trystan to tattle, but it's not my fault Trystan called when we were on our way to the Cages. I shrugged. "Did you rat Cam out too?"

I shrugged again before pointing at the still-ringing phone. "You should answer that, or he'll just keep calling." I spun around and strolled out of the room, closing the door behind me.

32

My gaze followed Jax as he slammed the door behind him. I knew he'd be mad, but I didn't realize he'd be this angry.

My phone buzzed again. "Shit." I held my phone in front of me. I could handle Trystan being mad at me, but the truth was they were both going to take it out on Cam when, in reality, it was my choice to go.

I swiped right, smiling for the camera as Trystan's face lit up the screen.

"What the fuck, Kai?" Trystan snapped, anger illuminating his face. "The Cages? Really?"

"I know it was stupid." I sighed.

His jaw flexed as he shook his head." Are you okay?"

I nodded. "I'm okay. I have to stay off my ankle for a few days, but then I'll be back to normal."

"Why would you go to the Cages?" I wasn't going to

answer that. I wasn't going to bring her into this. So I said nothing. "Cam, right?"

I tilted my head to the side. "This has nothing to do with her." If he wanted a reason to be angry with her, he wouldn't get it from me.

"Oh, no?" He rolled his eyes. "So it was your idea to go to the Cages?"

I rolled my eyes back, matching his energy. "You know what? This is your fault."

"My fault?" That surprised him.

"Yep." I said, popping the p. "Your fault. If you would just call Cam."

"Kaia." He cut me off. "We agreed that it would be easier not to talk every day."

"Tryst, she's been sad." I sighed. "Like really sad since you left, and I thought this would cheer her up."

"You both could have been hurt."

"I know, and I promise I will never do it again, but please don't be mad at us."

"How pissed is Jax?"

"He won't talk to me."

"He'll never admit it, but he was scared. He knows what happens to girls at those kinds of events."

"How long before he forgives me?"

Trystan shrugged. "A day or two, probably." Trystan looked left. "Hey, Kai, I have to go, but I'll call you tomorrow and check on you."

"Call Cam."

"I'll think about it." He flashed an all-white smile, and then the screen went black.

I dropped my phone on the bed beside me, blowing out a heavy sigh as my gaze flicked to the closed door that Jax slammed. I hated that he was angry with me, and I wasn't sure how to fix it.

My phone buzzed.

It was Cam.

I swiped right.

"Hello."

"Omigod, thank god you're okay," Cam said. "I'm so sorry, Kai. I should never have taken you there. You are okay, right?"

"I'm okay," I said, staring down at my bandaged ankle. "Are you okay?"

"Yeah, I wasn't near the fight when it went down, and by the time it was broken up, I couldn't find you."

"A really hot fighter pulled me out of it, took me to the back, and bandaged me up."

"No freaking way." I could hear the excitement in her voice. "Like how hot?"

"Really hot, and I gave him my number."

"Does Jax know?"

"Jax isn't really talking to me. I don't think I've ever seen him this mad."

"Yeah, Owen is pissed at me, and I'm sure as soon as Jax talks to Trystan, he'll be pissed too."

"He already knows."

"How mad is he?"

"He's..." I drew out the word. I didn't want to lie, but I also didn't want to upset her. "He's upset."

"Give it to me straight, Kai."

Blowing out a deep breath, I gave it to her straight. "He's fucking pissed."

"I can't blame him. I should never have taken you."

"You don't belong there either, Cam. He's not just mad you took me. He's mad you went, and I'm sure when he talked to Jax, he was worried about your safety, too. I don't know what's going to happen between you and Trystan, but you've been a part of this family for a long time."

"Well, I'm pretty sure Jax is going to disown me after this."

I had a feeling she was right. I had a feeling he was done with me, too.

THE NEXT FEW days flew by. The first morning, Jax brought me a pair of crutches so I could get around without him, and Syn and Harlow kept me company. On the second day, Cam showed up to visit, but Jax wouldn't let her in the house. I only knew this because Cam texted me that she was going to give him time and that she would come by later when he wasn't home. I didn't even know Jax was home. He'd avoided me since he handed me the crutches and walked out without saying a single word.

By the fifth day, my ankle was feeling better and not so tender, so I ditched the crutches but decided I still take it easy. Jax was still avoiding me. Tomorrow, everything would go back to normal, except it didn't seem like Jax would be part of my normal anymore.

33

Jaxtyn

I was still angry with Cam and Kaia, but forcing myself to stay away from her for five days ended up punishing me more than her. I missed her. I missed being around her so badly that I'd almost crawled into her bed the night before. The only thing stopping me was how furious I had been. But on day five, that boiling rage was down to a simmer, and one more day without her, it would probably go cold, and I would forget why I was ever mad.

Shoving my hands into the pockets of my black joggers, I strolled through the darkness of our connecting bathroom and into Kaia's room. A twinge of disappointment hit me when I spotted her asleep in her bed. Her TV was silent, but the screen flashed brightly, lighting her up, and before I realized it, I was standing next to her, brushing a strand of her blonde hair out of her face.

Kaia was beautiful, even asleep. I watched as her chest rose and fell with slow, shallow breaths. My gaze dropped lower. The corner of my lip curled up when I realized she was wearing my t-shirt. When it was Harlow or Syn's week to do laundry, Kaia always ended up with my clothes in her closet. My fingertips traced over her bare thigh.

Everything in me wanted to wake her up. To lean in and kiss her so hard, I stole her breath, but I didn't. Instead, I grabbed the blanket at the foot of her bed and pulled it over her before twisting to find the remote to her TV. I hit the power button, and the room went dark.

"Jax," Kaia whispered as her hand clasped onto mine. Swallowing hard, I closed my eyes as the heat from her hand sent a rush of blood straight to my groin. The only thing keeping me from responding was that I wasn't sure I could control myself. Thankfully, the room was dark, and she couldn't see my face.

Opening my eyes, I twisted to her as I cleared my throat. "I was just checking on you." My tongue swept across my mouth, wetting my dry lips. "I'm going to bed." I pulled lightly against her grip, hoping she didn't let go. She didn't. Her grip tightened.

"Please stay." She pulled gently. "I know you're still mad, but please stay." I wasn't mad anymore. Hell, I wasn't sure I ever was. I was terrified when the text came through that she was at the Cages. I'd heard stories, lots of stories, of the things that have happened to single women there, and I couldn't bear the thought of someone hurting her and not being there to protect her. "Jax?"

"Uh." I blew out a sigh. "Okay." I tapped the night light on the nightstand beside her bed, and the soft glow was enough to see her. I needed to see her. I needed to feel her heartbeat against me. Her sleepy gaze met mine as she released my hand, slid over, and lifted the blanket for me.

"Stay with me tonight."

I nodded, shoving down my black joggers and stepping out of them before I slid in beside her. I settled into the bed, and she settled into my side, curling tightly into me. Heat pulled at my groin as her heat surrounded me.

"Do you want to talk?" she whispered. I shook my head. I didn't want to talk. I'd missed her so fucking much that none of what happened mattered anymore. I just wanted her, and it hit me loud and clear. I wanted her.

"No," I said, my voice low and husky.

I shifted, not wasting any time. I swooped in, claiming her lips in a kiss so fierce it suffocated us both. She didn't hesitate in the slightest as her lips parted, and my tongue slid through, tasting and teasing her mouth. Her tongue met mine stroke for stroke as I rolled over her, settling between her thighs. She jerked back, gasping for air.

"Kai," I panted. "You are mine and only mine." Our eyes locked as her chest heaved. "Do you understand what I'm saying?" I didn't want to share her anymore. I never really did.

She nodded. "Yes."

I rose to my knees, grabbing the hem of her shirt and shoving it up as she lifted her body to let me pull it over her head and toss it across the room. I sucked in a sharp breath as my gaze raked over every perfect curve of her body. She didn't shy away from my gaze. I dropped to my hands, hovering over her.

I dropped my head. My mouth inches from hers. "Don't ever do that again."

"I promise."

My lips captured hers, and I kissed her hard as I ground my hips against hers, my cock settled between her thighs, straining and throbbing against her pussy lips. The only barrier between us was the thin material of her panties and my boxer briefs stopping my dick from sliding through her slick flesh.

I wanted her so fucking bad. To claim her. All of her. To make her mine.

"If you want me to stop, tell me now, Kai," I breathed against her lips. "Say it now."

"Don't stop." Her voice was a pleading whimper.

My mouth moved down her cheek to her jawline

and down her throat, kissing, tasting, and nipping her skin as I moved further and further down. I was so fucking desperate to slide inside her to feel her warmth to end this sweet fucking torture, but I'd waited this long, and I wanted to savor every minute of it.

My lips lowered, trailing kisses over her collarbone before shifting so I could kiss down her chest and over her tits. My mouth closed over her nipple sucking and flicking the taut bud with my tongue. She arched into my mouth, begging for more. My chest swelled with excitement. She was begging me for more.

I shifted to the side of her as my hand closed over her other tit. I massaged the sensitive flesh rolling the pebbled bud between my fingers as my mouth continued its slow torture of the other tit drawing it in between my teeth and tugging gently.

"Jax."

"Don't worry, baby," I murmured against her skin, letting the heat of my breath tease her skin. "You're going to come for me." My gaze met hers with a cocky smirk pulling at my lips. "And when your pussy is soaking wet for me. I'm going to fuck you until you come on me."

My hand raked down her stomach, teasing the skin just above her panty line with my fingertips. Another smug grin tugged at my lips when she shivered as I pressed my lips to her neck. "Do you have any idea how much it turns me on knowing no man has ever touched you," my hand slipped under her panties, dipping between her legs, "here?" I slid my finger through her slick flesh, groaning against her throat as she coated my fingers. "How much it turns me on that no man has ever been inside this sweet pussy?" She moaned, arching into my touch as my fingers teased her clit. I pressed my lips to her ear. "You are mine. This pussy is mine." My finger dipped, circling her entrance as I nipped at her earlobe. "Say it, Kai. Say you are mine."

"I'm yours," she breathed, her voice nothing more than a raspy whisper. "Please, Jax." She rocked her hips, chasing my finger.

"Tell me this pussy was made for me."

"It was made for you."

She gasped, gripping my shoulder as my finger slid inside. "You're so fucking wet for me, baby." My finger slid in and out, giving her time to adjust before adding a second finger. My mouth captured hers and kissed her hard, fast, and messy as my fingers pumped in and out, stretching her. Getting her ready for my cock. She moaned into my mouth when my thumb added pressure to her clit and found a rhythm that made her body tremble.

I wanted her so fucking bad. My dick throbbed painfully against her thigh.

My speed increased as she rocked against my hands. "Fuck, Kai. I need you to come for me. I need you to come all over my hand." My voice was rough. As if on cue, her pussy walls squeezed my fingers, and she cried out as she came all over my hand. I pulled my fingers out of her and dragged them across my mouth as my gaze held hers before slowly pulling them between my lips and sucking them clean.

Her chest rose and fell with deep, ragged breaths as she came down from her first high, and I shifted on the bed, pulling my boxers off and then ripping her panties off. I needed her now.

"You sure?" I asked as I climbed over her, settling between her thighs, careful not to let my cock touch her yet.

"I'm sure." Her eyes pleaded with me not to stop.

I pressed my cock to her center, groaning as I slid through her arousal, the orgasm I gave her. Positioning myself at her entrance, I guided my hips forward, careful not to go too fast. She was a virgin, and I didn't want to hurt her even though I was desperate to be balls deep inside her.

Her eyes squeezed shut as I pushed the head past her entrance and stilled when she sucked in a sharp breath and held it.

I pressed my lips to hers, kissing her softly. "Breathe, baby. Breathe." Her eyes eased open as she released her breath. I inched in deeper and deeper, slowly giving her time to adjust. A shiver ran down my spine with one last jut of my hips; I buried myself inside her, and her pussy tightened around me, and my cock throbbed inside her.

"You okay?" I rasped.

"Yes. More, please."

"You sure?" She rocked her hips, begging for more.

"I'm going to fuck you nice and slow until you tell me you want more." I withdrew completely and slowly entered her again and again until she was pleading for more. I pumped in and out, slowly picking up speed with each plea as she rocked her hips, meeting me thrust for thrust.

"Jax," she moaned, her body shaking beneath me.

"I need you to come on my cock, baby." My hips thrust forward, feeding her pussy more and more of my cock. Our bodies were slick with sweat as I slid against her, feeling her hardened nipples brush against my chest. Our labored breathing and wet sounds filled the quiet room. I was so fucking close, and so was she. Her pussy walls clenched around me, and her legs trembled. "That's it, baby. Don't fight it. Soak my fucking cock with your orgasm." Her abs tightened, and her back arched as she cried out, screaming my name. "Fuck." I shoved myself deep and then jerked out and slid my cock onto her stomach between us as I exploded.

I'd never had sex without a condom before, and I definitely didn't want to make a habit out of it. The last thing we needed was Kaia getting pregnant and having to explain that to our parents.

We used our clothes to clean up before settling into

her bed. She curled into my side, and I wrapped my arm around her.

"Did you mean what you said tonight?" she asked after we both finally caught our breath.

"Every single word. I don't want to share you anymore."

"So, are you my boyfriend?"

"We don't have to put a label on it. We don't have to complicate it. It's just you and me."

"So it's a secret."

I nodded. "For now."

I didn't know how to be a boyfriend, but I knew I didn't want to be with anyone but Kaia. I also couldn't imagine having that conversation with our parents. I wasn't sure what the future held, but right now, there was nowhere else I wanted to be. We'd figure the rest out later.

34

Kaia

Pulling open the bathroom door, I sucked in a deep breath inhaling the scent of greasy bacon. My gaze flicked over my room. Jax was gone. My mouth twisted with confusion. He was cooking breakfast? Jax didn't even know how to turn the stove on. Or at least I didn't think he knew how to turn it on.

Bouncing down the back staircase to the kitchen, I froze when I hit the tile kitchen floor. "Dad?"

His gaze flicked up to meet mine as his face spread into a smile. "There's my baby girl." My gaze flashed to Jax sitting at the breakfast bar, eating whatever my dad was cooking.

It wasn't that I wasn't happy to see my dad because I was. I hadn't seen him in over a month, but I wasn't expecting him back for another month. I also knew what this meant for Jax and me. It had only been a few days since Jax claimed me, and things were good, and the house was usually the only place we didn't have to hide. Who knew how it would go now? I didn't think we needed to be a secret, but Jax needed to do this in his own time, and I was okay with that.

Wiping the confusion off my face, I strolled further into the kitchen, pulling out the stool next to Jax and sliding in.

"Breakfast?" my dad asked without looking up from the bacon he was frying.

"Sure." I forced a smile. "What are you doing back so early?"

"We have to fly to Australia tomorrow, and Linda wanted to come home and check on everything first."

"What's in Australia?" Jax asked.

"Business stuff," my dad said, flipping the bacon in the pan.

"When did you get back?" I asked.

"Early this morning," my dad answered. "Everyone was sleeping, and we didn't want to wake you." Good thing they didn't because they would have found Jax in my bed naked, and there would be no turning back from that.

"Good morning, Ms. Fritz," Linda said, and my spine stiffened as I twisted to see Linda strolling into the kitchen with the phone to her ear.

They hadn't even been home twenty-four hours, and the community gossip was already calling. She was the neighbor from hell. The one who knew and saw everything, and if she'd seen Jax and me on the front lawn the night I found him in the driveway, Linda was about to know about it. Jax must have thought the same thing because his body stiffened as his gaze followed her.

"Uh huh," Linda hummed into the phone, smiling at my dad before leaning in for a kiss. "Well, Ms. Fritz, I would say that is their business." Linda's gaze flicked between Jax and me, offering a good morning smile. "I'm sure everything will work out in the end, but I do have to go. Perhaps we can catch up later." She grabbed a piece of bacon off the plate. "You too. Goodbye." She disconnected and dropped the phone on the counter.

"What was that about?" I asked, trying to sound disinterested.

"Apparently, Lacey Hall is pregnant."

"She's like fifteen," Jax said.

"I believe she's sixteen, but still," Linda said, raising her shoulders. "And apparently, the father is Christopher."

"Her stepbrother?" my dad cut in.

"Yes," Linda said with no judgment in her voice. "I'm just glad we never had to worry about that with our kids. You were all so responsible." I knew without a doubt she was referring to teen pregnancy and not a relationship between Jax and me.

"I have to go," Jax said, jumping off the stool, and I knew what she'd said had gotten to him. "I want to get in some ice time before school." Jax bolted out of the kitchen without another word.

"I need to go too," I said, sliding off the stool. "I'm meeting Cam at the rink this morning."

"Actually, Kai," Linda said. "We were hoping to talk to you for a minute this morning."

"To me?" I asked, my chest tightening. I wasn't opposed to telling them about Jax and me, but I didn't want to do it alone.

"Yes." My dad smiled. "Sit, please. Give us a few minutes before you leave."

Swallowing hard, I slid back onto the stool facing my dad and Linda as my chest rose and fell with long, deep breaths.

"Your dad and I were thinking maybe you would like to visit Australia with us."

"What?" My face twisted with confusion. That wasn't what I was expecting them to say. "I mean..." I paused. Did I want to go to Australia with them? I shook my head. No. Going to Australia sounded fun, but not with just my parents. Maybe if Jax, Syn, and Harlow were going, but they weren't because they all had school. "I have work."

"Quit," my dad suggested. "Or put in for vacation or a leave or something." He hated that I worked at that bar probably more than Jax and Trystan did.

"I..." I trailed off. I hadn't planned to tell him I was skating again yet. I don't know why. I knew he'd be excited. Maybe that was why. I didn't want to disappoint him if it didn't work out, but I didn't have a choice now. "I'm actually skating again. I have a new partner and a new coach."

"Kai, that's great," Linda said.

"We just started, and we are still working everything out."

"Maybe we can come see you skate this morning," my dad said.

"No." I shook my head. "Not yet. Maybe when you get back from Australia." I slid off the stool. "I really have to go through."

"Family dinner tonight," Linda said. "Six o'clock." I nodded, then bolted out of the house and into the garage to find Jax's car already gone.

He left me.

We rode to the rink every morning, but he freaked out again this morning and left me. Sighing, I rolled my eyes. Giving him time to work this out on his own was annoying.

My phone buzzed, and I jerked it out of my pocket, thinking it might be Jax explaining why he left me, but it was an unknown number.

Unknown number: Is this the pretty girl from the Cages?

Kaia: Maybe. Who's asking?

I knew who it was. I'd only given my number to one person that night, but I didn't want him to know that.

Unknown number: Alex, the man who saved you from being trampled on.

Alex: She told me her name was Kaia.

Kaia: That's me.

Alex: Can I take you out tonight?

A smile spread across my face. Even though I'd agreed to be Jax's, it still felt nice to be asked.

Kaia: Sorry, can't. Family dinner, and then I have to work.

Alex: You work at the East Side bar, don't you?

How did he know that?

Kaia: Well, that's creepy.

Alex: I was there a few nights before the fight and thought you were the prettiest girl I'd ever seen.

Kaia: You're a smooth talker.

Alex: There's more where that came from. Have dinner with me tomorrow night.

Kaia: I can't. I work.

I could end it by telling him I had a boyfriend, but Jax made it clear we didn't have labels. I hit the side button, making my screen black, and shoved it back into my back pocket, and when it didn't vibrate again, I figured he'd gotten the point.

Running into the house, I grabbed my purse and keys. Now, I had to go to the rink and see how badly his mom's words affected us because nothing was ever easy with Jax.

35

Kaia

Staring aimlessly into the distance, I rolled the silverware into a napkin. It was slow tonight, so I'd started my closing routine early. Thankfully, rolling silverware didn't require much thought because my mind was stuck on Jax.

I'd made it to the rink early for practice, but Jax wasn't there, and I was pretty sure he was avoiding me again. I was trying to be patient and understanding because this was all new to him, too, but it was getting harder and harder to understand why he did what he did.

"Hey," Anna shouted, pulling me from my thoughts. "A really hot guy just asked to be seated in your section out here."

I started to ask her if it was Jax, but I knew it wasn't because everyone here knew Jax. Since Trystan was gone, that meant it was probably Owen. I finished rolling the last silverware and placed it in my triangle stack before strolling out of the back through the bar and into the dining room.

But it wasn't Owen. It was the tall, dark-haired fighter who saved me from being trampled.

"Alex." I scowled.

"That wasn't the reaction I was hoping for."

"Sorry." I shook my head, shaking the surprised fog out. "I'm just... I mean... What are you doing here?"

"You said you were working, so I thought I would come and ask you out in person."

"You're persistent."

"I am. I won't go down without a fight." His lip curled into a grin. "Unless you give me a reason to."

"Like what?"

"Like you have a boyfriend, or you're married or something."

I shook my head. I wasn't sure what Jax and I were, but I knew this wasn't how I wanted to live: constantly worried about where I stood in someone's life, but I wasn't ready to give up on him yet, either. "No, I don't have a boyfriend, and I'm not married, but I'm still not interested."

"Yet." He smirked.

"Probably never."

"Probably?" I raised my brows. "You said probably. Which isn't a never."

"What can I get you?" I asked, fighting the grin tugging against my lips as I pulled my pad out of my apron and ignored his cocky grin.

"I'll have a burger and fries."

"Anything else?" I asked, jotting down his order.

"Yeah." My gaze flicked up as I pressed the tip of my pen to the pad, waiting for him to answer. He folded his arms in front of him and leaned forward on the table. "The time you get off."

"Not gonna happen." I smiled before spinning away.

This felt all sorts of weird. Here was this super hot guy begging to go out with me, and then there was Jax, the reason I was saying no, who wouldn't even return my call.

I punched his order into the system, fighting the urge to glance over my shoulder at the blue-eyed fighter.

"Kai," Joe shouted. My gaze flicked to my manager strolling up to me. "You're cut. Wrap up and clock out."

"I just got a table, but I can see if Anna can take it." He nodded as he passed me to help a customer at the opposite end of the bar.

Anna agreed to take my table, and I quickly grabbed my things and exited out the back so Alex wouldn't see me.

My jaw clenched when my gaze landed on Jax sitting on the hood of my car.

"Get off my car," I growled, my tone laced with anger.

He'd avoided me all day, ignored all my calls, and now he showed up here like nothing was wrong.

"Kai," he said, sliding off the hood and reaching for me.

"No," I said, dodging him, but I wasn't fast enough, and he caught me by the elbow. "Jax."

"Please, just give me five minutes, Kai," he pleaded, spinning me to face him and pushing my back into my car. "I know I fucked up."

"Yeah, well, you seem to do that a lot," I said, avoiding eye contact as I crossed my arms over my chest. "And this is getting to be exhausting."

"I know." His hands dropped to my waist. "I'm sorry."

I shook my head, shoving his hands off me. "You need to learn to use your words."

"I know," he said, putting his hands on the car hood behind me, blocking me in. "I've never been very good at this, but please let me try."

"You have two minutes," I muttered. "Talk fast."

He dropped his arms to his side. "Can we..."

"No," I cut him off. We weren't leaving this spot together until he explained. "One minute."

"I'm terrified of ending up like my parents."

"I know." I sighed. "Trystan told me it was bad."

"And I don't want to disappoint my mom either. I've put her through a lot over the years, and I'm trying to do better."

"And you think she would be disappointed in us?"

My brows furrowed in confusion. "Because I can't be your secret forever, Jax."

"That's not what I meant. I just think we need to know for sure that this is forever before we throw a grenade into the family."

I didn't believe that was the actual reason, but at least he was talking to me, and I understood his need for time. "You have to stop shutting me out."

"I know." His hands curled around my hips, and I didn't knock them away this time. He dropped his head, nuzzling my neck. "I'm really sorry, Kai."

"Okay." I sighed. "We can keep our distance while your mom and my dad are home for now, but eventually, this is going to come out, and it's better..."

"I know, Kai," he said, cutting me off as he stood back to look at me. "I just need time."

I nodded. "Where's your car?" I asked, scanning over the parking lot.

"I had Owen drop me off. So, can I catch a ride with you?"

Pulling my car door open, I tossed my purse inside. "You should probably walk. We wouldn't want them to get the wrong idea." I slid into the driver's side.

"Wait," he said. "Are you serious?"

I slammed the door shut and turned the key, starting the engine before rolling the window down.

"You can't have it both ways, Jax." Part of me understood why Jax was worried about our parents because neither of us knew how they would react, but the other part didn't care how they would react, and I wanted him not to care either. We were adults. "I'll see you at the house." I rolled up the window, put the car in drive, and drove away, my heart pounding so hard I thought it might explode.

My gaze flicked to the rearview mirror to see Jax still standing where I had left him.

36

Jaxtyn

Owen eased his white car up beside me in the bar parking lot where Kaia had left me, and I jerked the car door open and slid in. I wasn't angry with Kaia. I was angry with myself. I actually expected Kaia to leave me, which was why Owen wasn't far. I'd left her at the house that morning without a word, all because I panicked and didn't want our parents to see us leaving together, and it took me all day to realize that was irrational. Our parents wouldn't be suspicious because I gave her a ride. I deserved it, and she was right. I couldn't have it both ways, but I couldn't figure out how to get out of my old ways.

"She left you, huh?" Owen chuckled. He knew she'd probably leave me, too. I didn't bother answering because we both knew the answer. "That's what you get for bailing on her and then ignoring her all day."

"Shut up," I mumbled, sinking back in the seat, but I knew he was right.

Owen surged forward, pulling the car into traffic, quickly changing the subject to hockey and our upcoming game.

"So, are Cam and Kaia coming to the away game this weekend?"

My gaze flicked over to him as my mind reeled, and confusion surged forward. That was a weird question because Cam and Owen had a thing, and I would think he would know if she was coming this weekend.

"Why don't you ask Cam?"

"We haven't really talked since I dropped her off after the cages."

"Why?" I asked, dragging out the word.

"I don't know." He shrugged, not taking his eyes off the road. "She's called and texted a few times, but I haven't answered."

"Is this about the Cages or Trystan?"

"I don't know... Both... Maybe." Owen had it bad for Cam, and he never knew where he actually stood with her because Cam was in love with Trystan.

"Trystan's mad at her too," I said, turning to look out the window. "I think the only person not angry with her is Kai."

"So you haven't talked to her either?" I shook my head. I hadn't talked to Cam since I'd told her to leave the Cages, other than to tell her she wasn't welcome at the house, and I really didn't plan on it, but I also knew that cutting Cam from my life wasn't an option as long as Kaia was in my life.

Owen swerved his car into my driveway, stopping behind Kaia's black car. Shoving open the door, I shifted in my seat. "Go home, call Cam, and work your shit out. You need a clear head for the game."

"I could say the exact same thing to you." He winked. "See you in the a.m., bro." I slammed the door and watched him back out of the driveway. Owen was right; I needed to work out my shit.

Walking through the garage, I could hear the muffled laughter coming from the kitchen. Pushing open the door, I stepped inside to see my mom, Kaia's dad, Syn, and Harlow sitting around the small round kitchen table with a board game in the middle.

"Come play, Jax." My mom laughed. "We are about to start a new game."

There wasn't a place at the table for Kaia, but that didn't surprise me. Kaia hated board games. She'd never admit that it was because she was terrible at them, though, and she was a poor loser.

"I need a shower and sleep." I forced a smile. "Maybe next time."

I wasn't sure what I was going to do when I got upstairs. I wanted to crawl into Kaia's bed with her, but I knew I couldn't, not with our entire family downstairs.

Most of the time, it was just Kaia and me home, but everyone but Trystan was here tonight.

Both doors leading to Kaia's bedroom were not just closed but locked. Since the first night we moved into this house, Kaia had never locked the door from the bathroom to her room.

I showered quickly and then slipped into a pair of boxer briefs. My gaze flicked from my bed to the open double doors leading to the terrace overlooking the front yard. The same terrace that I shared with Kaia. Her bedroom had the same double doors as mine. I should go to bed, but I couldn't help but wonder if Kaia's doors were closed.

Stepping out onto the terrace, a gust of wind blew, and I sucked in a deep breath, inhaling her sweet scent. Kaia stood at the edge of the terrace, staring out into the darkness in nothing but one of my t-shirts that hung mid-thigh, and my fingers ached to touch her.

"Are you still mad at me?" I whispered.

"No." She glanced over her shoulder. "I'm sorry I left you."

I shrugged. "I would have left me too."

"So what now, Jax?"

37

Kaia

Jax and I sat on that terrace for hours that night, talking, laughing, and setting more ground rules. Well, he set more ground rules, like we behaved as long as our parents were in the house. Being with Jax was complicated, not just because we shared a home and our parents were married but because Jax was broken. Watching his parents go through their divorce destroyed his belief in a happily ever after, even though he'd seen how happy my dad and his mom were.

Even though I told Jax I agreed to his new rules, I didn't agree with him. We weren't kids anymore, and hiding like we were didn't make sense to me, but for now, it was okay.

Our parents were supposed to leave for Australia the following day, but something came up, and their plans changed, which kept them home for the next four weeks. That was the longest our parents had been home at one time in several years.

Even though I was desperate to have a place where we could be a normal couple, we managed to make it work; on the beach under the stars, in his car behind the bar, in the showers at the rink, he continuously found new places to be intimate. Still, Jax was always super careful that no one would see us even if we were in a public space, and after the third week, the sneaking around was starting to get old for me.

The night before our parents finally made their trip to Australia, I was in a better mood than I'd been in all year. I'd missed sharing a bed with him. It was always sex, then leaving because wherever we were, we couldn't stay. Then we'd go home, and he'd go to his room, and I'd go to mine.

I glanced over my shoulder to the bar where Cam and Owen stood drinking a beer and smiled. I wasn't sure if they were a couple, but I was happy they'd made up.

The bar had a live band, and it was packed.

"Kaia," Jeremy, the busboy, shouted over the music. "Table three needs you." I nodded and pushed my way through the crowd to table three.

It was Alex. Alex was here every night I worked, and every night, he asked me out. It had been four weeks, and he hadn't given up. I couldn't figure out if he was just that into me or liked the challenge.

"What can I get you, Alex?"

"A date tomorrow?" I shook my head. "Fine, I'll settle for a beer."

"What kind?"

"Surprise me."

From where I was standing, I could see the entire bar. Owen and Cam were still at the bar drinking, and Jax was standing with a group of college friends surrounded by Puck Bunnies. I was starting to hate the rule that we kept 'us' a secret. I hated that he wouldn't tell those girls he was off the market. Or maybe he wasn't. It was always hard to know where I stood with Jax until we were alone.

"Will anyone be joining you tonight?" I already knew the answer to that question. No one ever joined him. His routine was the same every night. He sat at the same table, asked me out when I took his order, and finally ordered something, and then every time I checked on him, he would ask me something about myself. It was like the longest first date ever.

"No. I can't stay long tonight. I have a fight."

"At the Cages?" He nodded. "You probably shouldn't be drinking then."

His lips curled into a grin. "I don't want the beer. I want the girl serving it to me."

Heat stung my cheeks, and my stomach fluttered.

"I'll get you that beer." I stumbled over my words. I stormed off, pushing through the crowd.

"Lex," I called across the bar. "Could you take table three a beer?" She nodded and narrowed her questioning eyes. "I need a break."

"What kind of beer?"

"Surprise him."

"I got ya!" She smiled.

Alex was getting bolder, and right then, I needed Jax to remind me that I was his. I pushed through the crowd, but Jax wasn't where I'd just seen him. The bar was too crowded, and I was too short to see over everyone without being on the elevated floor in the dining room.

I needed air. I pushed my way through the crowd toward the rear exit.

"I've had a few offers." I froze. It was Jax. I twisted around to see Jax standing off the dance floor in the darkness.

"You're really hot." The tall, thin blonde with him smiled. I shifted on my feet, turning to move towards them. "Do you have a girlfriend?"

"No." He smiled that flirtatious smile I loved so much at her. "I don't really do girlfriends." My heart twisted hearing him say it out loud. I knew in my head that it was him letting her know he wasn't interested, but I also knew that wouldn't stop her. The sparkle in her eyes said she wanted him.

Rolling my eyes, I twisted around and bolted for the rear exit. I was trying really hard not to be that girl—the jealous girlfriend who overreacts, especially when I didn't know if I was actually his girlfriend. Truthfully, Jax wasn't doing anything wrong, but I was so insecure in this relationship that it pulled out the worst emotions in me.

I sucked in a deep breath and slowly exhaled. The rear exit door clicked and then swung open.

"Hey," Jax said. "I thought I saw you disappearing out here."

"Yeah." I forced a smile. "I needed a break."

"What time do you get off?"

"I probably won't get cut tonight. It's too busy."

"The team wants to go to this party over near Saddle Creek. Call me when you're done, and I'll come pick you up and bring you to the party."

"I'm pretty tired. I think I'll just have Cam take me home."

"Oh, well, I don't have to go."

"Jax, don't be ridiculous. Go have fun with your team."

"Okay." He smiled, leaning forward and brushing his lips across mine. "The parents leave tomorrow morning, so maybe I can sneak in after."

"I think we should tell them before they leave," I blurted out without thinking before speaking. He stepped back, narrowing his eyes. "About us," I whispered, unsure what I was saying.

"Kai, I'm not telling our parents we're fucking." My lips parted in shock. That wasn't what I meant, but those words sliced through me, and I didn't know it then, but they left a painful permanent impression that told me exactly where I stood with him. "Kai, I thought we decided to keep this a secret." We didn't decide anything. He decided for us, and I agreed because I wanted him, and I thought that was enough, but as more time passed, I realized it wasn't.

"Yeah, you're right." I sighed, trying to hide my disappointment. "I should get back in."

"Oh, I forgot to tell you, Wicked Sinners is coming to Summerlin next weekend." Summerlin was two cities away but only an hour's drive, depending on where the concert was. "Trystan sent us tickets and booked us a room."

"No freaking way," I shouted. That news changed my mood almost instantly. I was always excited to see Trystan perform, and I was a huge fan of Wicked Sinners. "Cam will be so excited to see Trystan."

"Uh, actually," Jax said. "He didn't send her a ticket."

"Wait, what?"

"He sent four tickets." He shrugged. "Family only, I guess."

"That's bull shit." I snapped. "Cam is part of this family."

"I know, Kai, but we need to let them work this out." I knew he was right, but Cam was going to be devastated. "But I was thinking since it's only another twenty minutes, we could go to..."

"Long Key Island," we said simultaneously. Long Key Island was a special place for all of us. It was our home away from home as kids. We spent every summer and spring break in that beach house.

"We could spend the weekend." He smiled.

"Sounds amazing."

Maybe this was what we needed. We needed to get away from everything and see what happened in a place where we could just be ourselves.

38

Trystan's performance on a massive stage under neon lights with millions of fans cheering them on was epic. Trystan pulled out all the stops for us, making sure we were front and center for the performance with backstage passes for after. If I hadn't grown up with him, I'd have been star-struck backstage, but then I remembered this was once the boy who was so messed up he pissed in the fish tank at a party because one of the fish gave him a dirty look and that was after he told the fish he'd fuck him up.

We spent an hour backstage after the concert, hanging out with Trystan, his band, and Wicked Sinners before everyone moved the party to the beach house.

Sitting in the sand underneath the stars, I listened to the waves crashing around me. Between the three-hour concert, socializing backstage, and the first hour of the party, I was peopled out. Shoving my toes deeper into the cool sand, I stared silently into the darkness as I tried to drown out the raging party behind me. I hadn't anticipated everyone coming back to the beach house with us, and I meant everyone, including the entire crew and all the groupies.

"How did I know I'd find you out here by yourself?" Trystan chuckled, sinking into the sand beside me. I shrugged, not saying a word. "On a scale of one to ten, how mad are you at me?"

I cut a glance his way before twisting back to stare out into the endless darkness. "Probably a three," I mumbled as I wrapped my arms around my knees.

"I guess I deserve that."

"Just tell me that the reason you didn't invite Cam had nothing to do with me at the Cages."

He sucked in a deep breath through his nose before slowly exhaling. "I'm angry she went to the cages because she could have been hurt, and even if we aren't together, I still care about her. She went to the Cages to get back at me because she knew I wouldn't want her there. I'm even madder that she dragged you down with her, but..." He paused as his tongue swept out, wetting his dry lips. "No, that's not why I didn't invite her. There's a lot more to the story that you don't know, Kai, and I prefer to keep you out of it."

"Then I'll stay out of it." I had no doubt there was more to the story and that Cam was probably trying to keep me out of it, too, but I didn't believe Cam going to the Cages had anything to do with Trystan. "I was never mad because you didn't invite her. I was mad you left it up to me to tell her you didn't invite her."

"Sorry about that." He sighed. "I guess I didn't think about that."

"Maybe next time you will."

"So, what's up with you and Jax?" he asked, bumping my arm with his elbow.

"Not sure what you mean."

He laughed. "Is everyone still pretending you guys aren't a thing?"

My jaw dropped, and my eyes widened. "You know?" His lips curled into a grin as he nodded. "Does everyone know?"

"If by everyone you mean Harlow, Syn, Cam, Owen, and me." He smirked, nodding his head. "Then yes, everyone knows."

"Do you think your mom and my dad know?"

"Uh, no, probably not." He chuckled. "They're all blinded by love and lust and all that shit." I laughed. He was right. Our parents had that once-in-a-lifetime love that made you want to vomit because you knew the chances of you ever finding that kind of love were slim. "Plus, they're not around that much anymore."

"Jax thinks they'll freak out if they find out about us."

"Did you ever hear the story of the first time I met your dad?"

"Didn't we all meet at the same time at our first Thanksgiving together?"

He shook his head. "No, I actually met Bradley when my mother was admitted to the hospital because we thought she was having a heart attack."

"I didn't know about that." I also wasn't sure where we were going with this story.

"It turned out it was a panic attack, but it was pretty scary. She thought she was dying, and your dad showed up at the hospital and never left her side." He ran his hand through his hair, pushing it out of his face. "Jax was the only one home at the time. He thought he caused it when it was actually my dad."

"Why would Jax think that?"

"During the divorce, he turned into a little asshole who liked to get into trouble, and it probably didn't help the situation, but he didn't cause it. She and my dad had a huge fight that day, and my dad told her he wanted full custody." I shook my head in disbelief. Trystan's dad had always been so good to all of us. He treated me and my sister like part of his family. "He didn't want custody. He was angry because he found out my mother was dating your father."

"Ah," I said. "Your dad has always been so awesome."

"Yeah." He nodded. "After my mom's scare, everyone got their shit together. Jax stopped doing stupid shit, and my dad stopped being a dick."

"Does this have something to do with Jax and me?"

"Before you guys moved in, my mother made us both swear not to cross any lines, and she was pretty specific with what lines she was talking about, but that was a long time ago. I think Jax is terrified that he'll actually cause her to have a heart attack."

I understood that Jax went through a lot with his family before I ever met him, and I understood he didn't want to let his parents down, but I also knew that meant there was no future for us if he couldn't get past this. "I just don't understand why it has to be a secret from everyone. Like the puck bunnies." I muttered the last part under my breath.

"Kai," he said with a slight edge to his tone. "Please don't misunderstand me here." My eyes narrowed on him. "How do I say this?" He pressed his lips into a thin line. "Nothing that happened in Jax's past excuses his behavior now. I'm only telling you this so you understand where his head is."

"I'm not following."

"You need to stand up for yourself, Kai." I nodded. "Jax is my brother, and I love him, but he's an idiot." He shook his head like a thought just popped into his head. "I guess all men are idiots sometimes."

"Are you an idiot sometimes?" I laughed.

"Yeah." He nodded, throwing an arm across my shoulder, and I rested my head on his shoulder. "I'm gonna call Cam and work things out."

A slow smile spread across my face. "It's not my business."

"Right," he snorted.

"Tryst," I said.

"Hmm," he hummed.

"Do you think our parents will be angry or disappointed if they find out?"

"Nah," he said. "It may be a little awkward in the beginning, and they may worry about the gossip that's going to happen, but I really don't think they'll care." I agreed with Trystan; I didn't think they'd care.

Trystan and I sat silently on that beach for what felt like forever, and during that time, I decided that I was done letting Jax make all the decisions. Tomorrow morning, Trystan and his band would leave to go back on tour, and Syn and Harlow would head home because they had plans for the weekend. That left Jax and me alone.

Jax had this weekend to figure out whether it was me he wanted or not. When we got back on Monday, if he didn't choose me, I had to walk away.

39

Kaia

The following morning, everyone was gone before I woke up. This was surprising, considering the party didn't stop until four in the morning, and I was up before ten, but everyone had somewhere to be except Jax and me. I was incredibly stoked to have this weekend with him.

I sprang out of bed and bolted toward the smell of bacon sifting through the house. Stepping through the entranceway, my face spread into the biggest grin when my gaze landed on Jax working shirtless behind the large granite island.

"Morning." He smiled. "I made breakfast."

I opened my mouth but snapped it shut when I caught something in my peripheral vision. My gaze flashed to the doorway, and my smile faded. It was our suitcases sitting in front of the door.

My questioning gaze flashed up to him. "Coach called two mandatory practices this weekend." Sorrow laced his tone. "I'm sorry, Kai, but we have to go back."

"It's okay." I forced a smile, trying to hide my disappointment. We knew this was a possibility. During hockey season, Jax's life revolved around hockey, but this was the first time this season they had been forced to a mandatory practice, and go figure, it would be on our weekend away. "How fast do we have to be out of here?"

"We have to leave in thirty minutes." Sucking in a deep breath, I exhaled slowly in disappointment. "I promise I'll make it up to you."

Still forcing the same fake smile as I nodded. This weekend was important for our relationship to move forward, and now I didn't know what to do. I'd wanted to talk to him about how I felt without the pressure of worrying about who was around, but now that conversation may not happen.

We finished breakfast and made the long, quiet drive back to town.

I WAS PRETTY sure it was exhaustion mixed with disappointment that had Jax so quiet this morning, but I was so wrapped up in my thoughts that I hadn't said more than two words the entire hour and a half home. I knew I needed to talk to him but couldn't find the right words.

"Trystan knows," I said once we'd returned to town. "He said everyone knows."

"Knows what, Kai?" He flicked me a glance before turning back to the road.

"About us."

"He didn't know anything," Jax said. "He was guessing until you confirmed it for him."

"He knew Jax, and I think we should at least talk to our friends."

He swerved the car into the driveway and parked before saying another word. He sucked in a deep breath as he reached forward, killed the engine, and exhaled slowly as he twisted in the seat to face me. "Kai, I need you to let me do this at my own pace."

"Jax, I get not wanting your mom to know for now, but does everyone have to think you're single?" I shifted in the seat to face him. "Like all of the puck bunnies?"

He huffed out a laugh. "Is that what this is about?" It wasn't just about that, but that was a start. I nodded. "Kai, you have nothing to worry about. I'm not interested in those girls." Not yet, but as long as he was single, they'd continue to throw themselves at him. "I am yours, and you are mine, but for now, I don't want to risk the rumors that will fly getting back to my mom."

"How long is for now?"

"What's the rush?" he asked, shoving his door open and sliding out. That was a good question; what was the rush? We were still in the very new part of a relationship that didn't require our parents to know, but hiding it from our friends was silly.

"Okay, but I have one request," I said, sliding out of the car and meeting him at the trunk.

"What's that?" He huffed as he jerked one of the suitcases out.

"We tell our friends." I would be happy with baby steps. His face pinched as he opened his mouth like he would argue. "It's not negotiable, Jax." His mouth snapped shut. He held my gaze for what felt like forever before finally nodding.

"Okay. We will tell Cam and Owen." I knew they already knew, but I felt like this was a huge win for me, and I couldn't hold back my grin, which must have been contagious because he grinned, too, before leaning in and pressing his lips to mine in a quick, sweet kiss. I wanted more, but I knew we were standing in our driveway in direct sight of the nosiest neighbor ever. "We can invite them over tonight."

"Actually, I picked up a shift at the bar. Lacey texted me on the way home and asked if I could cover. She's sick."

"Okay then, Owen and I will meet you and Cam there tonight, and after your shift, we will tell them."

"Okay."

40

Kaia

Glancing at my watch, I rolled my eyes, slightly annoyed that Jax wasn't here yet. Of course, Cam hadn't made it yet either, so I was probably just being paranoid.

"Kai." My gaze flashed up to Lilly, popping her head through the service entrance doorway. My eyes widened, hoping she would tell me Jax was here. "You have a table." I knew it wasn't Jax because he never sat to eat, but Alex did every single time I worked.

I pushed through the service door leading into the dining room and spotted Alex sitting at his regular table.

"Don't you ever give up?" I chuckled, pulling my pad out of my apron.

"Not when there's something I want."

My cheeks heated, and my stomach fluttered. "That

must be extremely frustrating when it's not reciprocated," I teased.

He shrugged. "There is nothing better than the thrill of the fight and the win at the end. There's no better feeling than holding that prize in your arms after."

"And would I be that prize?" I wasn't entirely sure how to take that. Was I a challenge he wanted to conquer, and what would happen if he did conquer me?

"Nah." He shook his head. "That's just an analogy, but I'd be a lucky man to have a girl like you as my girlfriend."

My smile faded. He'd said a bad word, or at least that's what Jax made it feel like. "What can I get you?"

"I still want a date with my cute waitress."

"A burger and a beer?" He nodded, and I bolted for the bar to put in his order.

"Hey." My head snapped up to see Jax leaning against the bar.

"You made it." My eyes flashed around the bar. There was no Cam and no Owen. "Where's Owen and Cam?"

"They already had plans together tonight."

"When did you call to invite them out tonight?"

"What do you mean?"

"I mean, how late was it when you called and asked them to meet us here?" I crossed my arms over my chest and squared my shoulders.

He raised his shoulders. "I don't know, like..." He

paused as his tongue swept out, wetting his dry lips. "It was after seven."

I huffed out a humorless laugh. "You had no intentions of telling them, did you?" I kept my voice low, careful not to yell and make a scene.

"Kai." I threw out a hand, stopping his excuses. I'd heard enough.

"I have to work, Jax. Go home."

"I'll hang out, and we can talk when you get off," he said, his brows pinched and his gaze fixed over my shoulder. I turned around to follow his line of sight. "Isn't that the guy from the Cages?" I nodded. "He was here the other night, too."

"He's here every night."

"Every night." Jax laughed sarcastically. "The food here is terrible."

"Every night I work." His gaze snapped to me as his eyes widened in understanding. Jax's shoulders bowed in aggression as he shifted to move toward Alex, but I stepped in front of him, blocking his path. "No!"

"So you told him no, and what, he's not accepting no for an answer?"

"He doesn't see the harm in asking me out every night since I'm single."

"You're not single."

"But I am Jax. I am unless we are alone." His eyes narrowed on me, but he knew I was right. "You can't have it both ways. You tell the puck bunnies you're single and let them flirt with you." I shrugged. "I thought this was how we did this."

He blew out a defeated breath as his anger dissipated. "Jax," I sighed. "I can't be your dirty little secret anymore. Either you're all in, or I'm walking away." I wanted him to choose me so badly it hurt, but he didn't. He just stood there silent. Swallowing hard, I nodded. "This relationship served its purpose, and for that, I'm thankful."

"Kai."

"It's okay, Jax." I forced a smile. "Friends?" Hurt flashed across his face, but he didn't fight for me, and I knew I'd made the right decision. There was no future for Jax and me.

"Friends," he repeated.

"You should head home."

"I'll wait and give you a ride home."

My gaze flicked over my shoulder to Alex, who was watching the game on the big screen TV across from him. "No, thanks. I have a ride."

41

Jaxtyn

"Another one," I shouted, holding my shot glass up to the bartender as she passed by. She nodded, and I dropped my arm. It was getting near last call, and I wasn't even close to being drunk enough not to feel the aching pain in my chest.

What the fuck was wrong with me?

She wanted one thing from me, one, and I couldn't do it. She left an hour ago with her fighter, the one who was willing to fight for her because, for some stupid reason, I couldn't. I was terrified of love. I was terrified of being in love. I saw what love did to a person. I saw what it did to my mom. It destroyed her, and Kaia's dad was left to pick up the pieces.

I never wanted to do that to someone, to break them like my father broke my mother, but even more than that, I didn't want to feel the level of heartbreak that made you stop eating for so long that you dropped three pant sizes or made you cry everywhere... in the shower, in the car, cooking dinner. So, I went to extremes to protect my heart, and yet here I was, sitting at this bar alone with an ache so deep in my chest I was pretty sure my heart was shattered, and I still couldn't say the words 'I'm in love with Kaia.' I couldn't give her what she needed, which was true confirmation that she was mine and I was hers.

So, now, I sat alone at a bar, drowning my heartbreak in whatever clear liquid the bartender was serving.

"Jax?" My lip curled into a snarl as I groaned. It was Cam, and I wasn't in the mood for her right now. I wasn't in the mood for anybody. I wanted to be alone. "What's going on?" Her tone was thick with concern, like she already knew something was going on. She slid onto the stool next to me.

"Not now, Cam," I slurred.

"Where's Kaia?"

I twisted in my chair, my gaze locking with hers. "She left with her fighter boyfriend about an hour ago."

Her eyes widened. "And... You... Let her?"

"She dumped me." My head sank, and I twisted back to the bar in time for the bartender to slide me another one.

"What can I get you?" the bartender asked Cam.

"I'm good, thank you." The bartender smiled and

nodded before sliding to the next customer. "What happened?"

I shrugged. I didn't want to talk about it. I wanted to drink until I was so drunk that I forgot my name. "Jax." But I also knew she wouldn't give up, and I couldn't make her leave.

"I believe her words were, 'I can't be your dirty little secret anymore.'"

"Ahh." She twisted in her seat to lean on the bar.

"Did she tell you about us?"

"No. She didn't have to. Anyone with eyes can see the way you look at her." She paused momentarily, like she wasn't sure if she should keep talking. "Which is why I'm confused about why you let her leave with someone else."

"Because I'm fucked up." I spun in my seat again. "Did you know he was here every night? He asked her out every night, and I couldn't even step up and be a real boyfriend to her."

"Yeah, I knew, but I never thought she'd take him up on his offer because she was head-over-heels in love with you."

"Yeah, well, I pushed her right into his arms."

"Jax, this is still fixable." My gaze shifted up to hers. "But if you waste time sitting here drinking instead of fighting for her, and she falls for him, it's over." I knew she was right, but I couldn't help but feel like Kaia deserved better than me. She deserved a man who would fight for her, fight for her like he did. She didn't deserve this broken man with commitment issues.

"She's better off without me."

"And are you better off without her?"

I shrugged, but we both knew I wasn't. I had to move on with my life and let her move on with hers. If I wanted to get over Kaia, I needed to get under someone new. I whipped the spinning barstool around, searching the bar for an easy fix. "Kaia's moved on, and I need to do the same." Cam's eyes widened like I'd surprised her. "You should go."

"Yeah, no." She laughed, but there was no humor behind it. "You're trashed, and I'm taking you home. If you want to fuck someone else, you'll have to do it sober when you can think clearly because if you do this, it's game over. Kaia's gone, and there's no going back. So, if you want to fuck everything up, you'll have to do it sober."

"I'm thinking pretty clearly."

"You're not," she said, "because if you were, you'd choose to fight for Kaia instead of finding some random pussy to stick it in."

"That's who I am, Cam."

"It was," she sighed, "but it's not anymore."

She was wrong. This is who I still was. I couldn't commit to the one person I was in love with. I was destined for a life of random pussy to stick it in.

"Tonight, I take you home; tomorrow, if you still feel the same sober, do whatever you want."

"No." I was being irrationally stubborn, but that was what people did when their hearts were broken, especially when they didn't know they had a heart to break.

"Jax, please, don't make me lay you out here because I'm not sure I can carry you by myself." The look on her face and the threat in her tone said she would do it, and tonight, I was drunk enough that she'd have a pretty good chance.

"Fine." Part of me wondered if she thought my sober brain would change its mind. Hell, maybe I was worried it would, or maybe I was worried about how bad it would hurt to see Kaia tomorrow and act like she wasn't someone I loved.

"Jax, you will survive whatever you're feeling, and it will make you stronger. But not fighting for Kaia is something you will regret forever because, in the future, you'll have to sit across from her and her family during family functions and feel that pain all over again every time you see her with him because that's what real love does to you. You never get over that kind of love." She grabbed my shoulders, shaking me. "Fight for her, Jax."

Cam was wise beyond her years, and everything she said made sense. I needed to sleep.

"Just take me home."

42

Jaxtyn

<<BEEP>>

I jolted up, my head slamming into something hard. "Ow." I winced at the bright light surrounding me as my hand rubbed the throbbing in my head. My eyes eased open, and I struggled to focus through my drunken, foggy hangover. My gaze shifted to Cam in the front seat of her car, twisted around to the back seat, staring at me.

"What the fuck, Cam?" My gaze flashed around the car as I searched my memories from the night before. "Why am I in the back seat of your car?"

"Because you passed out there, and you're too big for me to carry," her mouth twisted with annoyance, "and since Owen wasn't available, I left you in my car to sleep it off."

I sank back into the seat and ran my hand down my face. "What time is it?"

"Late," she muttered, shifting back into her seat and buckling her seat belt. "Practice starts in fifteen minutes."

"Shit."

"We'll make it in eight minutes." She smiled through the rearview mirror as she started the engine. "Giving you enough time to brush the alcohol off your breath and get into your uniform."

Cam saved my ass not just last night but this morning. "Thanks, Cam."

"That's what friends are for," she said, putting the car in drive and swerving into traffic. "You were pretty messed up last night."

"I had too much to drink."

"That's not what I'm talking about, Jax." My gaze flicked up, meeting hers in the rearview mirror. "I'm talking about what happened with Kai." I hadn't remembered until just now that I'd poured my soul out to her. My heart clenched painfully tight. "I'm not going to get in the middle of this, but I am going to say this; I know you're hurting right now, and we all have a tendency to do dumb shit when we are hurting to try to ease the pain." She leaned forward, checking for oncoming traffic before surging forward. "But if you choose now not to fight for her and move on, it's over. There's no coming back from that."

Swallowing hard, I nodded. I knew she was right, but I didn't know what to do at this point. I needed to clear the fog out of my brain to figure out where to go from here.

She eased the car into the parking lot. "Kai is my best friend, and I don't want her to get hurt either, so if you know you don't want the same thing as her, move on, but I don't believe that's the case."

"I need some time to pull my head together, and then I will talk to Kai."

"Don't take too much time, Jaxy Boy. You'll miss your chance."

Cam and I walked into the rink together, quickly going our separate ways when we made it through the main entrance. I washed my face, brushed my teeth, added some fresh deodorant, dressed, and met them on the ice on time.

But I played like shit the entire practice.

"What the fuck, West?" Coached shouted when I missed the puck and tumbled to the ice. "Bench," he shoved his pointer finger dramatically toward the bench, "now!"

Shit.

I pushed off the ice, gliding towards the bench behind the wall, the last place I wanted to be right now.

"What is wrong with all of you today?" Coach shouted, this time louder. Thankfully I wasn't the only one playing like shit today. "Hit the showers." Coach stormed off the ice, and I knew we'd all pay for this tomorrow.

"What happened to you?" Owen said, skidding to a stop in front of me. I shook my head. "Not only are you playing like shit, you look like shit."

"I had too many drinks last night."

"By yourself?" He drew the words out. I nodded. "What happened with Kai?"

"What?" I scowled. "What makes you think anything happened with Kaia?"

"You only drink alone when something happens between you and Kai."

My gaze flicked up to the stands at the exact moment that Kaia, Cam, and the fighter bounced down the stairs with their skates in hand. Seeing her with him felt like a punch straight to the heart. I didn't expect it to feel this bad. Owen's brows pinched as he followed my line of sight. "Oh." His eyes went wide. "Who is that?"

"The fighter that rescued her at the Cages."

"And?" His gaze flicked back to me. "They are dating?" I shrugged. "I thought you were dating Kaia."

My eyes narrowed in confusion. "Why would you think that?" I don't know why I said that because, at this point, I knew that everyone knew, but old habits die hard.

He huffed out a humorless laugh. "Oh, are we still pretending you two weren't a thing?" I didn't respond. "I see why she left."

"She's my stepsister. How would I tell my mother that I'm not just dating but fucking my stepsister?"

"How do you let that," he pointed to Kaia in the stands, "get away because you're a grown man scared of his mother." He was right. How could I push Kaia into someone else's arms so easily?

"I just don't want to cause any more hurt for my mom."

"I've known your mom for a long time, and I think if sixteen-year-old Jax had started dating a much younger Kai, your mom would have flipped, but adult Jax dating adult Kaia isn't going to get the reaction you're expecting."

"Maybe." I sighed.

"I don't really believe this has anything to do with your mom." He shrugged. "If you can't commit to her the way she wants to be committed to, then move on, bro."

The problem was that I wanted to. I wanted to give her everything she wanted, and everything about that terrified me.

"We should go introduce ourselves," Owen suggested, and before I could stop him, he was pushing off the ice and heading their way. I dropped my helmet on the bench as I pushed to my feet to follow behind Owen.

I glided up behind Owen, and jealousy burst through my chest. The way she looked at him and smiled felt so intense that I thought someone had reached into my chest and ripped out my heart. I'd changed my mind; I wanted to run.

"Hey, Jax." Cam smiled, and I groaned. There was no backing out now. Kaia's gaze flicked up to me as her smile faded.

"What's up?" I asked, forcing a smile. "You guys getting in some ice time."

"Yes," Kaia said.

"Jax," Cam said. "Have you met Alex? He's here with Kaia." My jaw flexed as I flashed her a warning look before my gaze flicked to Alex.

"Yeah, we've met."

"We should get on the ice," Kaia said.

"You didn't have practice today?" I blurted out, not wanting her to go yet.

"Uh yeah." She smiled. "Early this morning before your practice." She paused for a minute, and I thought it was over. "I went in your room to see if you needed a ride, but I guess you didn't come home last night."

My gaze flashed to Cam and back to Kaia. My heart rate picked up. She thought I had spent the night with some random girl. I could see it in her eyes, and Cam must have realized it, too, because she blurted out, "He got trashed and passed out in my car."

"Oh," Kaia said, a hint of relief in her voice.

"Been there, man." Alex huffed out a laugh.

"We should hit the showers," I said, slapping Owen

on the arm, but I didn't wait for anyone to respond. I spun and skated away before I did something I couldn't take back, like punching Alex in the face.

43

Kaia

"I can't believe you brought Alex to Jax's game," Cam muttered. She'd said that four times since we'd made it to the arena, and I still didn't understand the big deal. Cam twisted around from the concession to hand me a large popcorn. "Is he staying at the hotel tonight?"

"Yes, but he has his own room." Cam and I drove three hours to watch Owen and Jax's game. We'd booked a room at the same hotel where the team was staying, mostly because Cam wanted to be near Owen and because it was the same thing we'd done since we were old enough to drive. "We should hurry; the game is about to start."

"Is Alex a hockey fan?" she asked as we pushed through the crowd back to our seats.

"No." I shook my head. Alex wasn't into sports at all other than fighting.

"Then why did you invite him?" I shrugged, popping a piece of popcorn in my mouth. "I didn't exactly invite him. I told him what I was doing, and he wanted to come."

"I think this is going to be an issue, Kai."

"An issue for who?" My brows pinched. She cocked her head to the side, her eyes screaming, 'really, Kaia?' "Jax?" I snorted a laugh. "Jax's doesn't want me, Cam."

"If you say so..." I did say so because if Jax wanted me, he would have fought for me, but he didn't. He wasn't willing to move forward, and the truth was I wasn't sure he ever would be able to. His commitment issues ran so much deeper than I realized.

We slid into our seats.

"I was starting to think you got lost," Alex said, flashing his perfect all-white smile.

"Concession lines are always terrible before the game," I said, matching his energy with my own smile. Our gazes flicked to the ice as the players emerged. My eyes immediately landed on #32, Jaxtyn West. Every game since he'd rescued me that night, he'd done the same thing when he hit the ice, and that was looking for me, but today he didn't. It was also the first time I wasn't wearing his jersey.

"So, hockey, huh?" Alex asked.

"You seem surprised?"

"Everything about you surprises." His tone was a mixture of flirtatious teasing with a hint of lust. "You are unlike any girl I've ever met."

"You mean boring." I chuckled.

The ref's whistle blew, drawing our attention to the ice. The puck dropped, and their sticks crashed together, fighting for the little black piece of rubber. Jax's team, the Lightning, vs. the home team, the Huskies. The Lightning took possession of the puck, and everyone was in place as they flew down the ice toward the goal.

Cam and I shot up from our seats, screaming with the rest of the crowd. They passed the puck down the ice, managing to evade the opposing team. Owen passed the puck to Jax. He dodged a player and took his shot, slamming the puck into the goal.

The crowds went crazy. That was one hell of a way to start the game, but too bad it didn't continue. By the end of the third period, the Lightning were so far behind that there was no catching up. I wasn't sure what changed, but it was obvious something had.

"So, what are the plans for tonight?" Alex asked as we made our way out of the arena.

"Typically, we'd go out with the team to celebrate their win," Cam answered. "But since they didn't win, I imagine there won't be a whole lot of that going on tonight."

"Okay," Alex sighed. "How about I take you two to dinner tonight?"

I nodded, a grin spreading across my face. "That sounds fun."

"Actually, I should check with Owen before I make plans," Cam said. Cam wasn't team Alex yet, and I couldn't understand why.

We made it back to the hotel, got checked in, and went our separate ways with a plan that Alex would pick me up at my room at six.

44

Staring into the hotel bathroom mirror, I was finishing my lip gloss when a knock sounded at the door.

"I'll get it," Cam said. Even though Owen told her they were hanging around the hotel, she'd decided to pass on dinner with Alex and me.

"It's okay. I'll get it." I stepped in front of her. "Don't wait up."

"You're coming back to this room tonight, right?"

I shrugged. "I hope not."

I could tell she wanted to stop me, but I flung the door open.

"Wow," Alex's eyes widened as his gaze trailed over me. "You look amazing."

"Thanks." I'd dressed in my sexist little black dress and strappy heels, hoping to impress him.

"Bye," I said, twisting to smile at Cam, and for the first time, she looked happy for me.

"What the fuck are you doing?" My gaze flashed forward to see Jax storming up, fist clenched at his sides. Owen and half his team were behind him.

"Woah, man," Alex held his hands out in front of him, sensing the aggression radiating off Jax. "We are..."

"You brought him here." Hurt and anger swirled in Jax's eyes as they flashed to me, and I instantly regretted the decision to let Alex come.

"I..." I didn't know what to say. I still didn't understand why I wouldn't bring him. Jax's gaze flicked from me to Cam standing in the doorway.

"Is this your room?" I opened my mouth to answer, but I realized he wasn't asking me. He was talking to Alex. "You're staying here with her?"

"Yes, but..."

"You're not fucking spending the night with her," Jax cut him off again.

"Jax," I snapped. "Calm down."

"Jax, man," Owen stepped up, placing an arm between Jax and Alex. "We should go."

"Yeah, we should all go," Alex said, his gaze flicking back to me as he reached out for my hand, but before I had the chance to touch Alex, Jax's fist slammed into the side of Alex's cheekbone. Chaos broke out in the small hallway as that one punch turned into a massive brawl.

Owen and the team tried to pull them apart, and

screaming echoed down the halls. Okay, the screaming was me, but I didn't know what else to do. They were going to kill each other.

It took what seemed like forever to pull the two men apart. Both their chests heaving with anger as they stared at each other with pure hatred.

"What the fuck are you even doing here, Kai?" Jax hissed through fast, rapid breaths.

"I..." I stuttered. "I'm always here."

"Maybe you shouldn't be anymore," Justin Blackwood said. "In fact, I think we should all call it a night." Justin's gaze was fixed on Alex.

"He's not fucking staying with her," Jax lurched forward, but Owen's grip tightened, and Justin jumped in to help.

"Bring him in here," Cam said, stepping out of the doorway to our room.

"I have my own fucking room," Alex growled, whipping the blood from his lip as they drug Jax into my room.

"She's not staying in your room either."

"Kaia, you should say goodnight," Cam said, her face so serious I nodded. She disappeared inside and slammed the door as Jax's team cleared the hallway.

I was so confused. What just happened?

"You should go deal with that." Alex pointed to the door before turning and storming away.

"Alex, wait."

He whipped around, shoving a hand through his dark hair. "Am I missing something?"

I knew what he was asking, but I didn't know the answer because whatever he was missing, I think I was missing it too. "I don't know."

He took a fast step forward into my space. His thumb pressed underneath my chin, and he cupped the back of my neck, forcing me to look at him. "Kaia, I like you, and I will fight every day for you, taking a thousand black eyes and bloody noses if there's something to fight for." He pressed his body into mine. "But if your heart belongs to someone else, then you're not mine to fight for."

My heart didn't belong to Jax anymore because he didn't want it, but he dropped his hands before I could tell him that. "You should go deal with whatever that was and text me once you make it back home. We can talk then."

He was giving me time to be sure that it was him I wanted. The truth was it seemed like an easy decision, like he was an obvious answer, but I didn't understand why Jax acted like he had a few minutes ago. Alex turned and strolled away, and I didn't stop him. He was right; I needed to deal with this before fully committing to him. Jax and I needed to close all the doors to move on.

45

Pushing through the cracked door to my hotel room, I tried to push down my anger. "Everyone out," I growled, pointing toward the door. "Now. I need to talk to Jax."

"Take it easy on him," Owen whispered as he passed. "He's still processing his emotions too." What the hell did that mean?

"Go, please."

"What the fuck was that, Jax?" I huffed out in one breath when the door slammed shut, and everyone was gone.

"Why the fuck would you come here with him?" he grunted, his tone laced with irritation and anger.

"Why wouldn't I?" I sneered. "I've come to every game since my dad met your mom. Just like I've gone to every event for everyone, and truthfully, I'd be at every one of Trystan's concerts right now if I could."

"Why did he have to be with you, Kai?" His tone was softer as hurt flashed behind his blue eyes. "Did you want me to be jealous?"

I blew out a heavy sigh as the anger I'd been harboring disappeared. "Why would you be jealous, Jax?" I shrugged, sinking onto the bed across from him. "This was your choice." I had no intention of making Jax jealous because I didn't think he cared enough to be jealous, but maybe everyone was right, and I'd been inconsiderate by bringing Alex to Jax's game.

"Me not being ready to tell people about us changes nothing about how I feel about you, Kai."

"And how do you feel about me, Jax? Because I thought you didn't care."

"I can't stand the thought of anyone touching you." That didn't answer my question.

"So you don't want me, but you don't want anyone else to have me either." I tried to control the tremble in my voice, but there was no use.

"Kai," he sighed, his eyes and jaw softening. I sat silently, pleading with him to tell me I was wrong. To tell me anything, but it never came.

"Just get out, Jax. Everyone was right; I shouldn't have come." He opened his mouth like he was going to argue. "Please, just go." I pointed to the door, and his mouth snapped shut as he nodded.

The door opened, and Jax disappeared, but before it closed, Cam pushed her way through.

"You okay?" she asked, climbing onto her bed.

I shrugged. I didn't know what I was. "I don't understand him."

"Jax is just as confused right now." She sighed. "He's in love with you but terrified of commitment, and that's why you shouldn't bring Alex to things like this."

"He asked if I was trying to make him jealous."

"I would ask the same thing if I didn't know you so well, but I do think you need to get your head out of your ass." She laughed. "How would you feel if you saw him with someone else at the bar?" I'd never looked at it that way.

"It would hurt."

"Just because you're not willing to wait for him to get his shit together doesn't mean he's over you."

"You think I was wrong for walking away?"

"Heck no." She scowled. "I think Jax needs to wake the fuck up and get his shit together. I'm just not sure rubbing it in his face at his game was the right way to do it." I nodded as everything sank in. She was right. "I like Alex, and it's obvious he's head over heels for you. He's the guy you deserve, but is he the guy you want?"

Sucking in a deep breath, I fell back on my bed before blowing it out slowly. "I like Alex, and I hate how Jax makes me feel."

"What do you mean?"

"I hate how he's all I can think about when I wake up. I hate how he's who I see every time I close my eyes. I hate how much I miss him when I'm not around him, but most of all, I hate that he doesn't feel the same."

"I think he does, Kai." She sighed. "I just think he's dealing with his own struggles, and no one would blame you for moving on if that's what you want to do."

I didn't know what I wanted to do, but I knew I needed sleep and time to process everything that happened. "Right now, I want to go to sleep and pretend this day never happened."

46

Jaxtyn

Pacing the tile floor outside my classroom, I couldn't think about anything but Kaia. I hadn't seen her since the night I'd walked out of her hotel room. When she was home, she stayed in her room with every door closed. She'd rearranged her schedule so that we wouldn't be at the rink at the same time anymore, and I hated it.

I hated not seeing her, and I hated that she'd changed her whole schedule to avoid me so she could be with him.

"You're making me dizzy," Owen said from the small bench against the wall. "Could you please sit down?"

We were early to class, like, really early. We usually hung back after practice to skate and see Kaia and Cam, but they didn't come until after we were gone.

"Why don't you just tell Kai how you feel and stop

torturing all of us?" My gaze flashed up to Owen as he fell back against the wall, rolling his eyes. "This is really getting old for everyone." He crossed his arms over his dark blue shirt, and my brows pinched. Owen always gave it to me straight, but he never looked annoyed. "Kaia is in love with you, and you're in love with her. Why are you making this so complicated?"

Because it was complicated. At least in my own head. It was like my head and heart were having this colossal fistfight. My head thought this was wrong. She's my stepsister and my heart—my poor stupid heart was raging its own battle. A battle between loving Kaia and knowing what love can do to a person.

I didn't want that to happen to either of us.

Blowing out a heavy sigh, I sank onto the bench beside him. "It's not that simple."

"It really is that simple, Jax. Kaia loves you, and you love her. Done." He leaned forward, propping himself up with his elbows on his knees. "Imagine being in love with someone who's in love with someone else." My gaze flicked over to him. He forced a tight smile, and I realized this was about Cam and Trystan. I nodded. He wanted someone he could never have, and I could have Kaia. I couldn't get out of my head long enough to realize what I was losing.

"Did you and Cam have a fight?"

He shook his head. "No, everything is great, but I know if Trystan calls, she'll be gone."

"That's kind of fucked up."

He shrugged, staring down at the ground. "Cam's never lied about her feelings." His tongue swept out as his gaze flicked up, meeting mine. "Maybe it's time you and Kaia stop lying to yourselves and each other." I ran my hand down my face. "Shit, or get off the pot, Jax." My face twisted with confusion. "I mean either love her or let her go, and by let her go, I mean move on with your life and stop pacing the freaking floor everywhere we go."

"It's too late." I sighed. "Kaia chose him. She changed her whole schedule to be with him and avoid me."

"You're a moron." He rolled his eyes. "She didn't choose him; she chose you. You didn't choose her back, and she didn't rearrange her schedule for him. She did it for you. So that she wouldn't hurt you."

I sucked in a heavy breath of realization as I nodded. "You're right." I pulled my phone out of my pocket.

Jaxtyn: I need to talk to you. Can you meet me after class?

I knew she was skating, so it would be a while before she responded, so I hit the button to close the screen.

The classroom door opened, and Owen and I rose from the bench. My phone vibrated in my hand, and I flipped it over. It was Cam. I hit the end button and shoved my phone into my pocket. I didn't have the energy for her words of wisdom, too.

Owen and I were partnered in different groups, so he went right to meet with his group, and I left to find mine.

The next hour dragged on and on. I tried to focus but could only think about everything I wanted to say to Kaia.

"Jax." My gaze flicked up to see Owen pushing through the class as everyone headed for the exit, worry etched on his face. I pushed out of my chair. "Where's your phone?"

"In my pocket," I said, already reaching to dig it out. "Why?"

"Cam's been trying to reach you." I rolled my eyes. Was that really an emergency?

I flipped my phone, and my eyes widened as panic whirled through me.

"Forty-six missed calls. What the fuck?" I had missed calls from Cam, Harlow, and Syn. Something was wrong.

"It's Kaia, Jax." The panic in his tone felt like it was crushing my soul. My chest tightened, and it was suddenly hard to breathe. I punched one of the missed calls, not caring who I talked to, as I stormed out of the classroom and bolted towards my motorcycle. I'd left everything behind.

"Jax," Cam said, and I could hear the sorrow and pain wrapped so tightly in her voice it immobilized me. "We've been trying to call you."

"Cam," I snapped. "Where's Kaia?" I needed her to tell me Kaia was fine.

"They took her by ambulance to Charity Regional Hospital."

"Ambulance," I repeated. A wave of nausea hit me, and my head spun. "What the fuck happened?"

"Get here now," she said, her voice cracking like she was trying to hold back her tears. "I'll explain everything once you are here."

"Is she okay?"

"I don't know," she choked, a sob breaking free, and I couldn't breathe.

"I'm on my way. Have Harlow or Syn call her dad now."

"We did." I disconnected the call and shoved my phone in my pocket as I grabbed my helmet and shoved it onto my head.

"Jax," Owen shouted from behind me.

"Meet me at CRH." I kicked my leg over my bike, kicked up the kickstand, started the engine, and surged forward.

I MADE the fifteen-minute drive to the hospital in eight minutes.

Cam was waiting for me at the entrance when I pulled in. Her eyes are red and swollen, and her face is streaked with tears.

"Where is she?" I asked, pushing past Cam. I needed to see Kaia.

"Jax."

I didn't stop. "Take me to Kaia."

"Jax," Cam said louder this time.

"What?" I whipped around. "I want to see Kaia." Anxiety pulled at me that wouldn't go away until I saw her. Until I knew she was okay.

"She's in surgery."

"What the fuck happened?" I managed to huff out in one breath.

"She was practicing with Parker, and during a lift, he lost his balance, and she fell." My chest clenched. "She hit her head pretty hard and somehow had a gash in her leg. We think maybe Parker's skate got her."

"How bad?"

"She was unconscious when EMS arrived. The entire rink was covered in blood."

"Where's Harlow and Syn?"

"I'll take you up."

I followed Cam through the entrance and to the elevator to the sixth floor. My heart hammered in my chest as the elevator doors chimed open, and we stepped into a waiting room where Harlow and Syn were pacing the floor.

"Has anyone called Trystan?"

"I called everyone," Syn said. "Mom and Robert are trying to get the next flight out, and Trystan too."

"I don't understand how this happened," I said. "Isn't Parker like one of the best figure skaters out there? How did he drop her and then skate over her."

"Because he was still drunk from the night before," Syn said. My gaze snapped up, narrowing on Syn.

"What do you mean, still drunk?"

"Harlow and I left the party over on Lexington Street early this morning, and Parker was still there drinking."

"I noticed his skating seemed off this morning," Cam said.

"He's fucking dead." I whipped around, anger burning in my chest. "Call me as soon as she's out of surgery." I stormed toward the elevator. Parker was a dead man walking.

"Jax. No," Cam shouted, grabbing at my arms.

"Go away, Cam." She wasn't going to stop me. I jerked myself free from her grasp. She didn't go away. She jumped on the elevator with me.

"Don't do this, Jax."

"Keep your phone on you." I hit button one. "My sister can help you get bail money together for me." The elevator chimed open, and when I stepped out, I nearly ran into Owen.

"Stop him, Owen," Cam ordered. "He's going to end up in jail."

"What the fuck?" Owen said, stepping into my path. I tried to side-step him, but he moved with me. "Jax, I don't know what's going on, but right now, Kaia needs you." I stopped, my gaze meeting his. "We can go to jail later. I'll even go with you."

He was right. I couldn't leave now. I'd never forgive myself if something happened to her.

I nodded on a heavy exhale, my shoulders sinking. "Fine, but once I know Kaia is okay, Parker's dead."

"Yeah, man," Owen said. "I'll start researching a place to bury the body while we wait." He was being funny, but I wasn't.

We rode the elevators back up, and when we stepped out, my eyes landed on Alex. He must have come up the back elevators because he never passed us in the main lobby. I didn't have time to react before Owen slammed his palm into my chest, shoving me back into the elevator. It was so unexpected that I didn't have time to fight against him.

"This isn't the time or place, Jax," Owen warned. "Whatever beef you two have is on hold for now. You two can work out your feelings when Kaia's all better, okay?"

I nodded. "I'm fine." He wasn't who my anger was directed towards at the moment. He released me, and we both stepped out of the elevator Camryn held open.

"Jax," Syn called out. My eyes shifted to meet hers. "She's out of surgery." I sucked in a deep breath holding it.

"Is she okay?" Cam asked.

"She's stable." A rush of air escaped my lungs, and I fell forward, grabbing my knees. She was going to be okay.

"The doctor said the surgery went well, and they successfully closed the gash in her leg, but the head trauma is a wait-and-see."

"What does that mean?"

Syn shrugged. "I don't know."

"He said there was minor swelling, and she's asleep now," Harlow continued. "He won't know the extent of the damage until she wakes."

I opened my mouth, but no words came out. This was too much.

"Is she going to wake up?" Cam asked.

"He said they have no reason to believe she won't, but head trauma is unpredictable sometimes."

I sank into a chair, leaning forward on my knees, and pressed my praying hands to my face.

"She's going to be okay," Harlow said, sounding more like she was trying to convince herself than us. "I know she's going to be okay."

"When can we see her?" Cam asked, sinking into the chair beside me.

"He said they'd let us back in once she's settled into her room," Alex said, and I tried to hide my irritation at him.

I didn't want him here, but because of me, he was

part of Kaia's life. If I had anything to do with it, though, he wouldn't be part of her future. Kaia was mine, and I planned to fix every stupid mistake I'd made if she'd let me.

"I love Kaia," I blurted out. "I'm in love with her."

Everyone's gaze shifted, stopping on me.

"Yeah, bro," Syn said, drawing out the words as her eyes narrowed on me. "We already knew that." Of course, they did.

I didn't bother looking at Alex. He'd gotten my message.

47

Jaxtyn

Three days.

It had been three days, and the doctors had no explanation for why Kaia hadn't woken up. It was clear that the doctors grew increasingly concerned each passing day that she didn't wake up, but no one was giving up on her yet. Even her medical team was still hopeful she'd wake soon.

The hospital room was a constant rotation of people. Kaia's dad and my mom returned early the following morning, and Trystan's flight landed about three hours later.

Cam and Alex were asleep in the waiting room. Syn and Harlow were at home showering before they came back. Trystan was sleeping on the small couch in Kaia's room, and her dad was in a chair directly across from me. I hadn't moved except to use the bathroom in three days. I ate, slept, and watched Kaia from this chair for three whole days, and I had zero intention of leaving until she was awake.

"Good morning." Dr. Torres smiled, stepping into the small hospital room. I straightened in my chair, and so did Robert, Kaia's dad. Trystan's eyes flashed open as he shot up to a sitting position. This had been our routine for three days.

"Any news, Doc?" Robert asked.

"All of her tests are normal." Dr. Torres shrugged. "I'm going to schedule another CT scan for this afternoon to check brain activity, but if it's still normal, we just have to wait."

"Is there a chance she won't wake up?" Trystan asked, pushing off the couch. "It's been three days; at what point do we get concerned that she's not going to wake up?"

He asked the question I'd been wondering but was too scared to ask.

"There's no reason she's not awake," Dr Torres explained. "Typically, with brain injuries, I would say the longer they are asleep, the less likely they are to wake, but this case is so rare." He forced a polite, sympathetic smile. "Let's talk again after her CT scan."

Trystan nodded, and the doctor left.

"Jax," Robert said, pushing out of his chair. "You should go home and get some sleep. I'll stay with her."

"No, I'm fine." I shook my head, sliding my hand into Kaia's.

"Jax," Trystan said. "You need a shower, man. You stink. Let me take you home, and we'll come right back after you get a little sleep."

I shook my head again, avoiding eye contact. "No. Syn is bringing me some clothes, and I'll shower here. I'm not leaving."

"Okay." Trystan sighed, pushing off the counter he was leaning on. "I'll be back in an hour, and I'll bring you some food."

I nodded. "Take Cam with you," I said, shifting in my seat. "She's been here for three days. She needs a break."

"So do you," Trystan said. I shook my head. I wasn't leaving. He rolled his eyes. "I'll see if she'll go with me."

Trystan left, leaving me alone with Robert. My gaze shifted up to Kaia, and my chest tightened. I hated seeing her like this.

"Is everything okay, Jax?" Robert asked, sinking into his chair across from me. "I know you and Kaia are close, but..." He trailed off.

Robert didn't know it, but he'd opened the door, and if I didn't take the opportunity now, I never would. It was now or never.

"I'm in love with her." My eyes shifted to meet his as my heart pounded in my chest. "Like really in love with her." His brows lifted, but he didn't look incredibly surprised. "It's my fault she's here. I talked her into skating again, and I'm terrified I'm going to lose her before I have the chance to tell her that I am in love with her."

"Okay," he interrupted me. "First, Kaia is going to wake up." He leaned forward. "Second, this isn't your fault. I'm glad you encouraged her to get back into skating because it is something she loves. This was an accident." Swallowing hard, I nodded. "Does Kaia love you back? And who is the man in the lobby that hasn't left?"

"She did." I blew out a heavy sigh. "And that's Alex. He's..." I paused. "I don't know what he is, maybe her boyfriend."

"Sounds complicated."

"It wasn't until I made it that way." My gaze shifted back to Kaia. "I was scared you and Mom would be angry. I was scared of how society would look at us. I was scared of ending up like my parents."

Pursing his lips, he nodded. "I can't tell you how society will look at you, but I don't think it matters as long as you're happy. Your mom already guessed something was going on. I was skeptical, but it was obvious when I saw the way you looked at her. I knew if you weren't together yet, it was only a matter of time because you look at her like I look at your mom."

I threw everything away to protect a secret that wasn't even a secret. I was so stupid.

"So, you guys don't care?"

"Jax, you and Kaia are adults. You're not blood siblings, but I'm not sure society will see it that way, and that is something you'll have to figure out how to deal with."

I nodded. "If she'll even take me back."

"I truly believe in the saying, what's meant to be will be." I'd freaked out about nothing. I still feared love and what happened when love faded, but there was no way I would let that stand in my way anymore.

"As far as what happened between your mom and dad," he said. "I know you kids got pulled through the mud in that divorce, but you can't let that stop you from living your life." He was right, and I wasn't going to let my fear of what might be ruin my life anymore.

I opened my mouth to respond but snapped it shut when the door pushed open, and Syn and Harlow pushed through.

"Here," Syn said, shoving a black bag at me. "Please go get a shower."

48

Jaxtyn

Five days...

Kaia still hadn't woken up, and the uneasiness in the room was heavy. No one had left the hospital in two days. Cam and Trystan were passed out on the small couch. Harlow was on the floor beside the couch, and Syn was curled into the chair across from me. Alex was sitting on the floor at the foot of Kaia's bed, flipping through his phone. My mom and Kaia's dad sat in the chairs outside the room, whispering low enough that I couldn't make out what they were saying, but I was sure they were discussing Kaia.

Alex and I hadn't had a conversation or really spoken to each other at all, but I knew it was inevitable. He'd only left the hospital twice since he'd gotten here, and that told me he was serious about Kaia and probably not going anywhere. Not that I could blame him, but it scared me because she could choose him and not me. I probably would if I were her. Why would she want someone who fought against this relationship every step of the way over someone who fought for her?

Movement in the doorway caught my attention, and I figured it would be Dr. Torres stopping in for his morning rounds. Every morning between 7:00 a.m. and 10:00 a.m., he stopped in, did a routine physical, checked on Kaia, and gave us an update. My gaze flashed up, and the anxiety twisting in my gut shifted to anger as my eyes locked with Parker.

"You have some fucking nerve," I growled, shoving out of my chair, fist clenching at my sides. Alex shoved off the ground, and I wasn't sure if he would stop me or join me, but if he got in my way, I'd hurt him too. I had so much built-up anger and resentment towards Parker I could kill him. Parker's gaze shifted around me to Kaia, and red-hot rage rushed through me. I surged forward, charging him. My fist connected with the side of his jaw, and he tumbled backward, falling to the ground. Jumping on him, I pounded my fist into whatever I could hit with multiple hands trying to stop me.

"Jax," Trystan hissed, jerking me off him and putting me in a death grip. "Chill."

"What is going on?" Robert yelled, helping Parker off the ground.

"Let me go," I growled, thrashing against his grip, but his grip tightened to the point it caused pain if I moved.

"I'm sor..." Parker started, but Alex stepped in between us.

"Shut your fucking mouth." Anger colored Alex's tone, and his protective stance screamed don't fuck with me. "Leave." Alex was a big guy, especially standing next to Parker.

"Let me have him," Syn said, stepping forward as she pulled her long black hair up into a ponytail, but Cam and Harlow grabbed her, pulling her back.

"What the fuck is going on?" Trystan said, tightening his grip around me.

"That's Kaia's skating partner," Syn snarled, pointing at Parker. "He's the reason she's hurt."

"I just needed to see that she was okay," Parker cried, wiping the blood from his lip with the back of his hand. "I didn't mean to hurt her."

"Fuck no, she's not okay," Trystan shouted. Kaia and Trystan were close. If Parker didn't leave soon, he wouldn't have just me to worry about. He'd have all of us to worry about. "You should leave before I let him go because I won't pull him off you next time."

"You should go," Robert said, pointing towards the door. "Now isn't the time for any of this."

Parker opened his mouth, and Alex twitched forward like he would hit him. Parker stumbled backward, throwing his hands up to protect his face.

"Stop it." It was a raspy whisper so low I almost didn't hear it. I froze, and so did everyone else. "Stop fighting." It was louder this time. Trystan turned with me still in his death grip. I thought I was hearing things, but it was Kaia. She was awake.

49

Kaia

My vision blurred, and my head pounded as my eyes eased open to the sound of shouting. "Stop it," I whispered, my throat sore. The room went silent. "Stop fighting." I blinked rapidly, trying to clear my vision as my gaze shifted.

I lay silent for a long moment, trying to remember where I was and what happened. I was in a bed under bright lights and surrounded by medical equipment. A loud beeping sounded behind me as something on my arm tightened: a blood pressure cuff. I was in the hospital. "Kaia," a deep voice said. It was my dad. Confusion twisted through me. He was with Liz in Australia. "Kaia, are you okay?"

"I—" I paused, my gaze shifting from person to person as they surrounded my bed. Everyone was here, and they all had the same concerned look etched into their faces. "I think so. What happened?"

"You don't remember?" Jax asked. I shook my head. "Do you remember all of us?"

"Dad," I said, starting at the left side and moving around the bed. "Trystan, Syn, Cam, Harlow, Jax, Alex, and Parker." I wasn't sure why I wouldn't remember who they were. Jax's gaze snapped over to Parker when I said his name. Anger illuminated his face.

"Parker and I are leaving," Alex said, his tone low and lethal as his large hand grabbed the back of Parker's neck. "I'll be back to check on you later." My gaze narrowed, following the two men as Alex led Parker out of the room. Alex looked angry, and Parker looked terrified.

"What's going on?" I was missing something. Why did everyone seem angry with Parker, and why was Alex here? We were friendly or closer to stalker/stalkee but not so close that he would come to the hospital to visit me after something happened.

"What's the last thing you remember?" Cam asked.

Sucking in a deep breath, I searched my memories. "I was working." I paused, trying hard to remember what was going on that night. "Jax was there, and we were..." I trailed off as my tongue swept across my bottom lip. What were we doing? "Oh, we were going to tell you and Owen we were dating." Oh shit, I wasn't supposed to say that. My gaze flashed to Jax. Panic surged through me as my eyes darted to my dad. "Oh, I wasn't supposed to..."

"It's okay." Jax smiled. "Everyone knows." He'd told them. All of that worry, and he'd already told them, and no one seemed mad or upset. However, everyone's face was pinched with concern. I was still missing something.

"Where's your mom?" My mind automatically assumed she wasn't here because she was angry when she found out.

"She's getting coffee." My dad smiled. "And she's not angry."

A wave of relief washed over me. "So why am I here?"

"You had an accident," Cam said. "During practice. You were doing a lift, and you fell." Ah, now it made sense. They were blaming Parker for my fall when who knows what actually happened. I could have lost my balance or been off on my timing. I'd deal with that later.

"Oh." I scowled, searching for the memories, but there were none. "Wait, so was this the night after we told you and Owen about us?"

Jax shook his head. "No, it was a few weeks after."

"Weeks?" Jax pressed his lips into a thin line as he nodded his head. "So, I've lost weeks of memories? How long have I been out?"

"I'm going to go get the doctor," my father said, twisting and bolting out of the room.

"How long have I been asleep?"

"Five days," Syn said.

The room stayed quiet while we waited for the doctor, and I continued to struggle with my brain to pull any memories I could, but there was nothing. It was like an endless black hole, and my memories were buried deep under all that blackness.

"Good morning, Ms. Cruz." An older doctor smiled. "I'm glad to get to meet you. How are you feeling?"

"My head is hurting, and I can't remember some things, but I feel okay." I shifted in the bed and realized there was a sharp pain in my leg. "And my leg hurts."

The doctor introduced himself, explained my injuries and treatment, did a quick exam, asked me a few questions, and then determined there was no explanation for my short-term memory loss and advised that it would probably come back after a few weeks. He also explained that I wouldn't be skating any time soon. This meant Parker would have to find a new partner, and as much as I didn't want to let him or my coach down, I was done skating professionally.

He ordered the IV and catheter to be removed and told me afterward to only get up with assistance until I regained my leg strength. He scheduled me for a CT scan and said that if everything came back clear, he would release me in the morning.

None of that made me feel any better about the fact that I'd lost weeks of memories.

The doctor left.

"I would like a moment with my daughter," my father told everyone, and the room slowly cleared out as he sank into the seat beside my bed. I hit the side button on the bed, lifting the back to a sitting position. "I'm so glad you are okay. You had everyone scared to death."

"I wish I could remember." I sighed.

"Don't dwell too much on what you can't remember." He smiled. "Because you are alive and awake to make lots of new memories."

I forced a smile. That was easier said than done. "Are you disappointed about Jax and me?"

He laughed. "No," he shook his head. "Jax was a rough kid, but he's become a good man. I've seen how he looks at you, and it's the same way I used to look at your mom." How had I been so blind that everyone could see how Jax felt about me but me? "He hasn't left this room since they let him back with you. We tried to get him to go home, even just to get a shower, and he wouldn't leave you."

"We were afraid you and Liz would be disappointed in us."

He shook his head. "Jax told me how he felt about you, and I could see how much he loves you. How could we be mad at that? I want my girls to find the kind of love I had with their mother."

"Thanks, Dad." I smiled.

He lifted from the chair and leaned forward, kissing

my forehead. "You are very loved, my dear girl." And that was the truth. I knew that before the accident.

My dad and I sat for another twenty minutes, catching up on everything. Or what I could remember anyway before Harlow joined us. In times like this, I missed my mom, but if I couldn't have her, I was thankful for the huge family I did have.

50

Jaxtyn

Pacing the hallway floor outside Kaia's hospital room, I impatiently waited for my turn to talk to her. She didn't remember the last few weeks. She didn't remember me letting her down, our fight, her relationship with Alex, and I had no idea how to handle this.

I could go in there and pretend none of it ever happened and move forward or tell her everything. I knew what I should do, but the thought of losing her again fought hard against my good conscience to do the right thing.

"How is she?" Alex asked behind me. I twisted around, my gaze freezing on the fresh bruise shining on his cheekbone. I thought about asking what happened, but I already knew. He'd made sure Parker never forgo the consequences of drinking and skating with Kaia again.

"She's okay," I said. "But she doesn't remember the last few weeks."

His brows pinched with confusion. "As in, she doesn't remember us?" I nodded. His throat flexed on a hard swallow as his gaze shifted past me like he was staring into space. "But she remembers the two of you?" I nodded again. A part of me felt bad for the guy. Obviously, he cared about Kaia, and I didn't hate him, but I didn't want her to pick him either. "And I suppose you don't want to tell her the truth?"

And here it was... That talk that I knew was coming but didn't want to have.

"What exactly is the truth?" I asked. "Are you her boyfriend?"

He squared his shoulders, crossing his arms over his chest. "No." He shook his head. "After what happened at the hotel, she realized she didn't know what she wanted. We talked the morning of her accident before practice. She told me she really liked me but needed to talk to you. She needed to close the door with you completely before she could move on."

"So, she was going to end everything with me forever?"

He dropped his arms, shoving his hands into his pocket. "I don't know." He shrugged. "I won't lie and say that I wasn't hoping she would, but honestly, that wasn't the feeling I got."

"And what feeling did you get?"

"That she wanted to give you one last chance to fix whatever it was between the two of you, but I don't know for sure." I nodded, and I couldn't help but wonder if he was right. Was she coming back to me, or was she going to tell me goodbye forever? "Look, if she loves you, I'll walk away because I only want her to be happy, but if there's even a sliver of a chance she'll choose me, I'm going to fight for her."

I nodded, understanding exactly how he felt. "If she chooses you, I will walk away. I will let her be happy with you." Even though I didn't want to, I would let her go if that's what she wanted. "I'm going to talk to her once her dad has his time with her, and I'm going to be honest about everything." I didn't want to tell her the truth, but I knew it was the right thing to do. I'd messed up, and I had to live with that regardless of her choice.

The door opened, and Robert and Harlow stepped out. "She's asking for you," Harlow smiled.

"Thanks."

I pushed through the door, and a slow smile spread across my face when my gaze locked with hers. My chest swelled with happiness to see her awake. It sucked that I had to break her heart all over again.

My hand cupped her face, and she leaned into my

touch. "You scared me." Her gaze lifted to meet mine, and I dropped my head, pressing my lips to hers, and every ounce of worry, sadness, fear, and anxiety left my body. Pulling from the kiss, I closed my eyes, dropped my forehead to hers, and sucked in a deep breath before slowly exhaling.

"I'm okay, Jax," she breathed. I knew she was okay, but I needed to feel the warmth of her skin against mine, even if it was just our foreheads. I stood like that for several long minutes before I finally released her and dropped into the chair beside her bed.

"So, I was hoping you could catch me up with everything I missed or am missing." Pursing my lips, I nodded. "Like, when did you tell everyone about us? The last thing I can remember was you were nervous about saying anything."

Sucking in a deep breath, I knew it was now or never, but I also didn't know where to start. She looked so happy knowing everyone knew I'd chosen her. How did I break her heart all over again? "You ended things with me the night we were supposed to meet with Cam and Owen to tell them about us." Her smile faded and twisted with confusion as her eyes flicked around like she was searching her memories. "I messed up because I was scared, and I let you down," I answered the question I knew she would ask. "I wasn't ready to tell everyone, and truthfully, I'm not sure I ever would have been if all of this hadn't gone down the way it did, but I know without a doubt that I want you, and I will never make that mistake again."

"Why is Alex here?"

"Because I was stupid and pushed you right into his arms."

"Wait, am I dating Alex?"

I nodded. "You were, I think." I paused, clearing my throat. "You brought him to my game, and things got heated. Maybe he can fill you in on what happened."

"Sounds like I'm missing more than just you telling everyone."

I nodded. "I told your Dad here at the hospital. I'm sorry I didn't tell him before that. You didn't deserve to be my dirty little secret, I believe, is how you put it." A smile twisted at the corners of her lips.

"So what happens now?" She raised her shoulders, holding them for a long moment before dropping them. "I don't remember Alex. I don't remember not being with you."

"Right now, we take it one day at a time." She nodded. "Between Alex and me, we can fill in the blanks."

"Yeah, but I don't know what I was feeling at that time. Did I hate you? Or was I still in love with you because right now I'm in love with you, and I don't even know Alex? Was I starting to fall for him? Was he falling for me? How do I tell him I don't remember?" My chest clenched painfully tight at the thought that she may have hated me and she might have moved on with him, but even more than that at the fear in her eyes.

"Alex knows," I said. "Maybe if we help fill in some of the blanks, it will help bring your memories back." I shrugged. "We'll just have to take it one day at a time." I honestly had no idea what was going to happen. If her memory came back, she could leave me, but if it didn't, she only remembered being in love with me. "Let's start with getting you home, and then we can work everything else out later."

Her gaze flicked past me to the small window. I twisted to see Alex pacing the floor like I'd done before him. "Jax," Kaia said. "I'm not ready to talk to him. Could you ask him just to give me a little time?"

"Are you sure?" She nodded. "Okay. I'll let him know." I pushed out of the chair and strolled out of the room.

"Is she okay?" Alex asked, and I nodded. "Did you tell her everything?"

I nodded again. "Yes, and she's confused right now. I suggested we both fill her in on everything, but she's asking for you to give her some time."

"She wants me to leave." His expression turned pained, and his voice dropped to a whisper. I couldn't help but feel bad for him. If it had been me, she didn't remember, I don't know how I would have reacted. "Okay. I'll go, and once she's released, I'll come by the house and check on her."

I stood silently, watching as Alex disappeared down the hall.

Cam rounded the corner with a bag of food I assumed was for Kaia, and that's when it hit me. If anyone could help her remember how she felt, it was Cam. She told Cam everything.

"Hey." Cam smiled. "How's she doing? Is she starving yet?" She held up the bag.

"She's struggling with her memory loss," I said. "She asked me to send Alex away."

"What did you tell her?"

"The truth, Cam. I told her the truth that I knew and that Alex could probably tell her more, but she doesn't remember. So maybe a chat with you will help her."

"You know my truth could end up hurting your chances of ever getting her back, right?"

I nodded. "If this is going to work, she has to know the whole truth."

"Okay. I will talk to her, but you need to go home and come back later." I perked up. I didn't want to leave. "Jax, I'm serious. You've been here for days. You need a real shower and sleep. I'll stay with her and call you anything changes."

On a heavy exhale, I nodded. Cam went into the room, and I headed home.

51

Kaia

Balling the wrapper in my hands, my eyes closed as I savored the last bite of the best burger I'd ever had. Or at least that's what it felt like in that moment.

"So, have they said when you can skate again?" Cam asked, holding her hand out for my garbage, and I handed her the balled-up wrapper. "I'm sure Petrov will be itching to get you back on the ice." She was right. Petrov would want me back on the ice the minute she knew I was cleared to skate again. Petrov wasn't a bad person, but she lived for the win, and there was no chance of a win if we weren't practicing. The problem was I didn't know if I wanted to do it anymore. Before Mattias died, it was all I wanted. My entire life revolved around skating and winning, but when I lost him, I lost my passion for sport. It suddenly didn't seem as important anymore. "She's been up here a few times to check on you. Your fall shook her up pretty bad."

"Can you do me a favor?" I asked, shifting to meet her gaze. She raised her eyebrows. "Could you let Petrov know that I'm done skating?"

"Kai." Cam's brows pinched as she shifted in her seat. "Don't let this ruin what you love doing. It was an accident an..."

"That's the thing." I shrugged. "I don't love it anymore. I love being on the ice, but when Mattias died, so did my love for professional skating. I only gave it another try for Jax, and I can, without a doubt, say I'm done skating. I want to try something else now."

"Like?"

"Like..." I shrugged. "Maybe going back to school. I've been thinking about getting into sports medicine for a long time. Maybe now's the time."

Cam nodded, a slow smile twitching at the corners of her mouth. "I will tell her as long as you promise to keep skating with me in the mornings."

My lips curled into a grin. "I promise." I didn't want to give up skating. I loved skating. I loved getting up early and swirling around the empty arena before anyone else even got out of bed. It was where I could think clearly.

"So what are you going to do about Jax and Alex?" That was a bigger issue.

My eyes shifted over her shoulder, and I sucked in a

deep breath as I shook my head before slowly exhaling. "I don't know." And I didn't know. I was so confused. "I don't remember how I felt about either of them before the accident." My eyes flicked down to her. "But you do. You could tell me."

"I could, but I think we both know that's not going to help." She forced a smile. "It's not going to change the fact that you don't remember or the way you feel right now."

"So what do I do?" My gaze flicked down to my fidgeting hands. "What would you do?"

She laughed. "You are not me, and I do not want to be the bad influence here." She shook her head and waved her finger. "Nope, not me."

I laughed. "Okay, then tell me what you think I should do. You know me better than anyone else in this world."

"Honestly, I don't know, Kai." She sighed. "But I think you'd be cutting yourself short if you didn't explore both of your options or at least give yourself time for your memories to return before making a decision."

"So I should date them both?"

"That's not exactly what I was saying." She chuckled. "But it's not a terrible idea." She shrugged. "Who knows how you'll feel once your memories come back."

"If they come back."

"They will." She smiled. "There's no reason to think they won't." I wished I could fall asleep and wake up without memory loss, but that also terrified me. I knew a lot went down from that night in the bar with Jax until I lost my memories, and it was scary how remembering would affect my life and how I felt about Jax.

"Enough about me." I smirked. "What's up with you and Trystan? Or are you and Owen a thing?" I felt like I was missing so much between the memory loss and being asleep for five days.

She pulled her legs into the chair and wrapped her arms around her legs. "It's complicated."

"I've got time, so spill the tea."

"Honestly, I don't know what's going on. Trystan's only here because of what happened to you, and now that you're better, he'll be leaving again soon, but..." She trailed off, pressing her lips into a thin line. "Since he's been here, it's like nothing changed. It's like he never left. It's like he never broke my heart by not inviting me to his show." I nodded, completely understanding where she was going. Knowing he didn't want to see her hurt her more than his leaving. "It's like we fell right back into our old routines without a word of what's going on between us."

"Why don't you ask him?"

"I guess I'm scared of his answer." She cocked her head to the side, forcing a smile. "That's one thing I've always loved and hated about Trystan; no matter how hard it is to hear, he will always give you the truth."

"Why do you keep putting yourself through this?"

My brows pinched. "Why don't you end it and give Owen a real shot?"

"Trystan is the right man, but it's the wrong time. He wants to go out on tour and be free, and if I'm still waiting when he gets back, then I guess we get to give this a real shot."

"Or he comes back only to leave again."

She nodded. "I could end up waiting forever for something that may never happen. I don't want to be his backup plan."

"Sounds like you have a pretty important decision to make, too."

She nodded. "Yeah." I knew Trystan cared about Cam, but I also knew he'd push the limits as long as she let him.

52

It felt good to be home and, even more than that, having a moment of quiet to collect my thoughts. My entire family had made it their mission to entertain me all day. While I did enjoy having everyone home and in one room for once, I was glad it was over.

Trystan had plans with Cam, my dad and Liz were going out for the evening, Syn and Harper had plans, and Jax... Well, I didn't know what Jax's plans were because he'd been the first to bail without saying a word.

My gaze flicked up when I heard the door from the kitchen to the living room open. "You hungry?" Trystan asked, strolling around the couch wearing a pair of black ripped skinny jeans and a white t-shirt. He didn't look dressed to go out with Cam tonight. "I can go pick something up or order something."

"I thought you had plans with Cam tonight?"

"I do, but I can cancel if you want company." He sank onto the couch next to me. There was no way I was going to be the reason Cam and Trystan didn't have a conversation that they both needed to have. "I'm sure Cam would understand." I knew she would, but they needed this time together, and I was okay with being alone.

"No..." I started.

"I'll keep her company." We both turned to see Jax standing with food in the doorway. "That is if you want pizza and wings from Fazzoli's." My mouth literally started to water. Fazzoli's was my favorite. Fazzoli's special wing sauce and homemade pizzas were to die for.

"Go." I smiled at Trystan. "Have fun tonight."

Trystan nodded and pushed off the couch. "I will see you two later then."

"Hey, Tryst," I said. "When do you leave to go back on tour?"

"Tomorrow unless you need me." I shook my head. I wasn't the one who needed him. "You two have fun." He winked and strolled out of the room.

My gaze followed Jax's as he set the food on the large coffee table. An awkward silence filled the room. Something I don't remember ever happening between us, even when he'd caught me watching him half-naked. Thankfully, Jax didn't let the silence last long, leaving me to wonder if I was the only one who sensed the situation's awkwardness. He had all his memories, so this probably wasn't weird for him; it was normal.

"I was thinking we could hang out tonight, eat, watch a movie, and maybe talk if you want."

Over the past few days, I'd done nothing but talk. I was talked out, or at least I felt like I was at that moment. Jax carefully lifted my legs and sank into the couch before setting my legs over his. He'd done it many times before, yet this time felt different, and I couldn't explain why.

Everything felt so right with Jax, like I could pick up where we left off in my memory, and it wouldn't feel like anything was missing except that I knew it was and that there was another man probably waiting to hear something from me.

"A movie sounds good." I smiled. "What did you have in mind?"

"What are you in the mood for?" He reached forward, grabbing the remote from the table. "Scary, romance, comedy, action?"

I thought about my choices, weighing each option carefully. I knew comedy or action were the safe choices. The choices that wouldn't leave me in Jax's arms before the end of the night, but for some reason, that was where I wanted to be. "Scary."

His gaze flicked up, meeting mine. His lips curled up into a smile. "You hate scary movies."

My brows pinched dramatically. "Wait, I do?"

His face softened with concern. "You don't remember?"

I laughed. "I'm kidding, Jax." He visibly relaxed, closing his eyes for a brief moment as he exhaled a heavy sigh. "Can we go to the theatre? Liz ordered a new chaise lounge couch the last time she was home that I haven't tried yet."

"Yeah." He smirked. "You eat, and I'll get the theatre ready."

Jax made me a plate, disappeared down the hall, and didn't return until I was completely done with my food.

"You ready?"

"What took so long?"

"I was getting the room ready." Ready for what? "Are you ready?" I nodded slowly, shifting on the couch, careful with my sore leg, but Jax swooped in and scooped me off the couch, cradling me in his arms. I wrapped my arms around his neck before he spun and carried me toward the back of the house.

"You know I can walk, right?"

"I know," he said, carefully weaving me down the hall and into the theatre. "I wanted to hold you. I've missed you."

"I was only asleep for five days."

He dropped me easily onto the oversized dark grey chaise lounge couch and strolled to the opposite side while I settled into the sofa he'd covered in pillows and a blanket. "First," he said, dropping onto the couch, "that was the longest five days of not knowing whether I would ever get to hold you again." I shifted my weight off my leg, twisting to face him, and he did the same. "Second, I'd lost you long before that because I couldn't get out of my own head."

It looked like this conversation was happening whether I was ready or not. "And what changed? The accident?" I knew the fear of death and losing someone forever was a powerful thing. It had the ability to not just completely change a person's feelings towards someone but bring every regret to the surface.

"Yes and no." He reached out, brushing a loose strand of hair behind my ear. "I knew that I fucked up before the accident. I just didn't know how or if I could fix it, but I was going to try. I texted you that morning before I went into class because I wanted to meet you after class to tell you everything, but I never got the chance."

"And what would you have said if you had gotten the chance?"

His tongue swept out, wetting his dry lips as his gaze searched my face, finally settling on my mouth. My heart fluttered, and my pulse raced. His chest rose and fell with slow, deep breaths. A shiver snaked up my spine as I fought back a whimper of anticipation so lost in the moment that I didn't even realize he'd moved closer. Our bodies flush against each other, he cupped my face as his gaze lifted to meet mine. His eyes silently begged for permission. My hand curled into his shirt, pulling him into me, and that was all he needed. His mouth covered mine in a desperate, hungry kiss like he'd been starved for days, and my mouth and tongue were what he needed to survive starvation.

I shifted my weight, pushing him to his back and climbing on top. My leg suddenly felt no pain. It could have been the 800 mg of Ibuprofen, but I'd like to think it was the adrenaline coursing through my veins. I rolled my hips against him, feeling every inch of him through my thin sleep shorts.

"Kai," he breathed, breaking from the kiss as his hand flew to my hips, stilling me.

"What?" My brows pinched. "What's wrong?"

"We can't."

"You don't want me?"

He huffed out a laugh. "You have no idea how bad I want you. It would be so easy for me to pick up like nothing ever happened and fuck you right here right now until you are screaming my name." He shifted carefully, putting me to his side. "But I don't want you to hate me when your memory comes back because I took advantage of the situation." There was no way that I would ever be mad about a mind-blowing orgasm, right? I was ready to explain that to him when I remembered Alex and realized Jax was right. I didn't know if I was dating Alex or not. Was I cheating on him? "I just feel like we should wait until you know what you want."

"What if I never remember?"

"Then you have to make the decision about what you want to do."

"Do you want me to date both of you?"

"No," he choked out. "I don't want to share you with anyone but..." He sucked in a deep breath and slowly exhaled. "I also want you to be 100% sure before you make your choice, and if that means you need to date both of us, then I won't punch him in the face again."

"Again?" I snapped. "You punched him in the face?"

"Yeah." He nodded. "It happened a week or so before your accident. I can tell you what happened, or you can let Alex tell you his side of the story."

I shook my head. "I want to move forward. If my memories come back, then we'll deal with it, but right now, I just want to move on."

His lips curled into a smirk. "What about Alex?"

"I'm going to text him tomorrow."

"What about Parker?" His brows furrowed, and there was something in his tone—worry, anger, aggravation. I couldn't quite put my finger on what, though.

"I need to text him too. I owe him an explanation."

"You don't owe him shit," Jax fumed. "And..."

"Jax," I cut him off. I had no idea what had gotten into him. Had I been dating Parker, too? "I don't want to date him, but we are partners."

"Kai," he said, pushing to a sitting position. "Did no one tell you who caused the accident?"

I shrugged. "Jax, it was an accident. I know every time I put my skates on and hit the ice, there was a chance something could happen, but it's no one's fault."

"You're right," he said. "In every sport, there's a chance of injury, but it increases by one hundred percent when your partner comes to practice after an all-night rager, still drunk."

My face twisted with confusion. "Wait, what?" My gaze flicked around the room, searching for any memories, but there was nothing. "He was drunk?" Had I known he was drunk? No. I shook my head. I never would have agreed to do lifts if I knew he was drunk. "How do you know?"

"Syn saw him at the party. She said he had to have gone straight from the party to practice."

"Why would he do that?" My chest tightened. "He's one of the best skaters alive. He knows better than that." My gaze flashed up to meet his, and I suddenly realized what was going on in the hospital. "That's why everyone was fighting when I woke up."

He nodded. "If I ever get my hands on him, I will kill him."

"Petrov will end his career if she finds out." If I didn't realize he was drunk, Petrov probably didn't either. Still, Parker would never skate professionally again if it ever came out.

"Petrov came up to check on you a couple times, and she knows what happened."

"You told her?"

He shook his head. "Syn did. She let Petrov have it. Told her if she couldn't tell that Parker was drunk, she should retire."

"I must not have realized either." I shook my head. "I just can't imagine letting him lift me knowing he was drunk."

"I don't know what you knew, and I don't care. Parker knew, and Petrov should have known." I mentally scratched Parker from my call list. I needed to remember before I dealt with him.

"Can we watch the movie now?" I sighed, both emotionally and mentally drained. I settled back into the couch and waited for Jax to settle before curling into his side as he flicked on the movie.

Not even ten minutes into the movie, we were both asleep.

53

Sitting in a dark corner booth in the back of the bar, I waited for Alex. I was early, but that didn't stop me from staring at the front door. I had no idea what I was going to say to Alex. How did I explain to someone I was close to that I didn't remember anything about them?

All I remembered was Jax.

I ran my sweaty palms down my jeans to stop my leg from rapidly bouncing up and down. The front door swung open, and Alex walked through. Whatever had been between us must have been good because I smiled, sucking in a deep breath like his presence sucked every ounce of oxygen out of the room at the sight of him. It could also be because he was crazy hot.

He paused, scanning the room until our gazes collided. The corners of his lips curved up, and my heart raced faster than two NASCAR cars closing in on the finish line as he got closer to the table.

"Hey." He leaned in, and I inadvertently retreated. His eyes widened as he snapped back. "I'm so sorry." He held up his hands. "I forgot."

"No." I shook my head, offering a polite smile. I wasn't sure why I'd retreated. It wasn't like I didn't know him, and what was the harm in a hello hug? I honestly didn't know what was wrong with me. This situation could have been so much worse. I was lucky; I only lost a few weeks of memories, not all of them. "I'm sorry. I'm not really sure how to act right now."

He slid into the booth across from me. "Yeah, I guess I don't either."

"I have some questions that I was hoping you could answer." I needed to know if Alex and I were friends or if he was my boyfriend. I needed to know where we left off. I thought I didn't want to know and wanted to start fresh, but it was making me crazy.

He nodded. "Ask anything."

"Are we dating?" I shook my head. That wasn't what I meant. "I mean, were you my boyfriend?"

His lips parted like he was going to answer, but instead, he sucked in a deep breath. Swallowing hard, he shook his head. "No, but not because I didn't want to be."

"Then why?"

"Because of him." The sadness in his tone made my

chest ache. I didn't have to ask who the 'him' was because I knew he was talking about Jax, mostly because there was no one else he could be talking about. "You were still in love with him."

"So we were just friends?" My eyebrows pulled together in confusion.

"No... I mean, yes..." He shook his head. "Honestly, I'm not sure we knew what we were doing. You had just finished shooting me down for the four hundredth time, and then ten minutes later, you slid in across from me, and after that, we spent all of our time together. I didn't even know about him until later, and I don't think you realized there were still feelings until the night at the hotel."

"I don't remember any of it."

"But you remember how you felt about him?" I nodded, flashing him a sympathetic look. I didn't want to hurt him. I didn't want to hurt anyone, but I didn't want to be dishonest either. "And you don't remember what happened between the two of you that made you walk away?"

"He told me, but no, I don't remember."

He nodded. "Is this where you end things with me?" There was a hint of sadness in his eyes.

When I walked into the bar, I didn't intend to say goodbye to him, but after hearing everything he said, I honestly didn't know what to do. It was obvious even with Alex, I was still in love with Jax, and it wasn't really fair to string Alex along, but the fear of making a rash decision that I would regret when I regained my memory was overwhelming.

"Honestly, I came here intending to start from scratch and see if you were willing to give me some time and a few dates to get to know you..."

"But?"

"But I feel like it may be unfair to ask you to wait for me when it seems like I need to figure out how I really feel about Jax."

"I'm going to say the same thing to you now that I told you at the hotel after Jax's game." He forced a smile. "I like you, and I will fight every day for you if there's something to fight for, but if your heart is with him, then you are not mine to fight for." His tongue swept out, and he shoved his hand through his dark hair. "And I believe your heart still belongs to him, right?" My lips parted, but nothing came out. My words lodged tightly in my throat. I didn't know how to answer that. "I think it always did."

"I wish I could remember something different, but I don't."

"I understand. I hope he treats you like you deserve to be treated this time, but if he doesn't, you have my number." His gaze shifted to the bar. "Looks like he's waiting for you to come back to him." He nodded his head toward the bar, and my gaze followed his line of sight to see Jax sitting at the bar with Owen and Cam.

Even though he knew I was out with Alex, he didn't know I was here. My gaze shifted between the three of them as they each threw back a shot and laughed about something Cam said, and I realized that was where I belonged.

54

Jaxtyn

Stumbling through the front door, I dropped my keys on the counter. I felt defeated, and no amount of alcohol could change that after watching Kaia leave the bar with Alex. Even worse, it was almost one a.m., and she still wasn't home. My chest ached, knowing there was a chance that she'd choose him after hearing his truth.

I strolled up the stairs and into my room, kicking the door closed behind me before twisting and falling onto my bed.

I pulled my phone out of my pocket, staring at the black screen. No new messages or calls. Pressing my lips into a tight line, I swiped up and clicked on Kaia's name. It was one in the morning, so I should just check on her to make sure she was okay.

Jaxtyn: Just checking on you.

I hit send. The message went through, and as soon as the 'delivered' popped up under the message, I heard a chime from her room. I shifted to a sitting position with my feet on the floor, narrowing my eyes on the bathroom door that led to her room.

My phone buzzed.

Kaia: Can I come in?

I didn't have time to respond. There was a tap on the bathroom door before the door slowly eased open. "Jax?"

"Kaia?" I pushed off the bed. "I didn't think you were home. Your car..." I trailed off as she stepped into the soft glow of the moonlight, sucking a sharp breath at the sight of her hair pulled up messily on top of her head and wearing one of my old oversized tees that came down to her mid-thigh showing off her bare legs and feet.

This girl had no idea what she did to me. My fingertips ached to trail over her bare, heated, silky skin. I clenched my twitching fists at my sides to keep them from reaching out to her.

"Harlow's battery was dead, so she borrowed mine."

"So you didn't go home with Alex?"

She cocked her pretty little face to the side, narrowing her eyes. "Did you think I went home with him?"

I shrugged. "I saw you leave the bar together, and then when your car wasn't here..." I trailed off because I didn't want to finish where I was going.

"Alex walked me to my car, and I came home. I needed a minute to process everything."

"And did you process everything?" Swallowing hard, I averted my gaze, knowing I might not want to hear what she was about to say.

She nodded. "I texted Alex about an hour ago that I hope we can stay friends."

My gaze snapped up, meeting hers. "What?" I wasn't sure I heard her right, and if I did, what did that mean for us? My heart pounded wildly in my chest.

"He said he would love to be my friend just in case you fucked up again." She released a nervous chuckle.

"What are you saying, Kai?" I slipped into her space so close she could feel the heat of my words. She didn't say anything as her gaze locked on my mouth, and her teeth sank into his bottom lip as my hands curled around her small waist before I slowly nudged her back. "Kai?" She didn't answer, but everything in the way she was looking at me said she wanted me to kiss her. I needed to hear her say it, though. I needed to hear her say she was mine.

Her back hit the wall, and my palms flattened on each side of her, completely caging her in.

"Kaia, what are you saying?"

"I'm saying," she whispered, "I don't want to play any more games, no more lessons, and no more second guessing what this is. I want you."

"Did your memory come back?" She shook her head.

A twinge of disappointment hit me, and I dropped my arms. "Then I can't do this."

"Why?" Her face pinched.

Cupping the side of her throat, I pressed my thumb to her lower lip, tugging it down. "Because when you come back to me this time, I'm never letting you go again." Her tongue swept out brush across the tip of my thumb, and I groaned, tugging down until it popped free. "I'm willing to wait until you're sure."

"I am."

"How?"

"Because it's always been you."

The hand on her throat slid back, gripping the back of her neck, and my other hand found her hip as I pressed my body into hers, holding her in place. "How could you possibly know if you can't remember?"

"Because he knew. He knew that my heart still belonged to you." My face twisted with confusion. He, as in Alex? Did Alex tell her she was still in love with me? She shifted her weight against me, and my grip eased. "Okay, never mind. I'll text him back." She teased as she moved to escape my grasp, but she wasn't fast enough. I grabbed, turned, and pinned her front to the wall. Her palms slapped flat against the wall. "If you don't want me anymore..."

Curling my fingers into her hips, I shoved my hips forward, pressing my throbbing erection hard against her ass. I dropped my mouth to her ear. "Does that feel like I don't want you?" I growled before pressing my lips to the spot just below her ear. My hand snaked around, slipping under the hem of her shirt as I pressed kisses down her neck, making my way to her shoulder. "I need you to be sure." I hummed against her heated skin as the tips of my fingers brushed against the lace of her panties. "Because the next time I slip my cock in this sweet pussy, it belongs to me. You are mine."

She whimpered as she dropped her hand and slid it over mine, so desperate for my touch that she was going to take matters into her own hands. My lips twitched with amusement as I cupped her pussy, letting her have control for only a second before I tore my hand away, grabbed her wrist, and slapped her flat palm against the cool wall. My hands slid up her arm, tangling her fingers in mine, pinning them tightly against the wall as I pushed my body harder into hers.

"Please, Jax," she begged. "I want you. I've always wanted you."

Releasing her hands, I stepped back, grabbed her waist, and twisted her around. Cupping her face, I searched her eyes for any signs of hesitation, but there was none. "Tell me you are mine."

Leaning into my touch, her eyes closed as she sucked in a soft breath. "I've always been yours," she smiled. "It just took a head injury for us both to realize."

"You sur—" She cut me off, slamming her lips to mine. That was all the reassurance I needed. Kaia Cruz was mine, and I would never make the mistake of letting her go again.

Her fingers curled into my shirt, bunching the thin material in her fingers as I slid my tongue past her parted lips. She met me stroke for stroke, tangling our tongues in erotic bliss.

My hands dropped, pulling at the hem of her shirt, tearing my mouth from hers to rip the shirt off her, and then quickly removing mine before filling my hands with her ass and hiking her up. She hooked her arms around my neck and her legs around my waist. My fingers tangled into the thin lace of her panties as I twisted the material around. With one hard pull, the panties shredded.

My mouth found hers again in a desperate, messy kiss as I strolled backward until my calves found the chair. Kaia loosened her legs as I dropped back into it.

My gaze shifted over her feminine curves as I reached between us, working to free myself. She watched, mesmerized, as I squeezed and adjusted cock until I was free. My hands looped around, gripping her ass and maneuvering her over me grinding her center over my cock. Her hands curled around the back of the chair.

"Fuck me, baby," I rasped, curling my fingertips into her ass and dropping my head back. "Fuck me like I'm yours, and you are mine."

She shifted until she found where she wanted to be

before rolling her hips and sliding herself over me, coating me with her arousal. My chest rose and fell with deep, ragged breaths as I watched her. Her teeth sank into her bottom lip, her eyes closed, and her head rolled back as she stroked her clit on the wide head of my cock.

Fuck she was hot!

"That's it, baby." I groaned. "Ride my cock and take what's yours."

"Jax," she cried out, and I thought I might come watching her falling apart on top of me.

"Come all over my lap, baby." My filthy words sent her over the edge. Her back arched, and her head fell back as she cried out. My cock twitched with excitement. I loved watching her come. My back flew off the chair as my arms wrapped around her trembling body, and my mouth covered her nipple, flicking the taut bud with my tongue.

Her hands cupped the sides of my face, pulling my gaze up to meet hers. "I love you," she whispered.

"I love you, too." I loved her more than I'd ever loved anyone, more than I ever thought I was capable of loving, and I hated that I had to lose her to figure that out.

"I need you to fuck me now." Her mouth captured mine. I kissed her slowly as her palms flatted on my chest. I reveled in the feeling of her, her touch, her mouth, her heat. The combination of it all was enough to send me over the edge.

I lifted from the chair, holding her at my waist, and moved to my bed.

Breaking from the kiss, I lifted my leg, kneeling before I lowered her on the bed and settled between her thighs as my forearms fell to the mattress. Pressing my weight into her, I slid myself through her slick flesh, soaking my cock in wetness.

I dropped my head. "Fuck, you're so fucking wet for me, baby," I purred against her throat, letting the heat of my breath and the hum of my words tease her skin. Her fingertips curled into my ass as she rocked her hips into me. My girl was so fucking ready to have me inside her.

My fingers curled into the blanket, fisting the material tightly to relieve some of my built-up sexual tension to slow myself down. I was so goddamn desperate to be inside her, to fill her with my cum. To claim her and make her mine, but I didn't want this moment to end. I wanted to take my time. I wanted to feel every inch of her.

"Jax, please..." But she wasn't going to let me. Not this time, anyway.

I pressed the head of my cock at her entrance. "Is this what you want?" I trailed my lips over her jaw and down her neck. "You want me to bury my cock deep in this sweet pussy?"

"Yes, please." She rocked her hips forward, teasing the head of my cock. My cock twitched with anticipation as her eager pussy threatened to swallow me whole. Her chest heaved, and her body vibrated with desire.

I guided my hips forward, slowly pushing into her. Her body tensed for a brief moment as her fingertips curled tightly into my biceps and her eyes squeezed closed. I paused, letting her adjust to me.

"Open your eyes, baby," I whispered against her lips as her grip loosened. "I'm going to go deeper, but I need to see your eyes." Her eyes eased open as I moved my hips forward an inch at a time until my pelvis was flush with hers. Her legs trembled, and a tense shiver ran down my spine as her pussy clenched around me.

I withdrew before driving back in, dropping my head to her shoulder. "More," she moaned. I pumped in and out of her at a steady pace. "Please." She bucked her hips forward, and I smiled against her shoulder. "I need more, Jax." Frustration colored her tone.

If my girl needed more, that's exactly what I'd give her. Lifting, I pinned her hands over her head with one of mine as I rolled my hips in a wave-like motion, each movement going deeper as I increased my speed. She arched into me as my fingertips trailed down her thigh until I reached her knee and pulled her leg up, hooking it over my shoulder as I pulled my knee up to her hip and drove back into her over and over again.

"Jax," she cried out, and I knew she was close, and I wasn't far behind her. My thrust grew more vicious with each snap of my hips.

"I need you to come for me, Kai." I grunted, and she cried out in ecstasy. "That's it, baby, come all over my cock." With one more deep thrust, I buried myself deep inside her as I exploded. I trembled as her pussy throbbed around my twitching cock.

I released her as I collapsed on top of her. I could have stayed like that forever, but after a few minutes, I shifted my weight and fell to the side of her.

"I need a shower." I sighed, flicking my gaze to her. "Want to join me?"

The corners of her lips lifted. "Yeah, if I can make my legs work."

I knew there was still more to discuss, but that could wait for later because, right now, my girl had come back to me.

55

"Happy birthday, Kai," Trystan said through the phone. "I'm sorry I couldn't be there, but I'll make it up to you when I get back."

Every birthday since I moved in with Jax and Trystan was the same. First, a family dinner, and then Jax, Trystan, Harlow, Syn, Cam, Owen, and I would do whatever I wanted for the evening.

This year was different.

This year, my dad and Jax's mom were gone on business, Trystan was still touring, Cam was on her way to visit Trystan, Harlow went with Syn to some convention in Redrock, and Jax planned a special surprise just the two of us for my birthday.

This would be the first birthday in years I didn't spend with everyone, and I couldn't help but feel a little disappointed, and I felt even guiltier about that.

Jax had gone out of his way to plan a special night for me, and I was appreciative. I just missed the way it used to be, but I guessed things couldn't stay the same forever.

Traditions had always been important to me. Even more so after losing my mom, but I knew as I aged and life changed, traditions had to, too. They had to account for new family and life changes, but it didn't change the fact that I missed the old traditions.

"It's okay," I said, trying to hide the disappointment in my tone. "When will you be home?"

"We have two more concerts, and the tour is over."

"And what happens after that?"

"We don't have any plans yet, so I'll be home for a little while." I thought about asking him about him and Cam but stopped myself. If he didn't offer the information, it wasn't my business. "Sorry, Kai, I gotta go, but happy birthday."

He disconnected, and I sighed.

"You ready?" Jax asked, popping his head through the doorway, and I couldn't help but smile at the sight of him. He was mine, and I was his, and there was no more confusion about where we stood with each other.

I followed him out of the living room and into the kitchen to exit through the garage, but I spotted a bright pink card with my name written in cursive on it and a small black box next to it on the counter. "What is that?" I pointed to the card.

"My mom and your dad left that for you." He swiped the card off the kitchen island and handed it to me. "You should open it."

Quickly ripping the envelope open, I pulled out the card that read: *Happy Birthday!* Flipping open the card, a white sheet of paper fell to the floor, but Jax caught it before it hit the floor and handed it to me. It was in Jax's mom's handwriting.

Dear Kaia,

We are so sorry we couldn't be there for your birthday, but we promise we will make it up to you when we get back.

Happy Birthday, Kaia. We love you!

PS the box is for you and Jax.

My gaze flicked up to the hand-sized square box. "It's for both of us."

Jax picked up the box and opened it to find two keys and another note.

"As you both know," Jax read his mother's words, "we had the pool house renovated this past week, and after careful consideration, we've decided to gift it to the both of you as a couple. You are adults, and you should have your privacy."

"I don't think they want to hear us having sex." I laughed.

"Your bedrooms will always be yours if you ever need them," he continued. "We love both of you. It's signed from my mom and your dad." My gaze raked over

Jax's face, and I wondered if he was having a mini panic attack because he had no reaction to the letter. His face was completely void of any emotion.

"Jax?" I said, and his gaze flicked up to meet mine. "Are you okay?"

I could visibly see the panic fade away when his gaze met mine as the corners of his lips curled up, and he nodded. "Yeah, we spend every night together anyway. We've shared a bathroom since we were kids." He slipped into my space, and his hands curled around my hips as he pulled his body flush against mine. Dropping his head, he brushed his lips against mine. "But you know what this means, right?" The heat of his breath sent a rush of heat over me and straight down, settling between my thighs.

"No," I hummed.

"It means that I have the privacy to do every disgustingly dirty thing I've ever fantasized about with you." My breath hitched, and I forgot all about any birthday plans we'd had. I wanted to spend all night exploring all of those fantasies.

"Th-that doesn't sound terrible," I stuttered. "In fact, we should..."

He released me, taking a step back. "Such a naughty girl," Jax teased. "We should go before I throw you over my shoulder, and we go break in the new bed."

"Or shower," I suggested. "Or kitchen countertop."

His tongue swept across his lips before sinking his

teeth into his bottom lip as his gaze raked over me. "We have reservations." He groaned, a strangled throaty sound. He was struggling with premade plans and new plans. "Let's go before I change my mind."

Jax and I slid into my car since I was in a dress and didn't want to deal with a dress on the bike.

"If you could have anything for your birthday," Jax started as he swerved into traffic. "What would it be?"

I considered the question for a minute as I stared out the passenger window. "To have just one more birthday with everyone. Like we used to before we all got lives that don't always coincide."

"Damn." He sighed. "I was hoping you were going to say a trip to some lavish exotic island or something I could actually give you."

"That would be nice too." I smiled.

Jax swerved the car into the bar parking lot, and my brows pinched. "Jax, the bar is closed tonight."

"The bar is never closed." Jax frowned.

"Monica said they had an inspection, and they failed or something, so it was closed for the night."

"Are you sure?" Jax scowled.

"Jax," I pointed to the bar, "the parking lot is empty, and the bar is dark. So, yeah, I'm pretty sure." This was his big birthday plans that he supposedly put a lot of thought into? The bar? This was my least favorite place in the world.

He opened his door and slid out. "Then I guess it will be quiet for just the two of us."

"Right," I said, pushing my door open and sliding out, not bothering to hide my annoyance. "Except it's closed, which means it's locked."

"Is there an alarm?"

"What?" Was he serious right now? "No, but I'm not committing a felony on my birthday."

"Trust me." He smiled, sliding into my space. His hands cupped my face, and I leaned into his touch. "No one will know." He dropped his lips to my ear. "How many times have you fantasized about me fucking you on top of that bar?" Never, until now. Now, I literally couldn't think of anything else. "About me bending you over a table and sliding my cock into your tight, soaking wet pussy." Excitement and arousal buzzed across my skin as I melted against him, and suddenly, a felony didn't seem so bad.

"Okay," I said with a shaky breath. Jax stepped back and slid his hand into mine. The minute the seductive heat of his breath left, so did the fearlessness, and the panic came back. "Omigod, I'm going to jail."

"You're not going to jail." He laughed. "No one will ever know we were here."

Jax pulled his hand out of mine as he fidgeted with the door knob. My gaze flicked over my shoulder like I was on the lookout. "Jax, are you sure about this?"

"Got it," he said, and my gaze snapped back to him as he pushed the door open.

"We're really doing this?" He placed his hand on the small of my back, giving me a gentle shove, and I stepped into the darkness. "Okay, we are really doing this."

"Stay here," he whispered. "I'll find the lights."

"What?" I reached into the darkness for him, but he was already gone. "Jax." He didn't answer. This was insane. He was going to turn on the lights, and we were going to get caught; I was going to go to jail, and I would lose my job. I turned to the door, changing my mind. This was a terrible idea. I winced as the lights flashed on and yelped when a crowd of people shouted, "Surprise."

As my eyes adjusted to the light, they swelled with tears. He'd planned a surprise party. My gaze scanned over the crowd. Everyone was here: Trystan, Cam, Owen, my dad and Jax's mom, Syn and Harper, the girls from work, and even my boss and Alex.

"Happy Birthday, Kai." Jax smiled as his hand curled around my hips.

"You did all this for me?"

"It wasn't easy, but of course. I knew you would want everyone here." He dropped his mouth to my ear so only I could hear him. "And maybe I can play out that bar fantasy later."

This was the best birthday present he could have given me.

56

Jaxtyn

It was close to two a.m., and the party was starting to dwindle down. My gaze followed Kaia as she said her goodbyes to friends and family, and all I could think about was getting her home and breaking in our new bed. The bar stool beside me moved, and I caught Alex in my peripheral vision as he slid onto the stool next to me.

"I'm surprised you came," I said without taking my eyes off Kaia.

"I'm surprised you invited me."

I shrugged. I honestly was, too, and if this situation had gone any differently, I wouldn't have, but Alex had been the bigger man, and I respected that. I knew Alex wasn't a threat, not as long as Kaia didn't have her memory back because she didn't remember how she felt about him, but I couldn't say I wasn't still a little worried about what would happen when her memories returned.

"Congrats, by the way," he said. "I heard you two made it official." I forced a smile but didn't say anything. "You know how lucky you are, right?" Sucking in a deep breath, I pushed off the bar before twisting to face him. He apparently needed to get something off his chest. Squaring my shoulders, I lifted my chin, ready to take whatever he was going to throw. "If this had happened just a few weeks later, she may have been mine. You get a second chance that you don't really deserve."

I wished I could argue with him and tell him he was wrong, but he wasn't. "You're right, and I do know how lucky I am, but I think we both know it was always going to be me." His jaw flexed, but he didn't look angry. "I know I fucked up, and all I can do now is move forward." I paused, glancing over my shoulder to where Kaia was dancing with Trystan. "I love her, and I will never hurt her like that again." My gaze shifted back to Alex, who was smiling.

"Good to hear, but you should know that even after I'm long gone, there will always be another me waiting to step in the next time you fuck up, and next time you may not get another chance."

"I won't need one."

"What are you two chatting about?" Cam slurred. I rolled my eyes when she didn't give us a chance to answer the question. "Jax, you mind if I chat with Alex for a minute?"

"About?" She raised her brows, giving me a none of your fucking business look. "Cam, this could only be about one of two things and..."

"Jax," she warned.

I shook my head. "No. Is this about Kaia?"

"What?" She frowned. "No."

"Then it could only be one other thing, and you have no business fighting in the cages, and you damn sure aren't dragging Kaia there again."

"Why would you think it has anything to do with me fighting?"

"Because you and Trystan haven't spoken once tonight, which means something happened, and you always want to do dumb shit when you're hurt."

"Mind your own business, Jax."

Gritting my teeth, I snarled, but I also knew I couldn't stop her. "Fine." I threw my hands up. "Do what you want, Cam." I had no intention of dropping it. She wasn't going to listen to me, but she'd listen to Trystan. I spun on my heels and strolled away.

"Hey," I said, stepping in beside Kaia. Kaia and Trystan's gazes flicked to me. "You need to go deal with your girl. I don't know what you did this time, but she's planning on fighting in the Cages again."

Trystan's gaze shifted over my shoulder to where I'd left Cam with Alex.

"Where is she?" Kaia asked.

"Discussing the Cages with Alex."

"Trust me," Trystan said. "I'm not the person you want help from. I believe her exact last words were, 'Don't ever fucking talk to me again.'" Our eyes went wide.

"What the fuck did you do?" I snapped.

"Happy Birthday, Kai," Trystan said. The sadness in his tone was painful. "I'll see you in a couple weeks." We stared silently as Trystan disappeared through the crowd and out of the building.

"What the fuck happened?" I asked, twisting to Kaia.

"I don't know." Kaia sighed. "All I know is Cam went up to surprise him at his last show. She hasn't said anything about it since she got back."

"That's not good."

She shook her head. "Nope, but I think we need to stay out of it. They need to figure this out on their own."

I nodded. "Let's go home." I sighed. Cam wasn't going to fight tonight, so we could try talking to her tomorrow when she was sober.

57

It was early, and the rink was empty and mostly dark, with only one of the overhead lights on. It had been almost two months since my skates hit the ice, and I didn't want anyone to be around if I made a fool out of myself. I didn't want to skate professionally anymore because my passion for making it to the Olympics died with Mattias, but my love for the ice was still as strong today as the first time my mom brought me ice skating with Harlow.

Stepping off the ledge and onto the ice, my legs shook with nerves. I'd spent almost my entire life on the ice. It shouldn't be something that I just forget how to do, and yet the thought of losing something else that was such a huge part of me was terrifying me.

The thought of losing the ability to skate would be like losing my mother all over again. My mother was the reason I started skating. She was at every practice, and when I didn't have practice, she skated with me. It was one of my earliest memories with her; I didn't want to lose that. It had always been her dream for me to make it to the Olympics, and up until Mattias died, I thought it was mine too, but it wasn't. I wasn't sure what I wanted to do with my life, but partner skating wasn't it anymore.

My gaze shifted down to where my skates were frozen to the ice, and my brain couldn't make my legs move. I knew I was being irrational. I had no reason to think that I wouldn't be able to skate again, but the fear was real. The doctor said I would return to normal use of my leg after six weeks of healing.

"Okay, Kaia, get a grip," I mumbled. "You can do this." Gazing forward, I focused on the ice in front of me, willing my legs to move, and they did. I pushed off the ice and glided to the opposite end of the rink. A sense of calm washed over me as I skated effortlessly around the ice. I spun and glided to a stop. I was building up the momentum to try a jump when something moved in my peripheral view. I spun quickly, throwing up the shaved ice all over the dark jeans that Parker was wearing.

"Hey, Kai," Parker said, an apology in his tone. I wasn't sure how I would feel seeing Parker again, probably because I hadn't decided how I wanted to handle the situation yet, but it looked like it was happening now whether I was ready or not. Frozen in front of him, I drew in long, deep breaths as my jaw flexed and my fist clenched. I was pissed.

Parker opened his mouth, and I knew an apology was about to come out. And everything about that sent anger radiating through me as I reared back and slammed my fist into his jaw. The sound of bone hitting bone filled the quiet arena before he stumbled back, gripping his jaw.

"Ah, fuck," I cried when pain shot through my hand into my wrist and up my arm. He flinched, but that definitely hurt me more than it did him.

"I deserved that," he said, rubbing his jaw.

"You deserve a broken jaw," I gritted out, cradling my hand. "What are you doing here anyway?"

"Cleaning out my locker." His voice was soft, almost sad, and I couldn't help but wonder if he was sad for himself or for everything he'd done. "Petrov dropped me this morning."

"I wish I could say I'm sorry, but I'm not." I crossed my arms over my chest. "What took her so long?"

"I just got out of rehab yesterday."

"You went to rehab?"

He nodded with a sad smile. "Yeah, I realized I had a problem and needed help. I wish I had realized before I destroyed my career and hurt you."

Sucking in a deep breath, I exhaled a heavy sigh. "What happened?" I was still furious with him but needed to know what had happened that day. I needed to know how I lost my memory. "I need to hear your side of the story."

"I went out partying with some friends," he said. "I don't remember much, but they called it a night, and I kept partying, and before I knew it, I had to be at practice in two hours. I don't know when I left. I don't remember making it to the arena, but I'm pretty sure I showered and changed and was on the ice on time."

"How didn't I know you were that drunk? How did Petrov not know?"

Raising his shoulders, he shook his head. "If you had asked me before the accident, I would have told you that I wasn't that drunk, but that's not true. I guess I just got really good at covering it up. To be honest, I don't remember much, but I do remember you asking if I was okay."

"And you told me you were?"

He nodded. "Petrov shouted for us to practice our step lift, and I lost my balance and..."

"I remember..." A wave of memories flooded back. I didn't know if I was remembering everything, but I remembered everything that happened on the day of the accident. "Omigod, Parker, I remember." I was so excited that I nearly jumped into a hug.

"What the fuck?" Jax's voice boomed from somewhere behind me. I whipped around as Jax and Owen hit the ice, racing toward us. "Get the fuck away from her."

"Jax," I shouted in warning. Even from the opposite side of the rink, you could see the anger radiating off him.

"I'm fucked," Parker muttered.

Jax and Owen sliced through the ice, stopping in front of me. "Get off this ice before I remove you." Owen was always the one to talk Jax down, but not this time. This time, they both looked like they were contemplating murder.

"Jax." I placed my hand on his heaving chest, trying to calm him. "Jax, please."

"I just came to clean out my locker," Parker said. "And..."

"Then clean it out and leave." The threatening tone in his voice didn't go unnoticed. "And if you come back or get stupid enough to try to talk to Kaia again, I'll rip your fucking throat out."

I shoved Jax backward to get his attention, but it wasn't working. His gaze was fixed on Parker, and if looks could kill, Parker would have spontaneously combusted when Jax's skates hit the ice.

I shoved Jax back again, and new memories flashed forward: the night in the bar, the fight at the hotel, and all the feelings and mix of emotions I'd felt for both Jax and Alex all came flooding back.

"Jax, I remember."

58

Jaxtyn

Her words hit me like a ton of bricks.

She remembered.

My chest tightened, and I suddenly found it hard to breathe. If she remembered everything, that meant she remembered her feelings for Alex and all the hurt I'd put her through. A bolt of sadness spiked through me.

"Let's go," Owen hissed, grabbing a hold of Parker's shirt and spinning him around. "I'm going to help you clean out that locker and personally escort you out of the building."

Kaia's gaze followed Parker as Owen led him off the ice. "Don't kill him, please," she shouted. "I don't think you get bail on premeditated murder." She was joking around. That was a good sign, right?

She spun on the ice, her gaze connecting with mine.

I couldn't read her. If she was upset or about to end everything, I couldn't tell. She opened her mouth.

"Skate with me," I cut her off.

Her mouth snapped shut, and her brows pinched. "But..."

"Skate with me, and let me take you out tonight. Tomorrow morning, we can go back to reality."

"So, you don't want to know what I remember?"

No, I didn't. I wanted everything to stay the same, but I knew that wasn't possible. "Yes, I just want one more night with you before..." I trailed off.

"Jax..."

"Please." I sighed. "Just give me tonight, and tomorrow, we go back to reality." The reality where I'd hurt her.

"Okay." She smiled, pushing off the ice and circling me. "I'll play you for it."

My face pinched with confusion. "Play me... For what?"

"If you win, we wait to talk." She sliced through the ice, stopping throwing the shaved ice onto my skates. "And if I win, we talk now."

My lips curled into a grin for the first time since my skates hit the ice. "What do you have in mind?"

"Hockey."

I huffed out a laugh. There was no way I heard her right. "You want to play a game of hockey?" She nodded, and I pushed off the ice, sliding to a stop behind her.

My hands curled around her hips as I dropped my mouth to her ear. "I think you're going to lose this one, Baby Cruz." I let the heat of my breath caress her skin, and she shivered against me as I pressed my lips to her neck.

She shoved out of my grasp, skating away from me before spinning back. A smug smile pulled at the corners of her mouth. "That, sir, is a penalty."

She was playing with me. "A major penalty?" I smirked, pushing off the ice. I wanted to touch her. "Will you be joining me in the penalty box?"

Shaking her head, she clicked her tongue, holding out her waving finger in front of her as she began skating backward. She kept enough distance between us that I couldn't reach out and touch her. "Are you ready to play? Or are you scared?"

"Oh, you're on, baby. What are the rules?"

"The first one to score wins."

"If I win, we do whatever I want today."

"Deal."

"Let's do this." I pushed off the ice, gliding to where I'd dropped my bag when I saw Parker near Kaia. I grabbed two sticks and a puck before gliding to the center of the rink, where Kaia was waiting for me. "You ready." I flashed her a grin, handing her a stick. Nodding, she took the stick, and I dropped the puck on the ice. I had no idea what she was doing, but there was no way I was going to let her win. Not this time. She was spending the night with me tonight, and tomorrow, we'd deal with whatever happened.

We positioned our sticks on each side of the puck. My gaze flicked up, locking on hers. Her cheeks were flushed, and I had the urge to warm her up, but first, I had to win. "Call it." I'd give her that head start. "You say go, and the games begin."

"Go," she shouted at the same time she hit the puck with her stick, sending it flying through my legs. She was already pushing off the ice to meet the puck with her stick and heading toward her goal before I even snapped out of the initial shock of her getting one over on me. I'd underestimated her, and that was my fault. I sped up behind her as she pushed the puck down the ice. She reared back to smack it into the goal, and I knocked it out of her aim and sped down the ice.

We went back and forth, fighting for control of the puck, and I didn't want it to end, so I was giving a little just to take it back. I knew I should just end it, but I loved being around her like this. I wasn't ready for it to be over. She slid in with some fancy ice skating move and stole the puck, but I hooked an arm around her waist and spun her away from the puck, leaving me in control again. I reared back, smacked the puck, and sent it flying into the goal.

"Hell yeah!"

"You cheated." She laughed.

I nodded. "Yeah, I did, and I'd do it again."

"That's a penalty, so that goal doesn't count."

I laughed. "The rules of the game were that the first person to sink the puck wins. I did that, so I win." I dropped my stick to the ice. Cupping her face, I forced her gaze to mine. "I win. You're mine tonight."

She opened her mouth to say something, and I slammed my mouth against hers, swallowing her words. I was done talking. She melted into me, and I wrapped my arms around her waist, lifting her off the ice. She wrapped her legs around me, and I thrust my tongue in and out of her mouth with greedy strokes. Her hands tangled into my hair as she met me stroke for stroke. I pushed off the ice, gliding toward the penalty box.

We had thirty minutes before the hockey team showed up for practice. Owen was here, but I knew he'd be invisible until practice since he knew Kaia and I were talking.

The penalty box was dark, with only a small amount of light shining from the one rink light that was on. Breaking from the kiss, I set her on the penalty bench, dropping to my knees in front of her.

"What are we doing?" she whispered.

"Whatever I want." I smirked. "And right now, I want to taste you." I hooked a finger into her black leggings.

"Wait, here? Now?"

"Right fucking now."

"Jax."

Ripping her legs apart, I ran my nose over the black

legging covering her pussy. "Just a taste before practice," I breathed. Her head fell back on a moan, and she rocked her hips into me. I smiled against her pussy. "I promise to make you come all over my face."

Hooking my fingers back into her leggings, I shifted so I could jerk them and her panties down to her skates in one fluid motion before settling back between her legs. I wanted to take my time and drag it out, but time wasn't on my side. There would be more time to worship every inch of her body tonight.

I dropped my face breathing in her sweet scent before I swept my tongue up, stopping to give her clit special attention with a long deep pull.

"Jax." Her tone was a desperate plea, a plea to make her come. Sucking on her clit, I slid a finger inside her, pumping in and out, working to find that perfect rhythm that set her on fire. One hand propped herself up, the other tangled into my hair, holding me right where she wanted me. "Fuck, Jax." Her pleas echoed through the empty rink. "Don't stop; I'm going to come."

"That's it, baby," I purred against her pussy, adding another finger. "Come all over my face. I want to wear your orgasm for practice." Her body started to vibrate against my mouth. "Every time I lick my lips, I want to taste exactly what we did in this penalty box."

"Fuck, Jax, I'm coming." I withdrew my fingers and replaced them with my tongue, lapping up every ounce of her orgasm.

"Fuck, you taste good." I groaned. She released my hair, and her heavy breaths filled the arena as she came down from her high.

It took us a few minutes to recover, but by the time the team hit the ice, we were decent.

"I'll see you after practice," Kaia said, flashing a flirtatious smile as she climbed the stairs heading out of the stadium. My gaze watched her perfect ass as she disappeared. Damn, it was going to be hard to concentrate on the game when all I could think about was her.

59

Jaxtyn

I had approximately fifteen minutes before Kaia got home, and I was almost ready. I'd racked my brain all day to devise the perfect date idea, only to realize Kaia was a homebody. She loved to get comfortable and relax. So, I decided to create the perfect date inside the privacy of our own home.

Cam and Kaia had already made plans for the day, and thankfully, Cam was now team Jaxtyn. Given the Cam and Trystan drama, I thought she would give me a harder time, but she didn't. She'd texted me throughout the day, giving me an update so I could have everything perfect by the time Kaia got home.

I'd ordered all of her favorite foods and found a list of different genres of movies to choose from. I didn't know if tonight would be my last night with her, but if it was, I was going out with a bang.

I finished the last-minute final touches by setting out the food across the kitchen island, lighting candles throughout the house, and adding pillows and blankets to the couch for the movie before quickly changing out of my jeans and into a pair of grey joggers and a t-shirt.

I was just rounding the corner out of the bedroom when Kaia pushed through the front door. Frozen, her lips parted, her gaze scanned the room, taking everything in.

"What is all this?"

"Our date." I started to get nervous as I second-guessed my decision to stay in tonight. "Do you like it?"

"It's literally my idea of a perfect date." She smiled, her tone filled with excitement, and I blew out a heavy sigh of relief.

"Why don't you change into something more comfortable, and I'll pour us a drink." I walked towards the refrigerator. "Do you want wine, beer, a mixed drink?"

"Actually, I think I'll just have something with some caffeine."

"Oh," my brows pinched, "are you tired?"

"A little," she said. "Nothing a little caffeine won't fix."

"We have Dr. Pepper or Coke."

"Coke, please," she called out, disappearing into our bedroom.

Jerking open the fridge, I scanned over all the drinks, trying to decide whether I wanted a beer or a

Coke. The door to the bedroom opened, pulling my attention away.

I froze; my heart rate spiked, and it was suddenly hard to breathe. Kaia stepped out of the bedroom in nothing but my t-shirt. Staring up at me through hooded eyes, she shyly tugged at the hem of my shirt. Heat pulled at my groin as my lips curled into a smirk. Even with her hair tied up in her messy bun and nothing but a t-shirt on, she was the prettiest girl I'd ever seen.

Releasing the refrigerator door, I gravitated toward her before realizing what I was doing. My hands ached with the need to touch her soft skin, and my mouth watered with the need to taste her again as my gaze raked up her bare, tanned, and toned legs to the thin white t-shirt that didn't leave much to the imagination, up to her soft blue eyes that said she had a different plan for tonight.

I wasn't hungry anymore. I didn't care about drinks. I wanted her.

I jerked my shirt off, and without stopping, I worked my pants down, tripping over them as I tried to step out of them, stumbling forward. If she was going to be half naked, so was I.

I reached out, gripping her hips and pulling her into me. "What are you doing, Kai?" My voice was a low, raspy whisper. Her hands curled around my biceps as her cheeks turned a pretty shade of pink. "Tell me what you want, baby."

"I want," she started, hesitating briefly as her tongue swept out, wetting her dry lips, "you to tell me what you want to do tonight."

"You want me to tell you all the disgustingly dirty things I want to do to you tonight?" I whispered against her lips. She nodded. My girl loved it when I talked dirty to her. "First, I'm going to carry you to our bed." Wrapping my arms around her waist, I jerked her up, and she locked her legs around my waist. Strolling into our room, I stopped at the foot of the bed. "Then I'm going to lay you on our bed, strip you naked, and admire what's mine before I taste every inch of you." Setting her at the edge of the bed where her feet were hanging over the side, I grabbed the hem of her shirt and slowly pulled it over her head, discarding it to the floor. I groaned, and my cock swelled as my gaze trailed over her naked body; she wasn't wearing anything under the shirt. Jerking down my boxer briefs, my cock sprang free. It was only fair that we were both naked.

Sucking in a ragged breath, my gaze lowered to her bare tits trailing over every curve and storing it in my memory in case I never saw her naked body again. Her nipples were tight, little peaks a few shades darker than her tanned skin. My eyes wandered down over her tight and toned stomach to the curve of her small waist and then lower to her bare pussy.

"Lay down." She did as she was told, falling back on the bed, pulling her knees up, and clenching them tightly together. My hands slid between her knees. "Spread wide for me, baby. I want to see everything that's mine." Her wide eyes locked on me; I easily pushed apart her thighs, spreading her wide. My gaze raked over her pussy, glistening with wetness. "My girl is already ready for me." She soaking wet, begging for me to slide inside her, but I wasn't ready yet.

My large hand wrapped around the base of my throbbing cock as I studied her body, trying not to think about the fact that this could be my last time with her and instead savor every moment, every memory, every taste, and erotic sound she makes.

"And when do we get to the tasting part?" She chuckled.

"Don't rush me, woman." I smirked, a playfulness in my tone. Releasing my cock, I lifted my knee onto the bed before climbing over her. I brushed my lips across her bare stomach. "I have all night and intend to take my time."

"Maybe I should have eaten first." I nipped at her nipple, and she squealed as she wiggled underneath me. "I just wanted a..." She trailed off.

"Wanted what, baby?" I dropped my mouth to her throat, kissing and nipping at her neck. "What did you need?"

"I needed you to fuck me and make me come."

I smiled against her throat. "I'll make a deal with you," I breathed against her throat, letting the heat of my breath feather across her sensitive skin. She responded with a raspy moan. "I'm going to slide inside this perfect pussy that belongs to me, and I'm going to fuck you until you come all over my cock, but after I feed you, you have to feed me." My lips trailed over her jaw and up to her lips. "And I'm not hungry for food."

"Deal," she breathed. "Now fuck m..."

My lips claimed her, stealing her words and kissing her. I kissed her frantically as I ground my hips against hers, sliding my erection through her slick flesh and stroking her clit with the broad head of my cock. "Is this what you want," I murmured into her mouth before pushing my tongue through her parted lips, fucking her mouth.

Positioning the head of my cock at the edge of her entrance, I teased her, pushing just the tip inside her. "Beg," I ordered, breaking from the kiss. "Beg me to fuck you."

"Jax, please," she moaned, rocking her hips against mine. "Please fuck me." Thrusting my hips forward, I filled her with one hard push. She cried out as her fingernail dug into my back. I paused, savoring the feeling as her pussy flexed around my cock, begging for more.

My hands fisted the sheets beside her head. Between the penalty box this morning and now, I was wound up and ready to explode. I pumped in and out slowly, dropping my lips to her ear. "This pussy is mine. It belongs to me." I rolled my hips in a wave-like motion in and out, up and down, grinding against as I moaned against her ear. "Say it, Kai, tell me this pussy is mine."

"It's yours," she panted, her body shaking beneath me. "I'm yours."

I groaned long and deep. "I need you to come for me, baby." I ground my hips against her, and she cried out in pleasure. My speed increased, and her thighs trembled as her pussy clenched around me.

"Fuck," she cried out as she exploded in ecstasy. "Jax."

"Come all over my cock, baby." My hips bucked forward faster. "Fuck." My abs tightened, and I filled her with my orgasm.

"That was exactly what I wanted." She panted. Her chest rose and fell with deep, ragged breaths as she came down from her high. We lay silent for several long minutes, savoring the feel of each other before she finally spoke.

"I know we said we would talk tomorrow, but I think we should talk now." My stomach dropped, and my lungs seized. "I'm starving." She smiled, and I said a silent prayer that it wasn't a pity smile. "Maybe we could eat and talk."

Swallowing hard, I nodded. I was about to find out the fate of my future.

60

Jaxtyn

Setting my beer on the table, I slid into the chair across from Kaia at the small round table in our kitchen nook, wishing I had something stronger, like tequila or whiskey or anything strong enough to numb the pain of Kaia telling me it was over. "Okay." I sighed, leaning back in my chair. "Let's do this." It was hard to mentally prepare yourself for what could possibly be the worst or the best day of your life.

She reached into the center of the table and grabbed a white napkin before cleaning the buffalo sauce off her fingers. I knew Kaia loved Buffalo wings, but she'd scarfed down half a dozen in three minutes. She hadn't been kidding when she said she was starving. "Where do I start?" There was a nervous tremble in her voice. Her gaze flicked up, meeting mine, nibbling her bottom lip. I was usually better at reading her, but at that moment, I couldn't read anything but the nervousness radiating off her and how fucking cute she looked with her 'just fucked hair' and buffalo sauce-tinted lips.

My eyes narrowed. "Are you okay?" Seeing her like this made me more nervous. Which I didn't think was possible.

"Yes." Her lips curved into a soft smile.

"Then let's start with what you remember." My chest clenched painfully tight, knowing I was asking her to recall all the hurt I'd put her through. All the pain I was hoping she'd be able to look past and forgive me for.

She nodded. "I remember the night at the bar," she said, staring off behind me. "I remember being so hurt and choosing to move on with Alex."

My eyes squeezed shut as I swallowed past the lump in my throat. I hated myself for making her feel like that, and even more than that, I hated that I forced her into the arms of another man. Forcing my eyes open, I pressed the bottle to my lips before taking a swig.

"I remember after your game at the hotel, you hit Alex, and I felt so confused because it seemed like you were fighting for me, but you didn't fight for me when I needed you to."

"I know that..." I started.

"What I need to know," she cut me off, holding her hand out to stop me, "is that you are in this now, for good, no matter what. That you are sure I am who you want forever and that whatever problems that come up, you're ready to face them with me. I need to know that you are ready to fight for us."

"Kai." I pushed out of my chair, moving in front of her and sinking to my knees, her gaze following me as I moved. "I'm in this." I grabbed her hand and held it with mine in her lap. "I want you and only you." The corners of her lips lifted as she reached out with her free hand, cupping the side of my face. "I love you, Kai. There is no one else for me."

"Good." She smiled. "Because it was always you, Jax, and I told Alex that the morning of the accident. I was going to text you after practice."

My lips curling into a grin. "So you're mine."

She nodded. "I'm yours." I pushed to my feet, pulling her with me as I wrapped my arms tightly around her, a massive wave of relief washing over me. "I was always yours."

"I'm sorry for everything I put you through. I watched my parents go through this terrible divorce, and I should have talked to you instead of running. I just didn't want us to end up like them."

"Then we don't." She sighed against my chest. "We make a promise to each other to always fight for each other instead of against each other. To fight for our happily ever after no matter how hard it gets."

I smiled against her head. "I will never stop fighting for us, Kai."

"Good," she whispered. "Because I'm pregnant."

Freezing, my smile faded, and my chest tightened.

"Jax?" She leaned back, her gaze meeting mine. "You're not about to panic again, are you?"

"Did you say you're pregnant?"

She nodded.

Holy fuck, she's pregnant.

61

Staring up at him, I couldn't tell whether he was about to throw up or bolt, but the panic covering his face was front and center. A wave of nervous nausea washed over me. That wasn't exactly how I'd planned to tell him, but I was scared, and the look on his face at that moment was why.

He stepped back, sinking into one of the dining room chairs as he stared off into space. "Are you sure?" His gaze shifted to mine.

I'd asked the same question three times to the doctor, so I understood his shock. I'd had time to come to terms with the news; he hadn't.

"Yes." I smiled, nodding. I strolled to the front door, where my purse was sitting on an entryway stand. I dug through it, fishing out the ultrasound photo before returning to Jax and handing him the picture. He took the picture, his lips parting as he stared at it. "Cam took me to the doctor this morning and then to lunch."

"Wait," he said, his head snapping up, and his gaze met mine. His brows furrowed. "So, Cam knows?"

"Yeah, I wasn't feeling good, and I was late, so she bought me a home test. I took three, and they were all positive. I was in shock, and I didn't believe it, so she offered to take me in to be sure. I am sure now. We saw the baby's heartbeat."

"Kai, why didn't you tell me?" I could hear the hurt in his words as he pushed out of the chair, setting the picture on the table. "Why didn't you tell me you were late? Or that you didn't feel good?"

"I guess I was scared of how you would react." I held my hand out, gesturing to him. "Can you blame me? Look at how you're handling it now."

"Kai." He sighed. "I'm in shock and still trying to wrap my head around the idea of being a dad, but I'm in this with you, and I would have been there for you today. You should have told me. You should have given me the opportunity to be there for you and my baby."

"I'm sorry." I sighed. My stomach churned with regret and sadness. I hadn't meant to take anything away from him. I was scared he'd do what he always did: panic, shut down, and run, but that wasn't fair. I should have given him the opportunity to be there if he wanted to. "A baby is a huge commitment, and I was afraid of throwing too much at you all at once."

He huffed out a laugh. "I guess I deserved that." He glanced back at the picture and then at me. "So, I'm going to be a dad?" His lips curved into a smile, and I nodded. "Okay." His gaze flicked around the small living space. "We are going to have a baby." I smiled. "We should probably start looking for a bigger place."

"So, you're okay?"

"Yeah," he said. "I never wanted to have a family until you Kai. It's a little sooner than planned, but I love you and can't wait to see what our future holds." He pulled me in for a hug, wrapping his arms tightly around me and holding me against him. "Are you okay?"

"I was in a bit of shock, and I was a little scared to tell you, but..."

"Kaia," he cut me off. "You don't ever have to be scared to tell me anything. I'm in this with you, and I don't want to miss anything. I know I messed up before your accident, but I never plan on making those mistakes again."

"I'm sorry I didn't tell you. I should have."

"We're in this together," he said. "So we figure this out together."

"Like telling our parents."

He cleared his throat as he nodded. "Yeah." He sighed. "My mom will be stoked, but I'm afraid your dad might kill me."

I huffed out a laugh. "No, my dad will be excited too, but I would like to wait to tell anyone. I want to get used to the idea before everyone else finds out."

"Okay." He nodded.

62

Jaxtyn

Two months later...

"Are you sure about this?" Trystan asked, staring at the tiny black box with the two-carat princess-cut diamond engagement ring inside.

I nodded, a smile pulling at the corners of my lips. I was sure, and I knew this was the absolute perfect time. Camryn, Trystan, Owen, Kaia, Syn, Harlow, and I were all at the beach house for a long weekend. Kaia had just hit the three-month mark, and she was ready to tell everyone we were having a baby, and I was going to propose in front of everyone. Once my mom and her dad got back in town, we would share the good news with them, along with the news we were moving out because we bought a house in North Carolina, where I was drafted to play pro for the Carolina Predators.

"So when are you doing it?" Trystan pulled open the top drawer of his nightstand and shoved the black box inside before pushing it shut.

"Tonight at the bonfire." I leaned over the second-floor terrace as I searched the beach for Kaia. Trystan stepped up beside me, mocking my movement.

"You think she'll say yes?"

"I hope so."

He sucked in a deep breath and slowly exhaled. My gaze shifted following his line of sight to Cam and Owen sitting on the pool's edge with their feet in the water, talking and laughing.

"You going to tell me what happened?"

Trystan shook his head. "Nothing." My brows furrowed. "She's better off with him anyway."

"Okay," I said, dragging the word out. "Owen is my best friend, and you're my brother, so I don't want to get in the middle of this, but I'm pretty sure you don't actually believe that." He shrugged like he was shrugging me off. I huffed out a laugh. "The man of so much wisdom doesn't know how to take his own advice." I shook my head.

"All I seem to do is hurt her."

"Then get your shit together."

His lips curled into a smirk. "I'm working on it."

"Are you two going to be able to get along for the weekend?"

He flicked a glance down to Cam and Owen. "She hasn't said a word to me since I got here, so I think we'll be fine, but I'll probably leave tomorrow morning." I opened my mouth to argue, but he cut me off. "Are they official?" I raised my brows. "Is she his girlfriend?"

I shook my head. "No. She's in love with you."

"Trust me," he sighed, "she's not. I fucked up."

I raised my shoulders. "Then fix it before Owen does become her boyfriend, and your chance is gone forever." I dropped my shoulders.

"Your girl's alone on the beach," Trystan said, nodding towards the beach. My gaze shifted to where Kaia stood at the water's edge.

She was breathtaking. "Give me the ring." I threw my plans out the window.

I was proposing now.

"You doing it now?" Trystan asked, moving to the nightstand. I nodded. He grabbed the ring. "Good luck, bro." He handed me the box, and I shoved it in my pocket.

"Thanks." I smiled before I strolled out to the beach.

My heart pounded wildly as I approached her. I knew Kaia loved me and was excited about our future together, but I also knew she didn't want to get married just because of the baby. But I knew without a doubt that I wanted to be her husband. I wanted to slide this ring on her finger and claim her as mine forever. I just hoped she knew that because if for one second she thought I was only proposing because of the baby, she'd say no.

"Hey." She smiled, wrapping her cardigan tightly around her when a gust of cool air blew past us. "I thought you were chatting with Trystan."

"I was."

"Did you figure out what happened between him and Cam?"

I shook my head. "No. Whatever happened, neither of them wants to talk about it."

"I hope they figure it out." She sighed. "I hate seeing both of them so sad."

"I actually came out here because I wanted to talk to you." I swallowed, and Kaia raised a brow as she twisted to face me.

"If you're not ready to tell everyone yet," she smiled, "we can wait."

"What?" My brows pulled together before I shook my head. "No, that's not it. I'm ready. I'm ready to share this," I gestured between us before pointing down to her stomach, "us, with everyone."

Her gaze softened, and a small smile pulled at her lips. "Okay, then what is it?"

I cleared my throat and reached for her hands, holding them in mine. "I know the plan was to come out here with our family and friends to surprise them with the baby news, but I was hoping we could surprise them with something else, too."

She cocked her head and narrowed her eyes. "Like, what?"

"That we are engaged." Her brows snapped together in confusion, and her gaze followed me as I dropped down to one knee in the sand. "Kaia Cruz, will you be mine forever?" I released her hands, pulled the black box out of my pocket, and opened it.

Her lips parted as her gaze shifted from me to the ring and back to me. "I..." She was rendered speechless. "Are you sure because if this is because of the bab—"

"It's not," I cut her off. "You are mine, and this makes it official. I love you, Kai, and I want you to be my wife."

Tears pooled in her eyes as she started nodding frantically. "Yes, yes, I'll marry you." I pushed to my feet, working the ring out of the box before sliding it on her finger. Her arms wrapped around my neck in excitement.

Cheers erupted, and still embracing, we turned to see the crew on the second-floor terrace chanting for us. They watched the whole thing.

"Cats out of the bag." She laughed.

Our parents showed up, surprising us that night, and

sitting around the bonfire, we shared our news with everyone.

As I stood back, watching my soon-to-be wife, the mother of my child, my chest swelled with happiness, and I smiled at the thought of how it all started.

EPILOGUE

One year later...

"Twist your shoulders this way," the cameraman directed Jax. "And hold the hockey stick out." My lips involuntarily curled into a smirk as I stood off to the side with my arms crossed, wearing a white robe with very little underneath, trying not to let the nerves get the best of me.

Jax twisted and turned shirtless in front of the white backdrop, smiling as people shouted orders and cameras flashed in his face. He was a pro at this. I was not. He enjoyed the spotlight, and I preferred hiding in the background.

Our lives looked so much different this last year. We moved halfway across the country for Jax to play with one of the best teams in the world, The Red River Renegades, leaving our friends and family behind three days after our wedding. Jax's career took off pretty quickly, and we welcomed our perfect baby girl, Kailyn West, into the world on the same day Jax was voted the sexiest man in sports. I'd found a passion for working with troubled youth who had a passion for skating, but I hadn't quite mastered WAG lifestyle. I didn't fit in with most of the wives and girlfriends. I hated all the extra attention, and I refused to sit in the box. I wanted to sit in the stands with the fans because that's what I was. I was Jax's biggest fan.

But today was Jax's sexiest man-in-sports photo shoot for the cover of Sports Illustrated magazine, and somehow, he'd talked me into being a part of it mostly naked with our new baby. The magazine didn't want me. They wanted him to pose with America's sweetheart of sports, Brooke Davis, who was at the top of her game in women's volleyball. She was young, beautiful, and fit. She was who should be on the cover of this magazine naked, not me.

Jax refused the offer to pose naked with another woman, and I loved him for that, but that left me standing in a robe waiting for Jax's solo shoot to end.

"That's a wrap," the cameraman shouted, lifting from kneeling. "Bring out the wife and kid." My stomach churned with anxiety as I let my insecurities get the best of me.

"You ready?" Syn whispered, strolling up beside me with Kailyn bundled snuggly in her pink blanket, sleeping peacefully in her arms.

Three months ago, Syn moved to Red River to escape a toxic relationship and get a fresh start. She moved in with Jax and me with the expectation that she would only be there for a month or two until she got on her feet, but Syn had been the blessing we didn't know we needed after we had Kailyn, and now I wasn't sure we could live without her.

I still giggled, thinking about the craziness of the entire situation. I would have laughed if someone had asked me six months ago if I would leave my newborn daughter alone with Syn. Not because I thought Syn would hurt her or be irresponsible but because I didn't think Syn had a maternal bone in her body. She was wild and careless, which was okay because she was young and single, but her love for Kailyn changed her. She was still young and free, but she loved being with Kailyn, and sometimes, we had to remind her that she didn't have to stay home. We encouraged her to get out and date. She always replied I'd rather be here. I assumed she just wasn't ready to date again after her last relationship, so we didn't push it.

During the day, Syn helped around the house with Kailyn, and at night, she worked in her brand new tattoo and body piercing parlor that Jax invested in to help her accomplish her goals.

"Kai," Syn said, bumping my arm with her elbow. "You okay?"

"Kai," Jax shouted, waving me over. "You ready?"

Swallowing hard, my heart pounded wildly against my rib cage.

"Kai," Syn said again, but she sounded so far away this time because of the pounding in my ears.

I shook my head. "I can't do this." I turned, storming off towards the empty dressing room I'd gotten ready in, slamming the door behind me. Sucking in a deep breath, I stood in front of the full-length mirror, letting my gaze rake over me.

Jax was in his prime. He somehow managed to get better looking with age, and I wasn't as lucky. I was a new mom, and even the forty pounds of makeup couldn't hide the exhaustion on my face, the extra weight I hadn't lost in the eight weeks since Kailyn was born, and all the new stress lines appearing.

My head jerked over my shoulder when a soft knock tapped on the door, and then it slowly opened. "Kaia," Syn said, slowly sticking her head in the door.

"I can't do this," I said, wrapping my arms tightly around myself.

Syn shut the door. "You don't have to do anything you don't want to, but tell me why?"

I shook my head. "Because I'm scared he's going to

wake up and realize he could have done so much better." The fear may or may not have been irrational, but regardless, it was real.

"Girl," Syn snapped. "Are you crazy? He's the lucky one, and he knows it."

"He's around these beautiful women who throw themselves at him."

"And I haven't seen him give them a second look. Hell, I'm not sure he even gives them a first look. Your husband is obsessed with you and the tiny little miracle your body carried."

"People are so cruel on the internet, and they already say mean things like I don't know why he's with her. He could do so much better."

Syn raised her shoulders. "Then show them why he's with you. Show them how obsessed he is with you. Stop hiding and show them. Shut them bitches up."

I snorted out a laugh. "How do I do that?"

"Go out there and let your husband worship your body and your tiny family for the whole world to see."

"And what if..."

"Haters gonna hate." Syn snickered, cutting me off. "Let them hate. They are jealous."

The corners of my twitched with amusement. "When did you get so smart?"

"I saw it on a meme or something." She shrugged me off. "So what's it going to be? You going to show these bitches who's boss, or are you getting dressed."

"Well, when you put it that way." I laughed. Sucking in a deep breath, I nodded. "Let's do this."

The door eased open, and Jax popped his head through the cracked opening. "Are you okay?" I nod, smiling. "I'm sorry. I shouldn't have pressured you into doing this. We don't have to do this if you're not comfortable."

I wasn't completely comfortable with my new mommy's body, but I was ready to embrace it.

"I'm ready." I smiled.

"Are you sure?" I nodded. "Can you tell me what happened?"

Biting down on my bottom lip, I shifted, flicking a glance at Syn. She smiled. "I was worried that after you saw the magazine, you would realize you picked the wrong woman."

His brows creased with worry. "What? Kai, I..."

"I know," I cut him off. "I was letting my insecurities get the best of me."

"Have I done something to make you feel insecure because..."

"No." I huffed out a laugh. Jax always made me feel like the most beautiful woman in the world.

Stepping into my space, his hands curled around my hips. "I love this body," he said, raking his hands up my ribs and around my back. "I love everything about it. The way it looks. The way it tastes."

"Oh gross." Syn sneered. "T.M.I." Jax and I both

laughed. "It's bad enough I have to hear you two fucking like rabbits every single freaking night."

"You could move out," Jax teased.

"Maybe it's not that bad." Syn laughed.

"You ready?" Jax asked, and I nodded. He slipped his hand into mine, leading me out of the dressing room and back to the white backdrop. "Let's do this."

The photo shoot went off without a hitch; the more time I spent in front of the camera, the more comfortable I got. Six months later, when the Sports Illustrated issue dropped, I almost cried because it was such a beautiful cover with my perfect little family.

Surprisingly, while there were a few haters, the outpour of supportive women was so amazing it encouraged me to start a Vlog on the reality of the life of a wife and mother of the sexist man in sports, and the response was ninety percent positive.

That experience made me realize I wasn't alone. Regardless of whether your man was voted the sexiest man alive or not, the insecurities that came with mommyhood were the same across the board. Women of all shapes and sizes, including supermodels, pop stars, and athletes, came forward to discuss how they learned to embrace not just mommyhood, but their new mommy bodies. As well as things like postpartum depression and many other issues women face.

Before long, I had my own PodCast that Jax made a special appearance too often, and between that and opening my new skating rink to help at-risk kids get off the streets and involved in something positive. Plus, being a mommy and a wife, my days were full.

Jax started a nonprofit working with youth and eventually started a youth hockey team.

I couldn't wait to see what else our future had in store.

STAY CONNECTED

Follow me for the latest updates on new releases!

Website: www.michaelasawyerauthor.com

Facebook Page: Michaela Sawyer

Instagram: @michaela.sawyer.author

TikTok: @michaela.sawyer.author

Amazon: Michaela_Sawyer

Made in the USA
Middletown, DE
07 March 2024

51041145R00216